The Actress

The Actress

VIVIENNE LAFAY

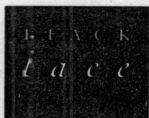

BLACK
lace

Black Lace novels are sexual fantasies.
In real life, make sure you practise safe sex.

First published in 1996 by
Black Lace
332 Ladbroke Grove
London W10 5AH

Typeset by CentraCet Limited, Cambridge
Printed and bound by Mackays of Chatham PLC

ISBN 0 352 33119 4

Chapter One

It was a perfect day in June, and a lone punt was making its way along the Cambridge Backs, the river Cam now restored to its normal tranquillity after all the hectic excitement of May Week. In the flat-bottomed boat Milly Belfort was reclining, an enigmatic smile on her pretty young face. She knew what an attractive picture she and her three companions made as they glided towards the aptly-named Mid-summer Common, propelled by the long pole that Piers Lascelles was so expertly wielding. As they passed by the stately college buildings she waved and smiled at the dons strolling around in their gowns and mortar boards, giggling to herself as she contemplated the purpose of their expedition.

'Penny for them, Milly!' said Bob Drew, as he stood to take over the navigation from Piers. His brown eyes glinted mischievously at her from beneath his auburn brows and she felt a brief twinge of desire catch her unawares.

'I was just wondering what all those learned dons would say if they knew what we plan to do this afternoon.'

Caroline James swung her bobbed fair hair and gave her friend a wink. 'But it's going to be Art, isn't it? Everyone knows that there's nothing wrong with a bit of nudity provided you dress it up as High Culture!'

Piers picked up the camera from the bottom of the boat and studied Caroline through the viewfinder. A lock of his gold hair fell across the lens and he brushed it away with a casual gesture. 'I don't think our photograph will end up in the Royal Academy, chaps!'

'Oh, I don't know,' Milly said, trailing her hand in the limpid green water. 'Evadne says she wouldn't be surprised if photography didn't become an art form eventually.'

'How about *porn*ography?' Caroline giggled. 'Could that be an art form too?'

'Why not?' said Bob. 'Poetry is considered art because it moves the heart, so if words can move other parts of you . . .'

'It doesn't take much to move your parts, old man!' Piers chortled, staring pointedly at the bulge in Bob's white slacks. He leaned over and seized Milly's free hand, pressing it to his lips. 'Honestly, Milly, you do devise the most wicked wheezes!'

'I suppose I must take that as a compliment. I try to keep you all amused, but it requires a great deal of forethought, I can assure you.'

Piers began to kiss her fingers, sending delightful tickling sensations all up her bare arm. Milly shivered, anticipating further delights. It wasn't the first time that she and her broad-minded companions had ventured out in search of sensual adventure but it promised to be the most exciting. The powers-that-be permitted young people to go out unchaperoned providing they remained in a foursome, and Milly always made sure that she and her partner ventured out in the company of like-minded couples!

Overhead the sky was an unbroken blue, and the spot they had chosen for their picnic, a copse near the small village of Horningsea, would provide just the right background for the tableau she had in mind. They moored the punt at the University boathouses and proceeded on foot, each of them carrying some useful item. Milly held the wicker basket of fruit and pale blue gown that she would change into for the picture. For the time being, however, she was wearing something more fashionable: a short-sleeved dress in flowery yellow chiffon with a matching sash slung around her slim hips. The low round neck revealed the creamy skin of her chest and shoulders, but the bodice disguised the fullness of her rounded breasts, making her seem almost flat in front. White strappy sandals and a cream straw hat with a yellow ribbon completed her outfit. Beneath the brim a pair of vivid blue eyes darted with intelligent interest at her surroundings and her soft, full lips were constantly moulding themselves into a smile, whilst tendrils of glossy dark hair fell around her dainty ears, which were adorned with tiny, diamond clips making her look as pretty as a picture. Evadne told her she always did.

With Piers bringing up the rear carrying his camera and tripod, the small party made for the clump of trees in the distance.

'Oh Milly, it's so nice to have something to *do* now finals are over!' Caroline exclaimed, plucking a grass stalk and pushing it between her teeth. 'I've been going half mad worrying about my degree. The May Ball was fun, but I hardly remember it now.'

'That's because you were tight on champagne most of the time!' Piers grinned.

She threw the half-chewed stalk at him. 'You can talk! Trying to seduce the Dean's wife – whatever

3

next! It's a wonder they didn't throw you out of King's without letting you graduate.'

'They wouldn't dare. Pa and Hunters were at Eton together and he's given loads of loot to the place. Anyway, Beryl was a good sport. She gave me a sloppy kiss, patted me on the backside and told me to trot off to bed like a good boy.'

'And off you went, meek as a lamb!' Bob laughed.

Piers' handsome face took on a sly expression. 'That's all you know!'

'What d'you mean?'

'Aha! Wouldn't you like to know, old chum?'

'We'd all like to know,' Milly insisted. 'Just what did you get up to after the May Ball, Piers?'

He flashed his even white teeth at them and hoisted the tripod from his shoulder to the path. 'If Bob will take a turn carrying this clobber so I'm not puffing so much, I'll tell you.'

Bob willingly took the load so the three of them could hear Piers' story. 'Well I went out on to the lawn, just for some air you know, and who should I see there but prissy Missy Edgington-Smythe, all dressed up in that dreadful frock her ma had sent her for the ball, and looking really sorry for herself.'

Caroline chuckled. 'I knew Tubby wouldn't stick her for long. He was bribed into partnering her, you know.'

'I know. Anyway, I was feeling randy as hell after that luscious kiss from Buxom Beryl and it was a case of anything in a skirt. So I asked her if she wanted some champagne and she sort of simpered at me in that ghastly way, like she does, and so I poured her a generous measure and watched her gulp it down. She went all flushed and bright-eyed, so I reckoned I was in with a chance.'

Bob gave a snort of derision. 'Not with prissy-lips, surely! You must have been desperate.'

4

'I was! Anyway, she took my arm and we went for a stroll around the shrubbery. There were plenty of other couples round there that night, I can tell you. But I was amazed when she drew me right into the centre of these rhododendron bushes and began kissing me with a kind of desperation, as if this was her one and only lifetime chance of a bit of the other.'

'It probably was!' Bob quipped.

'Don't be horrid,' Caroline intervened, though her eyes glinted wickedly. 'She can't help it. If you had a mother like hers you'd probably throw yourself at anyone just to get away from her.'

'Thanks a lot!' Piers said, wryly.

'So what happened?' Milly prompted. 'How far did she let you go?'

'It wasn't exactly a case of letting me, more of forcing me.'

'What, you let her rape you? Shame! Why didn't you cross your legs like Mater told you?'

'Shut up, the lot of you, or I won't tell.' They fell silent, suppressing their laughter in their eagerness to hear the whole story. Piers continued. 'Anyway, there we were in the rhododendron bushes and she started to undo my fly and pull out my tadger. No preliminaries or anything. I was flabbergasted, I can tell you. I didn't think she even knew I had one! She started to pat and stroke it as if it were her pet rabbit or something, and of course it grew even bigger. I started to think she was a lot more experienced than we'd imagined.'

'Did she let you get into her knickers then?' Bob asked.

'Don't be so impatient, I'm coming to that. Well by now I was all steamed up, ready to grope and kiss and squeeze whatever and wherever I could. While she fondled me I put my hand up her party skirt and that's when I had the surprise of my life. She was

5

wearing silk stockings with garters, but when I put my hand up a bit further expecting to find some fearfully old-fashioned bloomers or something all I could feel was her hairy quim!'

Milly stared at him, laughter bubbling up inside her. 'You mean she had no knickers on?'

He nodded. 'Exactly.'

The four of them fell into helpless laughter. Eventually, through her tears, Milly said, 'You mean ... all the time she was prancing around with Tubby, trying to look as if she was enjoying herself, with her silly made-up face and her awful hair-do she had ... she had ... a bare bottom?'

'Must have had! Unless she took them off later, which I doubt.'

'Talk about being prepared. She must have been a good Girl Guide!'

'What did you do next?' Caroline asked, pruriently. 'How far did she let you go?'

'Further than I would have dreamed. I started to stroke her hairy lower lips and soon my finger slipped in, right into her tight little cunny. I was sure she would slap me down but she did quite the reverse. She kissed me passionately as she pulled away at my dickory dock and then began saying things like, "Give it to me good and hard, naughty boy!" and "Rub my little button till it's hot and throbbing!" I tell you, I couldn't believe my ears!'

'*Prissy* lips?' Milly gasped. 'Are you sure we're talking about the right girl here? Maybe we should re-christen her "kissy lips"!'

'What else did you do?' Caroline prompted, her cheeks flushed.

'She wouldn't let me fuck her, if that's what you're wondering. But I did a good job on her with my fingers, and she did an equally good job on me with

6

hers. Let's just say we were both fully satisfied by the end of the evening.'

'"After the Ball", you mean!' Milly giggled, and they all broke into singing the rude version of 'After the Ball was Over', laughing and joking as they headed across the field towards the trees.

In the middle of the copse was a small clearing which Milly declared to be just right for their purposes. She pulled a postcard out of her bag and the others crowded round to examine it. The picture was of Manet's famous *Déjeuner sur L'Herbe* which Milly had seen when she had visited the Louvre museum in Paris that Easter. She'd had the idea of making a photograph to parody it.

Carefully they arranged the basket on the ground with the fruit spilling out of it, just as in the painting. They placed a mortar board beside it, in place of the straw hat discarded by Manet's model, and then the two men began to undress while Milly pulled the plain blue dress over the yellow one she was wearing. When the two men were entirely nude, Piers set up his Kodak camera at a distance and set out the lead and squeeze trigger that would enable him to take a photograph by delayed action.

Already Bob's erection was fully in evidence, and as he busied himself with his preparations Piers started to become aroused too. Milly felt a rush of desire welling up in her and grew impatient for the photography session to get under way. For only when they had taken the pictures would the real fun begin.

Caroline took up her background position to imitate the woman gathering flowers on the river bank, with the boat moored behind. Milly sat posed with her elbow on her knee and her hand supporting her chin. They were bent on reproducing the original scene as faithfully as possible so that the reference to Manet's work was immediately obvious. The difference would

7

be that this time both women were fully clothed, while the men were in the altogether. It was Milly's intention to make a 'feminist' version, reversing the sexual implications in order to make her point about the exploitation of the female form in art, a subject that she had often debated with Evadne Parker, her tutor.

When they were all ready, Piers pulled the string several times to make sure of getting a good shot. He was lying on the ground like the figure on the right of the painting, gesturing towards Milly with his right hand and wielding a short ebony cane in his left. This gave her an idea. 'How much more film do you have in your camera, Piers?'

'Oh, just a few more exposures.'

She gave a mischievous grin. 'Then I think we should use them to good effect. Caroline, come here a minute!'

Soon the two women had the men across their knees. Milly began smacking Piers' naked buttocks with her hand while Caroline chastised Bob with the cane, and the scene was faithfully recorded by the trusty box on legs. The lusty action, after so much inaction, had sent all their adrenaline levels soaring and they regarded each other with bright cheeks and brighter eyes. Beneath her layers of skirts Milly could feel her secret parts clamouring for attention.

'Now it's your turn, ladies!' Bob declared, rubbing his smarting bottom.

Milly nodded. 'All right, but not for a spanking. Let's try something a bit more interesting.'

'What do you have in that dirty little mind of yours, Milly?' Piers asked, his grey eyes sparkling at her with lecherous glee. She noticed that his penis was now completely hard, lifting its domed head away from his hairy stomach as if awakening after a long sleep.

'You will be developing this film yourself, won't you?'

'Of course! Don't worry, darling, the results will be for our eyes only.'

'Fine. In that case it's time to strip off, Caroline!'

The two women took off their dresses, discarding them in a casual heap, and were soon as naked as the men. They made a handsome foursome. Both the men were strapping types who rowed for their colleges, and Piers was also a cricket blue. Their muscular torsos and strong legs gave them a manly presence when clothed, but when stripped of their garments it was obvious that they were red-blooded males in every way. The pair had most impressive erections, Piers' long, rather elegant organ rearing up in pale contrast to Bob's more robust, ruddy one.

Of the two women, Milly knew she had the more voluptuous figure. Her breasts sat high and round upon her chest, perfect globes with delicate pink nipples that jutted proudly. Her dark bush was thick and curled, but the slitted pouch of her sex could still be seen beneath the thicket. Her stomach was flat and smooth, but her bottom was rounded as firmly as her bosom. Caroline was altogether more lean, and her bosom had a tendency to sag, but her long legs and slim waist were assets that women envied and men admired.

Milly and Caroline knelt back-to-back on the grass with the men standing before them, then each woman took the tip of her partner's cock between her lips and glanced towards the camera. There was a click as Piers surreptitiously pulled the cord that worked the shutter and then the girls stood up laughing.

'I say, that's pretty unfair!' Bob complained. 'Is that all the pleasure we chaps are going to get this afternoon, just a quick lick?'

Milly smiled. 'Just wait till we've done the photography then you won't be disappointed, I promise you.'

'There's two more photos on the film,' Piers declared. 'How about you girls getting down on all fours while we pretend to take you from behind?'

Milly wriggled her buttocks appreciatively as the wet nose of Piers' prick nuzzled against her slit. She was feeling quite achingly randy and longed to proceed to some mutual pleasuring, but there was one last tableau to arrange first.

'Let's stage an orgy!' she suggested.

They tried out various positions and finally settled on one where Caroline lay on the ground with Piers mouthing her parts while Milly did the same to his, and Bob sat astride Caroline's chest with his cock between her lips, his fingers playing with Milly's pert nipples.

After the shutter had clicked, the foursome were disinclined to stop what they were doing and so the 'orgy' proceeded in earnest. Milly closed her eyes in bliss as Piers' fingers reached for her pussy and dabbled in her sweet juices. She could already taste his, seeping from the slit in his glans. His long shaft filled her mouth and she caressed it lovingly with her tongue while he slowly brought her towards a climax, his hand deep inside her now and pushing hard against her protruding love-button with rhythmic strokes.

Opening her eyes again she could see Bob thrusting in and out of Caroline's willing mouth, as the girl made the little cries that preceded her orgasm, cries that intensified to low moans as the crisis approached. Blindly Milly reached out and touched the erect knob of her nipple, tweaking it fiercely until her friend was in the throes of a wild climax.

Aware that Bob was shooting his stream between Caroline's ecstatically opened lips, Milly gave Piers' bollocks a squeeze and had the satisfaction of experiencing a similar hot jet as it squirted inside her own mouth. The very idea of them all coming together in such a spectacular way brought her finally to her own consummation. With a surprised cry she gave herself up to the dancing waves of energy that were flooding her with bright sensation, making her buck and wriggle to wrest every last spasm of sensual pleasure from Piers' helping hand.

Soon the four of them lay exhausted in a heap, panting and laughing in equal proportions. Suddenly they were all ravenous and swigged from a bottle of wine then devoured the fruit they had brought with them as props.

'Oh Lord, why can't this go on forever?' Caroline sighed, her head on Bob's chest as she gazed up at the blue scraps of sky between the trees.

'What will you do when you go down, Bob?' Piers asked, evoking sniggers from the girls.

'Train for the Bar,' he answered. 'Not that I'm keen, but it's what my parents want. I suppose you'll take over the old estate, what?'

'Not for a while. Pater wants me to go to the Colonies – India, probably. Says I should get some experience before he lets me loose at home.'

'Practise on the poor old natives first, eh? Never mind. They say those Indian women worship men's whatsits, you know. They've got big stone dildoes in their temple and when they go down on you they treat it as a form of worship. I reckon you'll be in clover there, old chap!'

'How about you, Milly?' Caroline asked. 'What are your plans?'

Milly sighed. It had been a relief to forget all about the future for a while but she knew she must face it soon. 'I honestly don't know. Ma would like it if I went straight into a teaching post but I just can't face it. I feel I haven't seen nearly enough of life. What I'd really like to do is travel.'

'Why not go to India with me?' Piers grinned. 'We could scandalise them by making love in a *howdah* on an elephant's back!'

'That's a tempting offer, Piers, but it's Europe I really want to visit. I just loved being in Paris with my godmother this spring.'

Caroline's eyes lit up. 'Your godmother, isn't she that amazing woman who believes in free love and teaches girls how to practise it?'

'That's right. Emma had an academy in Florence, although she's retired now. I'm hoping to stay in her villa. The trouble is, she and Ma don't really see eye to eye.'

'You're twenty-four, Milly,' Caroline reminded her. 'Surely you're old enough to know your own mind by now.'

Milly sighed. 'It's easy for you to say that, Caroline, when your parents are dead. But I don't want to upset my mother. She's had a hard life and I really admire the way she's always fought for women's rights. But she thinks I'm like her, and I'm not.'

'Parents always think you're a chip off the old block,' Piers said. 'I'm toying with the idea of becoming the black sheep of my family, gambling and whoring my fortune away.'

The others laughed, but Bob pointed out that Piers was far too fond of his mother and sisters to do anything of the sort.

With the sun beginning to wane the four friends dressed themselves and cleared up, then walked back to the boat. Their discussion had brought on a sombre mood, far removed from the abandoned exhibitionism they had shown earlier, and they boated back to the lawn of King's in almost complete silence. Tomorrow the examination results would be posted and they would know their fate. Whatever plans they might or might not have for the future were for the time being obscured by that imminent and daunting prospect.

After taking leave of the men, Caroline and Milly cycled back to Girton. The women's training college had been deliberately sited far from the men's colleges to enable them to avoid 'temptation'. This had not proved sufficient deterrent in Milly's case. She'd made the most of her time at Cambridge in every way, often indulging in clandestine visits to men's rooms which had resulted in much scaling of the college walls after midnight. Fortunately Milly was of an athletic build and disposition, and she counted the two occasions when she had been caught and punished as a price worth paying for the furtherance of her education in unorthodox extra-curricular activities.

After supper that evening the two women met in Milly's room once again. They were both in melancholy mood. The following morning Caroline would be leaving Cambridge and going to live with the widowed aunt, whose fortune had paid for her studies. A job in a local school had been found for her, but there the freedom she had enjoyed as a student would certainly be curtailed.

'Never mind, Caro, you're sure to find some nice young headmaster who will make an honest woman of you,' Milly smiled, hugging her close.

Caroline gave her a rueful grin. 'I knew I'd have to face this some day, it was all part of the bargain. But I shall miss our wonderful life here, Milly. And you, of course.' She suddenly brightened. 'Why don't you visit us in Suffolk? I'm sure Aunt Maud would love to have you, and it would give you a chance to think about what you wanted to do with your life. Oh, do come!'

'It's very kind of you, but Eva would be upset if I didn't stay in her cottage for a while.'

13

'Oh, her! Honestly, Milly, I don't know why you put up with that woman's whims and tantrums. You don't really love her, do you?'

It was a conversation they'd had many times. Caroline just couldn't understand the nature of Milly's relationship with Evadne Parker, her Classics tutor. She was a confirmed lesbian, with an unrequited passion for her favourite student. Milly had often tried to end their affair. They had gone through 'platonic' phases where they tried to be just good friends, but always Evadne had succeeded in emotionally blackmailing her so that she gave in to her advances one more time – and then regretted it. Milly knew there was something unhealthy in the older woman's personality, something that might well get her into real trouble one day, but she also felt a deep admiration for her intellect.

'I feel sorry for her,' she admitted. 'She knows it will have to end between us sometime, but I can't walk out on her cold-bloodedly. I've been beastly to her while I've been studying for exams, making excuses not to see her and acting moody when we were together. So now I feel I must make it up to her. For a few weeks, at least.'

'So it's honeymoon time at Fen Cottage, is it?' Caroline sneered. 'Frankly, I can't see you putting up with it for long, Milly. You're too keen on men to give them up altogether.'

'She doesn't insist on me giving up men, you know.'

'Yes, but she hates it when you go with them, doesn't she? Don't give in to her, sweetie, you're far too good-natured. She'll swallow you whole if you're not careful, and only spit you out when you're too old and tired to make a new life for yourself. I know the type. Aunt Maud was just like that with poor Uncle Tom.'

'Don't be ridiculous!' Milly rose to close the curtains

and pour more wine. 'I may not be sure what I want to do yet, but I *am* sure about what I don't want.'

'Then tell that woman you are going away for good. It'll be for the best, believe me.'

Milly stared silently at her friend for a few moments before answering. It occurred to her for the first time that Caroline might be jealous of Evadne. Not in a physical way, since they were both far more interested in men's bodies than women's, but envious of the close intellectual bond that existed between them. Although Milly was eight years younger than her tutor they debated as equals, with Milly often surpassing Evadne in insight where the older woman had the advantage in knowledge.

'I think I am the best judge of how to deal with her,' Milly said, quietly.

'I'm sorry, I know I shouldn't interfere. I just don't want to see you waste yourself, that's all. You're so pretty, and clever and talented, Milly.'

'Now you're starting to sound like my mother!'

'Ah, the famous suffragette! What is she doing these days, Milly, now that we all have the vote?'

'Oh, it's by no means over yet! She's campaigning for women to be allowed to vote at twenty-one, like the men.'

'Well I, for one, am quite content to wait until I'm thirty. I don't want to bother my head with politics. I shall have quite enough trouble thinking about how to manage a career in education, and whether I'm prepared to give it all up if I meet the right man.'

Milly sighed. 'It's a choice I never want to make. Why should men be able to have wives *and* careers, while women can only have one or the other?'

'Children, I suppose.'

'And if you don't want, or can't have, children?'

'Then they should bend the rules, but I bet they don't. Still, I'm not convinced I shall make much of a teacher. If I meet the love of my life I'm sure I'll gladly give up chalk and talk for wedded bliss!'

'Don't you be so sure!' Milly laughed. 'I can easily see you as a dedicated teacher who won't be distracted from the line of duty.'

As they teased each other and chatted away into the night there was an underlying sadness between them still, and when Caroline finally rose to leave the two women hugged tearfully.

'Good luck for tomorrow!' Milly whispered, opening the door.

'Thanks. I won't wish you the same because you don't need it, while I need all the luck I can get! My train's at ten. Will you come to the station with me?'

'Of course!'

Left alone in her room, Milly felt disinclined to sleep. She was nervous about tomorrow's results. Everyone expected her to do well, but what if she didn't? The exam papers had been gruelling, and she had felt unprepared for one or two of the questions. Then there was the sense of impending anti-climax. For four years she had worked hard at her studies – played hard, too, she reminded herself with a smile. But now it was all drawing to a close and the future was a blank slate on which she might sketch out for herself almost any kind of life she pleased. She knew she was privileged to have education and a private income, and she was grateful to her father for settling so generously in her favour. Yet now she felt it was almost as much of a burden to have too much freedom as to have none.

She undressed and washed herself at the marble wash-stand before getting into her narrow bed. The thought of that afternoon's romp brought a warmth to her flesh, but her mood remained sombre. How would a free spirit such as hers fare in a world peopled by narrow-minded souls who believed that one should toe the line and live a life of respectable drudgery? That could never be her way. If she had to move abroad to be free and live according to her impulses that's what she would do, and without regret.

Just before she fell asleep, Milly found herself thinking of her godmother once again. She knew that Emma Longmore had left England years ago, to live with a handsome Italian who was half her age. Maybe she should let her spiritual guardian be her inspiration and follow her example!

Chapter Two

The sunny evening lifted Milly's heart as she cycled towards the cottage where Evadne, her tutor and lover, lived in rustic seclusion. There was a feeling of relief now that she knew she had passed her exams with distinction, putting her in a carefree mood. It would be nice to take a walk along the river, she decided, but that all depended on what kind of mood she would find Eva in. Just lately she had shown a tendency towards petulance. Dismounting at the gate, she wheeled her bicycle up the path of the pretty garden and stationed it against the porch.

Eva opened the door wearing her usual mannish attire, a cigar butt sticking from her rosy mouth. 'Darling! I've been expecting you since tea-time. What have you been doing?'

Milly frowned. 'Just collecting some photographs to show you. We didn't say a precise time, did we?'

'Of course not, but you're generally here by five. Never mind, we'll forego tea even though I baked some scones.'

'Oh Evie, I'm sorry!'

Milly allowed herself to be swept into her lover's

arms although she still felt uneasy. Eva never used to be such a stickler for punctuality. Was she getting nervous because term was almost at an end? Be kind to her, Milly cautioned herself as a wave of cigar smoke enveloped her. The kiss that followed was rough and passionate, but she needed to be wooed.

'Don't, Eva,' she complained, pulling away. 'Let's save all that till later.'

'You torture me, you know!' the older woman sulked, her brown eyes darkening. 'I dream of your body day and night, but sometimes I wonder if you think of me at all when you're not in my company.'

'Don't be silly, of course I do! Anyway, I've brought you a treat.' She moved into the tiny cottage and took off her straw boater. From the bag slung over her shoulder she produced a packet. 'Remember how we were talking about the way women were portrayed in Art? As passive nude figures, and all that?'

'Yes?' Eva answered gruffly.

'Well Caro and I decided to do something about it. And this is the result!'

She handed Eva the photograph, showing her and Caroline with the two men posing in the woods. 'Isn't it a scream?' she giggled, encouragingly.

But Evadne was not amused. 'If this is what you get up to in your spare time, Milly, I would rather not know about it.'

'Oh don't be so stuffy!' Milly snatched the photo back and replaced it in the packet with the others. 'You're no fun to be with any more, Evie! You take everything so seriously.'

'I take you seriously.' Eva took her into her arms again and stared soulfully into her eyes. 'I can't bear to think of you sharing your beautiful body with anyone else, you know that. But I cannot deny you that right. Just don't rub my nose in it please, sweetheart.'

She began to kiss her again, but Milly knew that if she didn't put a stop to it they would end up making love and the evening was too nice to waste. She gently extricated herself.

'Can't we go for a walk now, please? It's such a beautiful evening.'

'Oh, very well,' Eva sighed. 'I know you would rather be listening to birdsong than my idle chatter.'

'No, that's not true! Besides, I would not describe your conversation so. I have always found our discussions very stimulating.'

Evadne grinned, stubbing out her acrid cigar. 'In that case, I shall hope for better things. If I may first stimulate you mentally, perhaps later you'll let me stimulate you physically.'

Milly gave her an arch look then wandered about the room while Eva put on her walking shoes. Pausing at the mantelpiece she reached out and stroked the smooth figurine of a nude girl dancing on a marble plinth. 'You cannot call this *objet d'art* passive,' she commented. 'It reminds me of when I saw Isadora Duncan. My godmother took me to see her troupe dancing when I was a girl. I was entranced!'

'I have a lot to thank your godmother for, it seems. She helped turn you into a free-thinking woman, didn't she?'

'You could say that. She certainly set a remarkable example. In some ways I admire her more than my mother. Ma didn't want me to come to Girton, you know. She said I was not cut out to be a teacher. I fear she was right.'

'Nonsense! You've a fine brain, Milly. It's such a shame that Oxford has only just allowed women to take degrees. The higher academic life would have suited you, I'm sure.'

'Maybe, but I am so impatient!' She raised her arms

above her head in a long stretch. 'I want to see everything the world has to offer before I settle down.'

The two women left the cottage and began to walk along the riverside path, arm in arm. When a man cycled by he raised his hat saying, 'Evenin' Miss, Evenin' Sir!' and Milly giggled. But she was used to people mistaking her lover's gender. With her hair in an Eton crop, and wearing Oxford bags with a tweed jacket, Evadne often passed for male. She even, on occasions, affected a monocle.

'What are your immediate plans, dearest?' Eva wanted to know, as they neared the weir. 'Now you have your certificate will you be looking for a teaching post straight away?'

Milly was aware of the apprehension behind the question. She wanted to be kind, but it was such a temptation to be cruel. 'Oh, I'm not sure,' she said, vaguely. 'Mother may have plans for me.'

Eva halted, took both of Milly's hands in hers and squeezed them. 'Please, my dearest, say you will spend some time with me in the cottage. I shall die if you leave me so soon!'

'Well, I may be able to spare a week . . .'

'A week!' Eva groaned. 'Is that all?'

'I should be bored if I stayed longer. Cambridge is lovely, but I know every inch of it. I long for fresh fields and pastures new!'

She twirled around on the path then strayed into the adjacent meadow, where she performed her own version of Greek dancing for a few minutes while Eva stood watching reproachfully on the path. At last Milly came up with a cheeky grin and hugged her friend. 'Don't mind me, Evie! I'm just jubilant now exams are over, that's all!'

'I've been thinking. How would you like to come to Italy with me?'

'Italy?' Her blue eyes shone at the suggestion. 'Oh,

how marvellous! I'd absolutely love it. Do you mean it, Eva dear?'

'Well I'm sure we could arrange it. I thought maybe Florence . . .'

'Florence, oh yes, yes! That's where Emma lives!'

'Emma?'

'My dear godmother – the one you feel indebted to, remember? She'd be so happy to see me again. You too, of course. She lives just outside Florence and might be able to put us up.'

Her tutor frowned. 'I want to study Renaissance art and history.'

'Anything you like! When can we go?'

'You will have to write to your godmother. And I shall see about the travel arrangements. With luck we could set out in, say, two weeks?'

'Perfect! I shall stay a week here with you, then go to see Ma in London. We can meet up again at Victoria, to take the boat train.'

Eva smiled broadly and her whole face was transformed, making Milly feel even more happy. She was fond of her female lover, despite her often churlish manner, and wanted her to be happy – although not at her own expense. This new plan promised to make both of them very happy indeed.

I wonder what Emma will make of her? Milly couldn't help speculating, as they strolled back along the twilit path towards the cottage with bats swooping overhead. The prospect of seeing her again made her feel excitingly warm inside. Last time they'd met, in Paris four years ago, her godmother had fully satisfied her curiosity about the male sex, answering all her questions in detail. She had arrived at Girton with a great desire to put all this knowledge into practice and, so far, had succeeded pretty well. Although she was still technically a virgin she knew how to pleasure a man in a variety of ways.

22

Yet if sex was not so much of a mystery to her any more, love certainly was. Milly had never been in love, although she'd had a 'crush' on some older girls at school. She could not understand the way Evadne felt about her, all those slushy poems and flowery phrases that she liked to scribble down while they were apart. The woman's libido she could more readily comprehend, since she knew the pleasures of the orgasm and when neither Eva nor some biddable male was present to make love to her she could produce one for herself. But all those elevated feelings were as strange to her as a foreign language.

'I have two fine trout waiting for us,' Eva smiled as the cottage came into view. 'They shan't take long to fry. But if you'd rather go to bed first . . .'

'Oh no, I'm starving! Besides, you'll need energy later. Better eat to keep your stamina up!'

'Wicked girl!'

'Yes, but don't you just love it when I'm naughty?'

Milly could tell from the flush in her cheeks that her lover was fired up and would do anything to please her. Sometimes she felt guilty for taking advantage of her, but it had been Eva who had made all the running.

By the time she was in the second term of her second year at college, Milly had already suspected that her tutor had taken a special interest in her. All those cosy after-hours chats in the senior common room, the invitations to spend weekends at the cottage which she'd turned down at first in case the other students suspected her of currying favour. Then there were those numerous 'chance' meetings, on the library steps or in the book shop, after which a cup of coffee or tea in a nearby café seemed inevitable.

Although Milly had made full use of her opportunities at Cambridge for mixing with the opposite sex, she was still naive as far as lesbian love was concerned. She had felt attracted to other girls at Cheltenham, but their adolescent experiments had been furtive, unsubtle. Now, while she sat in the easy chair listening to the gramophone with the smell of frying fish drifting through from the kitchen, Milly remembered how her relationship with Evadne had progressed from that of tutor and student to lovers.

It had been a fine summer's evening, much like this one, and Eva had invited her to the cottage to discuss some literary topic – the evolution of Romance, she believed it was. Certainly they had covered Troubadours, and Keats. Milly had been led to believe that there would be other students present. When she arrived, however, Eva had laughingly told her there was a party on in town, and that the others – shallowminded creatures to a woman – all preferred the pleasures of the senses to those of the mind. There had been wine at Honeysuckle Cottage, and plenty of it, together with macaroons and chocolates.

'I have been wooed with wine and sweets and poetry,' Milly remembered saying to herself, as she lay in her tutor's ample wooden bed.

But first they had talked into the night, flushed with alcohol and excited by each other. The discussion had proceeded along carefully structured lines, leading up to Evadne producing some of her poetry. The gushing sentimentality of it had been embarrassing to read, especially as much of it had been read aloud, and it had slowly dawned on Milly that the 'sweet nymph' in 'I hunger for Thee' and the 'bird of paradise' in 'Heaven's Gate' were metaphors for herself.

Evadne was not unattractive to her, with her soft voice and caressing hands, telling her how lovely she was, and how clever. After the way some of the other tutors had tried to squash her bright intelligence in tutorials Milly was flattered to have someone boost her confidence. By the time Milly realised it was far too late to go back to her digs, she was also too drunk to resist her tutor's offer to share her bed. There was no spare room in the cottage, so it was that or sleep on the rickety, uncomfortable sofa. Besides, Milly had never been made love to by a woman before and she was curious.

They had gone upstairs to the candle-lit room with the creaky bed and spooky shadows, giggling like schoolgirls as they frightened each other with tales of ghosts. Eva had made her lie down and had then slowly, reverently undressed her while she lay perfectly still, with her head on the lace-trimmed pillow, a strange excitement gushing through her veins along with the wine. The bedroom had been hushed, and the undressing had taken on the atmosphere of a ritual, as if Eva were laying out a corpse. Milly remembered the dream-like, hypnotic state she had been in, letting the older woman strip her to her underwear.

'I have often imagined how your body would look completely naked,' Eva confessed, her voice hoarse with emotion. 'But now I can hardly bear to uncover it.'

Her eyes travelled all over the skimpy undergarment, leaving a trail of fire on the flesh beneath. Milly wanted to be stripped and naked, wanted to feel Eva's adoring hands and lips as they moved intimately about her body. So she began unbuttoning her lace-trimmed camiknickers. Eva still wore her shirt and trousers, but with trembling fingers she pulled the straps down over Milly's shoulder until the rounded tops of her breasts were exposed.

The scent of tobacco wafted into Milly's nostrils as her lover's lips travelled down the valley between her breasts, awakening the warm currents of her desire and making her shudder with sweet expectation. At the same time she felt hands gently caressing her inner thighs, moving near to the opening where her secret flower waited, with dew-laden petals, for those searching fingers. She moaned softly as the top of her camisole was pulled open and her ripe, stiff nipples reared in longing.

'Exquisite!' Eva breathed, her warm lips and tongue enclosing the hard bud of her nipple.

Now Milly could feel the rough trousers against her legs as the other woman moved against her. Her mind was racing, wondering how they were going to reach their consummation, wondering how skilled and experienced her tutor was in the ways of Sappho. At last Eva's fingers parted her pouting lower lips and found the pearl within. Milly groaned aloud as a slick fingertip coaxed her clitoris out of its niche and gently stimulated it, making the juices gush from her.

'Such a dear little pussy!' Eva crooned, softly. 'I'm going to give it a nice big kiss!'

The teasing words set up a spiral of longing in Milly, so intense that by the time she felt the first touch of Eva's lips against her vulva she began to climax. Her body thrilled to the rhythmic waves of bliss and her lover, realising what was happening, drank thirstily at her brimming vulva as if she were trying to suck her dry.

After that Milly had stripped completely, letting the older woman caress her all over. She seemed to particularly favour her round, pert bottom. It wasn't long before the tide of desire started to flow in her again, and this time Eva did more than just stimulate her externally. The fingers that had played so exquisitely with her breasts and labia now ventured right inside her, slowly at first and just around the entrance, then inch by inch until Milly was squirming with arousal and silently begging her lover to penetrate her completely.

At the first long thrust of her digit, Milly sighed out

her relief and clenched tightly, making her lover chuckle. 'Such an eager little pussy!' she murmured. 'We shall stroke you, my pet, until you're purring with pleasure.'

It didn't take much 'stroking' to bring on a second orgasm, making Milly gasp and thrash with ecstasy as she was completely taken over by the sensations. Afterwards she was happy to lie in Eva's arms against her cotton-clad bosom. She had no curiosity about her lover's body, and somehow sensed that the woman had no desire to remove her own clothes, and so it had remained ever since. Although their love-making had progressed over the months, with Eva finding ever more ingenious ways to satisfy her beloved, she always remained fully clothed. They never discussed it, but Milly sensed that the poor woman hated her female form and would rather have been born a man.

'Here we are, darling. *Truite aux amandes* and some of those nice potatoes from the garden,' Eva announced, shaking Milly out of her reverie as she came in from the kitchen.

They ate well at Honeysuckle Cottage, since Eva loved to cook and produced some new treat every time. During the meal they drank white wine and, by the time they sat cuddling on the sofa before the fire, Milly was such in a mellow, sensual mood that she knew she would submit to her lover's caresses without complaint.

When there were tensions between them, as there had been over the last few weeks, Evadne seemed to demand total passivity from her partner during love-making. It was her way of keeping her in line, Milly decided. Sometimes she chafed against it and refused to submit, and then the proceedings could become rough. More than once the older woman had slapped her, but afterwards she had been so tearful and contrite that Milly could not bear it. Well tonight she

27

would do anything Eva wanted. The promise of a trip to Italy had sweetened her, turning her mood into one of happy expectation.

They made their way up to the bedroom and while Milly kicked off her shoes and lay down on the bed Eva lit the oil lamp. With careful hands the older woman rolled down Milly's stockings until her legs were bare and then began to caress her feet. Milly stretched voluptuously, enjoying the warm tingling that spread upwards past her knees to her thighs, making her feel beautifully relaxed. Her eyes were closed, so she didn't notice her lover reach over and pluck a long georgette scarf from the dresser.

Milly only became aware of what was happening when she felt her arms being lifted above her head and her wrists tightly bound. Her eyes snapped open in alarm. 'What on earth are you doing, Eva?'

'Ssh, darling! Don't be afraid. I'm tying you to the bed, sweetheart. Trust me, I know what I am doing. You will be my little dolly, and I shall play with you.'

Milly stared up into her brown eyes but they were dark and inscrutable. Somewhere deep inside her was a thrill of fear, but she hardly dared acknowledge it. This was her own dear, familiar Evadne. She wouldn't harm a hair of her head – or would she?

But then Milly began to remember how mean she had been to her tutor lately, sometimes refusing invitations to go to the cottage on the pretence of having to study for her exams while, in reality, she was seeing a young man. Had Eva found out about her deceptions? Was she going to punish her? As the ends of the scarf were tied to the bedhead Milly was disconcerted to find that the thought of being disciplined physically by her tutor was not altogether unpleasant.

'Now, you are entirely my plaything!' Eva said, but it was impossible to tell exactly what was behind that knowing smile. 'Just lie back and enjoy yourself, Milly dear, while I undress you. Let yourself go limp, just like a rag doll.'

Since she had no option, Milly did as she was told. First her tweed skirt was removed, then her petticoat. Eva unbuttoned her blouse but, since her arms were tied, could not remove it completely. It hung open, exposing her camisole which was also unbuttoned to display her naked breasts. Gently her knickers were pulled down over her thighs until her lower half was completely bare.

'Now I can do just what I like with you,' Eva whispered, her eyes gleaming bright in the mellow glow. Again Milly felt a sharp stab of fear that made her squirm inside, and she felt her clitoris start to throb urgently. What did her lover intend to do next?

For what seemed like ages Eva just sat there observing her, evidently enjoying the spectacle of her help-lessness. Then she produced Milly's own leather bag and began rummaging in it. 'You don't mind, do you? It's for your own good, precious.'

Mystified, Milly watched her take out her small cosmetic bag and open it. She withdrew the pot of lip-rouge, Scarlet Flame. It was only recently that Milly had begun to wear 'war-paint' as the male students called it, and then she reserved it for special occasions. Her mother would most definitely not approve. She watched curiously as Eva opened the small china pot to reveal the bright red sticky paste, then smeared some on her fingertip.

With her left hand she squeezed Milly's right breast, making the nipple stick out. Then she began to dab the rouge over it. When it was covered she did the other one. Milly could see herself in the wardrobe mirror and she giggled to see her pink nipples trans-formed into blatant red buttons. 'Now I really do look like a "scarlet woman!" Honestly, Evie, you do have some weird ideas!'

She remembered how Eva loved to make her wear outlandish combinations of clothes such as riding boots and camiknickers, or a boater and stockings with garters and nothing else. This game with cosmetics looked like being a variation on that theme.

But Evadne just smiled at her, wiping her fingers on the georgette scarf that still held Milly prisoner. She returned to her handbag and picked out her new box of face powder, opening it with a smile.

'I've watched you powdering your nose, precious. You like it, don't you? The softness of the puff against your face, the smell of the powder.' She lifted the lid and the familiar scent filled the room. Lifting up the inner compartment, Eva dabbed the swansdown puff in the pale beige powder letting a small cloud into the air.

Milly felt the soft touch of the puff against her cheeks and sighed. Just why her lover felt the need to make her up she had no idea, but there was something very soothing about it so she submitted gladly. The fluffy ball travelled down her neck to her shoulders and soon she realised that Eva intended to powder her all over her body, as if she were a baby. She dipped the swansdown into the powder again and began to flick it around her breasts, carefully avoiding her sticky nipples, then down around her stomach. It tickled her skin in a delightful, arousing manner that soon had her sighing with pleasure.

When Eva continued on down to her legs Milly spread her legs apart so that her sensitive inner thighs could benefit from the gentle stimulation. In the mirror she looked strange, pale and yellowish all over with the glaringly bright nipples rearing aggressively from her tumid breasts. She felt as if her body were being as finely tuned as a violin string, prepared for

some new experience, and her slightly fearful anticipation increased.

'Now, my little dolly, we are going to play a game
of Blind Girl's Buff.'

Milly saw the silk scarf in Eva's hand and knew she
was about to be blindfolded. A shiver went down her
spine when she realised how much more apprehensive she would feel being kept in the dark. But still
she did not resist. The scarf was bound tightly about
her head, and then she heard Eva opening drawers
and rummaging around, evidently with some new
surprise in mind. She felt exposed and vulnerable,
clinging to the belief that her tutor loved her dearly
but with just enough doubt at the back of her mind to
add spice to her situation.

Now Eva was brushing her shiny cap of hair, with
rhythmic, even strokes. After a while she let the brush
hairs caress her neck and on down to her breasts. The
slightly abrasive feeling against her tender flesh made
her shiver. Eva applied the hairbrush to the under-
sides of her breasts and then to her stomach, in a
circular motion. She brushed out her small, neat bush
of pubic hair and then passed on to the soft skin of
her inner thighs, making her squirm and squeal. 'Ooh,
Evie! That does feel ticklish!'

No reply came, but soon the brush was being put
to service on the soles of her feet, making her wriggle
even more. Then she could hear the lid of another pot
being unscrewed. The tension in the room increased
as she smelt something familiar, and eventually iden-
tified it as her rose-scented face cream. What on earth
was her lover planning to do with that?

Gentle fingers parted her labia and anointed her
inner lips with the cool cream, rubbing it in until all
her folds were thoroughly moistened and the nub of
her clitoris stood out firm and tingling. Eva probed
into her with a well-lubricated forefinger but did not

linger, proceeding to do the same with her rear entrance. At first Milly contracted her muscles tightly, unused to such familiarity, but as the soothing cream took effect she relaxed and allowed her lover's finger to penetrate her more deeply.

'There's a good little girl,' Evadne crooned, withdrawing her finger at last.

Milly lay in suspense, feeling loose and open back and front. She knew that Eva had been preparing her for something, but what? She could hear her fiddling around, and guessed that it would require implements of some kind. This wouldn't be the first time that her lover had done strange things to her naked body. Indulging her love of gastronomy, Eva had tried unsuccessfully to make blancmange moulds of her breasts at New Year, covered her belly with lemon pancakes on Shrove Tuesday and stuffed her pussy full of strawberries and cream after the May Ball.

This time, though, she sensed that things were different. Her legs were being lifted up, and her ankles tied to the foot of the bed with her thighs spread wide apart. For the first time Milly felt really frightened. 'What are you going to do?' she whispered.

'Never you mind, my sweet. You're going to enjoy this, I can promise you. And when you're happy, little dolly, Evadne is happy too. Just relax, now.'

Milly did her best, but it was difficult to feel at ease with her hands tied behind her head and her legs splayed open and immobile. She was at her lover's mercy now, and she knew it. When she felt the first touch of her oily hands on her pussy she couldn't help but flinch. Eva spoke in soothing tones, as if she were addressing a baby.

'There, there now. Easy does it. In we go!'

Something was being pushed in between her buttocks, something slick and smooth. She tried not to tighten up, but it felt strange. Slowly the soft, alien object was inserted into her and then, when it was securely lodged, she heard a pumping sound and her arse began to fill up. The sensation was extraordinary, but after a few seconds Milly found she really liked the feeling. She squeezed on the air-filled thing with her muscles and felt it give then spring back when she relaxed again.

'Lovely!' Eva murmured. 'Now the front. We'll soon have you completely filled up, darling.'

Something was being inserted into her pussy, something long and hard. Eva pushed it in up to the hilt and left it there for a few seconds. She seemed to be making adjustments. Milly felt some kind of cup being put over first one breast then the other, and then a sucking feeling at her nipples. At the same time she felt the bladder in her rectum begin to fill with air and whatever was inside her vagina started to move in and out.

Eva was obviously manipulating the instruments and it took her a while to get them synchronised, with a good rhythm going. At last she managed it, and Milly relaxed into the strangely sensual feelings that swept through her. Her front and back passages were being stimulated with perfect timing, the inflated bladder filling her arse as the probe reached the farthest depths of her pussy, and deflating as whatever Eva was using as a dildo was withdrawn. This to-ing and fro-ing, filling and emptying, was slow to begin with but soon gathered speed.

The procedure, bizarre as it was, soon evoked sensations of earthy delight throughout her lower regions, while her breasts were responding to the rhythmic suction on her nipples, increasing her arousal. Soon her whole body was caught up in the swirling ecstasy which was leading her on towards the ultimate gratification. 'What are you doing to me?'

she moaned, as the increase in her desire became almost unbearable. 'What are you using on me?'

'Ssh, don't you worry about anything. Just lie back and enjoy it,' came the soft reply.

The climax was not long in arriving. When she came, Milly writhed and twisted her spasming body, which only seemed to make her orgasm more violent, more prolonged. She was vaguely aware of her lover's encouraging chuckles, and the sudden acceleration of the stimulation which almost made her scream with the overloading of her senses.

When her own shuddering ecstasies subsided, Milly longed to flop down on the bed and ease her pained muscles. She sighed with relief as she felt her lover untie first her ankles and then her wrists, allowing her to move on to her side and curl up into a more comfortable position. No move was made to remove her blindfold, but she felt her chafed skin being gently treated with some ointment and then Eva's heavy form lay down on the mattress beside her, with her strong arms taking her into an embrace.

In a few seconds Milly was asleep. When she awoke it was early morning, and she was tucked naked in the bedclothes. Her blindfold had been removed. Eva was still lying at her side fully clothed. She was watching her awaken, with a smile on her face.

'Morning, dearest. I've been looking at you for at least an hour. You're so lovely when you're sleeping.'

Milly stretched and yawned, wondering why she felt so stiff. Then she remembered, and a blush crept into her cheeks. How strangely Evadne had made love to her yesterday, and with such mechanical ingenuity!

'I see you're remembering how it was for you last night,' her lover grinned, rising from the bed. 'Perhaps you'd like to see what brought you such bliss. I didn't want you to see it last night in case you were frightened and couldn't relax. But now you can see it all.'

Curious, Milly sat up in the big bed and watched her bring the things over from the dressing-table. She stared at the motley collection of rubber tubes and cups with disbelief. 'But what are they? Where did they come from?'

'They're surgical instruments. I borrowed them from one of the medics. Two breast pumps, some enema tubing and bulbs and a gynaecological probe. I thought you'd be amused to see them!'

But Milly felt rather nauseated. There was something just too weird about using objects intended for medical purposes to give sexual pleasure. She began to wonder, not for the first time, if her lover was entirely sane.

Eva noticed her distaste and hugged her. 'Don't worry, dear, there's nothing wrong in it. You enjoyed what I did, didn't you?'

'Yes, of course. But . . .'

'Well then, but give me no buts. I'd go to any lengths to make your lovely body quiver with pleasure. You know that, don't you dear?'

'Of course. But I'd rather we didn't do it in quite that way again, if you don't mind.'

'We shan't be able to. I have to hand these back today. Never mind, I'm sure there are a million other ways I can make you happy.'

'Oh yes, and we thought of one way last night.' Milly's face lit up as she remembered what they had decided on their riverside walk. 'We're going to Italy together! Oh Evie, I can't tell you how happy that makes me feel! To be in that wonderful sunny land, with that beautiful scenery and those kind, gay people! You're going to love it, Eva darling. And the best thing of all is that I'm going to see my dear godmother again!'

But, to her dismay, Evadne was scowling. 'I think

you've forgotten that I shall be going there solely for the Historical Monuments and Art Treasures.'

'That too, of course!' Milly tried to hug her, but her tutor's body was stiff and unyielding. For the first time it occurred to her that Evadne might be jealous of her love for Emma, the woman who had first taught her about life, and love.

Chapter Three

Milly was surprised at how relieved she was to be going away from Evadne for a week. The hot-house intensity of the older woman's passion was very wearing. It made her wonder how she was going to manage in Italy. At least her Aunt Emma would be there too.

First, though, she had to face her own mother. As Milly saw her waiting at Paddington station she was full of conflicting emotions. She was proud to be the daughter of Kitty Belfort, one of that brave band of suffragettes who had secured the vote for some women at least after the Great War. Yet she couldn't help wishing her mother had retired gracefully after that.

Kitty's life was still a frantic round of political activity and Milly knew that now she was expected to follow in her footsteps. But she couldn't be less like her mother in temperament and attitude, and resented any attempt to push her into the same mould. Nevertheless, she would have to face questioning about her future soon. Maybe her godmother could help her decide which path to take in life for, surely, that was one of her duties.

Milly suspected that she took after her feckless father, although she hadn't seem much of him since her parents had separated years ago. Being a lawyer he had drawn up a settlement, although he hadn't wriggled out of his responsibilities entirely, having supported his daughter through college after taking her side against her mother. Kitty saw herself as a champion of working women and had little time for 'blue-stockings'. As she descended from the train, however, Milly put aside all resentment and responded to her mother's welcoming smile.

In the hustle of getting themselves and the two suitcases into the waiting cab Milly had no time to observe how her mother was looking, but once she was sitting opposite her in the stuffy vehicle she was shocked to see her looking so down-at heel in a shabby coat and hand-knitted cloche hat, with shoes that had seen better days. She knew there was no hope of taking her in hand over her wardrobe, as Kitty Belfort believed she was above such trivialities as fashion. She was still an attractive woman, although her complexion bore no hint of powder, but her manner was very down-to-earth, gruff even at times, and she thought women's heads should not be filled with thoughts of romance but with practical matters.

'I was glad to hear you did well in your examinations, Milly,' she began, stiffly, obviously making an effort to overcome her prejudice against academic study.

'Thanks, Ma. I hope it was all worth it.'

'What are you going to do now? Look for teaching posts, I suppose.'

Milly had hoped for time to break the news of her Italian holiday to her mother. Still, there was no point in prevaricating. 'Actually, my tutor – who has become quite a friend – has invited me to visit Florence with her.'

Kitty's face darkened. 'And what's that all about, pray? Does she think you have the time to go gallivanting on the Continent?'

'Well, I thought I might visit Aunt Emma. She might be able to fix me up with some sort of job.' Her mother huffed, crossing her arms firmly over her chest and glaring out of the window at the slow-moving London traffic. Milly tried to mollify her. 'I know you think I'm not cut out for teaching, Ma, so I thought something else might be more suitable. Exactly what I'm afraid I don't know.'

'We always need secretaries,' Kitty said, shortly. Her daughter knew that 'We' meant that devoted band who had not rested on their laurels but were still campaigning.

Milly knew better than to refuse outright. 'I shall certainly consider that when I return from Florence. It might be useful to tide me over for a while.'

'Tide you over? What kind of attitude is that, my girl? We need someone with commitment and dedication, not the dilettante sort you find in West End offices nowadays!'

Milly sighed, wishing they could have persuaded the driver to open the roof of the taxi. The heat was stifling and, seated in close confinement with her mother, she was already perspiring. If it hadn't been for her luggage they could have travelled to Kennington on one of the open-topped buses. Her mother now lived in a terraced house south of the river with two other like-minded women, and Milly disliked the idea of staying in the cramped dark rooms that were so different from her digs in Cambridge, surrounded by lawns and trees. Still, in a week's time she would be setting out for sunny Italy, so she could afford to be cooped up for a week with a bunch of earnest women's rights campaigners. Milly was determined to behave well and not give her mother any cause for complaint while she was with her.

The other women were out when they arrived, so Milly was able to sit in the small living-room and drink tea with her mother in peace. It saddened her that there was an awkwardness between them. Since she had gone away to school at Cheltenham when she was twelve and then on to Girton, she had only seen her mother in the holidays. Even then she had often been left in the care of her nurse or godmother since Kitty was always off on business.

Her mother put down her cup with a determined air. 'Well my dear, you might be considered an adult woman now, but you still don't have the vote. Doesn't that infuriate you?'

'Not particularly,' Milly admitted. 'Until there are women standing for Parliament in droves I don't see that it will make a ha'porth of difference to the way the country is run.'

'But we have to start somewhere!' Kitty said, peevishly. 'Honestly, Milly, sometimes I feel ashamed to have you as a daughter. How I envy the wonderful Mrs Pankhurst! All three of her girls joined the Cause to fight alongside their mother.'

'I wish I could be more interested in politics for your sake, Ma.'

'Well what *are* you interested in, for heaven's sake?'

It was hardly possible to reply 'men, mostly' which would have been the truth but not one which her mother wanted to hear. 'Oh, I like art and music and books,' she said, vaguely.

'All very well if you have the leisure for them. But your father didn't want you educated to be a lady of leisure, Milly. He expects you to either take up some worthwhile occupation or marry some good, solid man who will take you in hand.'

'I don't want to be "taken in hand" mother. But

please, if I'm to stay here can't we call a truce? I worked really hard this term and now all I want to do is take a rest.'

'You don't know what hard work is!' her mother grumbled, but she poured her more tea and handed her the plate of scones so Milly knew she wasn't too angry with her.

Since her mother was busy as usual for most of the week, Milly spent a good deal of time visiting the museums and art galleries alone. She drew the gaze of many a good-looking young man, as well as some not-so-young ones, which pleased her even though she wasn't in a position to encourage any advances. Although Cambridge had provided her with many opportunities for love affairs she felt a new thrill at being out in the wide world, and the prospect of travelling abroad was even more exciting.

Milly felt it even more keenly when she set out to meet Evadne on the first leg of their long journey. She stood under the ornate black and gilt station clock with her mother, waiting for Evadne to appear. Kitty had taken the morning off to accompany her daughter, and although she was grateful she still worried about what she would make of her female lover.

'There she is!' Milly cried at last, waving to attract her tutor's attention.

Evadne came striding over wearing a beige alpaca jacket and white open-necked shirt with black twill trousers. She carried a straw boater and on the porter's trolley behind her was a shabby brown suitcase. Milly was ashamed of the way her heart sank to see her lover looking so uncompromisingly masculine. She forced a smile. 'Mother, this is Evadne Parker, my tutor.'

The two women shook hands stiffly and Milly could tell that they disliked each other on sight. If they were better acquainted they would get on, she told herself, since they were both champions of women's rights. Yet the antipathy between them had nothing to do with politics. Kitty's was the gut reaction of a mother who sensed that her only daughter was being preyed upon emotionally and sexually, while Eva resented that protective maternal instinct, preferring to see Milly as free to choose her own lovers. All this Milly understood at some gut level, although she preferred not to think any more about it.

'Come on, Milly, or we'll miss the train!' Eva said imperiously, after a few polite remarks.

Milly embraced her mother. 'I shall send you a postcard as soon as I arrive.'

'Give my best wishes to Emma, won't you? I am sure she will help if you get into any trouble, financial or otherwise. But if not, don't hesitate to wire me or your father.'

Much to Milly's surprise there were tears glistening in her mother's eyes as she turned away. Kitty did not often show her feelings and it was sometimes hard to believe that she had a heart beneath that stoical, practical exterior. Hurrying to the steaming train, Milly found Eva waiting impatiently by the door of their carriage.

The journey seemed interminable, but the sea was not too rough and by the time they reached Paris where they had to change trains Milly was in a kind of comfortable daze. They took a sleeping compartment to Florence, which was great fun. Milly had won top bunk at the toss of a coin, and when she awoke next morning and lifted a corner of the blind she was amazed by the brightness of the sunlight.

'Nearly there!' Eva told her, looking at her watch. Already they could hear the guard going down the corridor awakening the passengers in his Italian accent.

Milly was delighted to see Emma waiting on the

platform when they arrived. She threw herself into her godmother's arms and gave her a big hug.

'My, you are quite a young lady now!' Emma smiled, but her bright eyes soon looked past her god-daughter to the strange figure of Evadne. Her reaction was not the same as Kitty's had been, however. She put out her hand with an open smile saying, 'You must be Eva. I've heard so much about you from Milly's letters.'

They drove through the streets of Florence, which were already bustling with early-morning life, in a horse-drawn carriage. Milly marvelled at the beautiful old buildings in yellowish-pink stone, many of them adorned with coats of arms, the huge cathedral striped in white and green and the great sweeping square of the Signoria, lorded over by an impressive town hall resplendent with crenellations and tall bell tower.

Eventually they reached the outskirts of the city and then slowly ambled along country lanes between charming hills dotted with cypress and umbrella pines. Every so often a smallholding with a yard full of chickens and pigs would appear, surrounded by olive groves and small meadows where goats grazed. On the way Emma chatted amiably about life in Italy, and listened with polite attention to Evadne's account of life in Cambridge. Milly felt relieved. She had been afraid that the two women would dislike each other, especially after the way her mother had reacted, but now it looked as though they might be friends.

Seated opposite her godmother, Milly had a chance to examine her more closely. Emma had aged in the four years since they were last together, but she was ageing gracefully and had lost none of her old style. Today she wore a wide-brimmed hat with a blue grosgrain riband into which she had fixed a small posy of wild flowers. Her calf-length navy skirt and cream lace blouse were rather old-fashioned it was

43

true, but for life in the country they seemed very suitable, as did her stout-heeled brogues.

At last the horse ambled in through a pair of wrought-iron gates and up to an old villa which Milly knew belonged to the family of Marco Donelli, Emma's constant companion for the past ten years or so. He was there at the door to meet them, his ruddy face smiling broadly and his dark hair threaded with silver streaks. A slight thrill passed through Milly at the sight of him. She had always thought him extremely handsome, and his broken Italian accent and *olde worlde* manners only added to his charm.

As soon as they met he gave a low bow and kissed her hand, sending shivers of delight up her spine at the touch of those full, soft lips. 'Milly! How grown-up you are looking these days! I know you break many a young man's heart, yes? Now don't try to deny it!'

Milly glanced nervously at Evadne, who was pursing her lips in disapproval. When she introduced them Marco's manner was more circumspect. He took her hand, but did not kiss it, and she addressed him coldly. Milly felt dismayed. Since she hardly ever saw Evadne in the company of men it was easy to forget how much of a man-hater her lover was.

They went into the cool hallway, full of statues and plants in pots, then the two guests were shown to their adjoining bedrooms. A connecting door between them made it possible for midnight trysts to take place easily, much to Evadne's relief.

'I was so afraid we should be separated, you at one end of the house at me at the other,' she admitted, taking Milly into her arms and showering her with kisses the minute they were alone. 'But now I shall be able to creep in like a little mouse and make love to you without the rest of the household suspecting anything.'

It was certainly convenient, but Milly couldn't help wondering whether Emma had guessed at the nature of their relationship and ordered things to suit them. She knew that her godmother was very broad-minded and used to run an academy for young ladies in Florence whose curriculum was, to say the least, avant-garde. Although she had now retired, Emma was well in with certain sections of Florentine society and Milly was looking forward to making some useful connections during her stay.

While the maid was unpacking their cases, Emma took them on a tour of the old Tuscan farmhouse. Charming as it was, Milly sensed a certain restlessness about Evadne which boded ill. After lunch, which they took on a shady terrace overlooking the vineyard, Eva said she would go upstairs for a 'siesta' and obviously expected Milly to go with her. But, to her lover's obvious chagrin, she preferred to talk with her godmother alone.

In the quiet sitting-room Emma at last faced Milly with the truth about her relationship with her tutor. 'I know you are lovers, Milly dear,' she said, with unabashed frankness. 'And I've no wish to pass judgement of any kind, but are you perfectly happy with Evadne?'

'I was,' Milly asserted with a sigh. 'But just lately things have become more difficult. She hates me having other lovers.'

'Male lovers?'

'Yes. I told her at the start that I would not stop having men friends and she said she could not stop me. But she minds terribly, and I feel so guilty.'

Emma took her hand and squeezed it. 'You are still young, my dear, and very pretty. You have the right to enjoy yourself with whoever you choose. If Evadne cannot accept that then she is in the wrong to imagine that she can steal your youth from you.'

'Aunt Em, if I were one of the girls at your Academy, how would you advise me?'

She released her hand with a sigh. 'I'd probably advise you to have no more to do with that woman. But it would be the same if it were a man. Where there is an imbalance in love, there cannot be true happiness for both parties. And I suspect you don't love her, am I right?'

Milly felt awkward. Her godmother had the knack of asking the very questions that, if answered truthfully, would lay bare her soul. 'I'm very fond of her,' she hedged.

'And does she satisfy you physically?'

Milly knew she need not be embarrassed about speaking freely to a woman of the world like Emma Longmore. Yet she was still diffident. 'Most of the time, yes.'

'But you prefer the love-making of young men?'

'It seems more . . . dangerous. And that makes it more thrilling. But I have rarely spent much time alone with men. In Cambridge we used to go out in a foursome, my friend Caroline and I with two male companions.' Suddenly she remembered the photographs she still had in her bag. She handed one to Emma. 'We used to have such fun together! See what high jinks we used to get up to. This is our feminist version of the *Déjeuner sur l'Herbe*.'

Emma's eyes twinkled with amusement when she saw it. 'How splendid! But I'll hazard a guess you haven't shown this to your mother, staunch feminist as she is.'

Milly giggled. 'Oh no! Ma thinks my time at Cambridge was spent exclusively in study!'

Emma smiled wryly. 'You have a right to further your education in any way you choose, Milly. I have always maintained that, as you know.'

They began to chat about what the future might

hold for Milly, a subject which she usually found depressing. However, Emma had some interesting ideas. 'If you'll let me keep this photograph I might be able to get you some modelling work on the strength of it.'

'Modelling? For the camera?'

'Yes. Marco has some friends who are photographers, and some of them are also involved with cinematography. Nowadays you never know where the career of a pretty girl like you may take her in that field.'

'You mean, making films?'

Suddenly Milly was very excited. She loved going to the pictures, and had pinned photographs of her favourite Hollywood star, Douglas Fairbanks, to the walls of her Cambridge room.

'I can't promise anything, mind,' Emma cautioned. 'But I'll do my best.'

The next few days were spent getting acclimatised. Once she was used to the heat, Milly was glad to take the carriage, led by its ambling horse, into Florence for the day and see the sights with Evadne who, armed with a Baedeker, was a mine of information about the Renaissance. Yet when they returned to the *Villa Donelli* for the evening meal, Milly could sense that her lover was dissatisfied.

'Your godmother is very hospitable,' she said at last. 'But I find the journey back and forth wearying, and the stillness of the countryside tedious. I should prefer us to find some small *pensione* in the city.'

Milly was unhappy about this. She loved the old villa and the cosy evening meals in the company of Emma and Marco. 'Evie, why don't you take a room by yourself?' she suggested. 'I'm sure you don't want to be with me every minute of the day, and you would be welcome to visit me at any time. I know you wish to make a more intensive study of the art and architecture than I do, so it seems only right that you should be in the heart of the city.'

The relief on Evadne's face was plain to see. 'Are you sure you don't mind?'

'Not at all. Let us make some enquiries and see if we can't find you somewhere nice.'

Milly suspected that Eva would be glad not to have to make conversation with Marco any more. The hostility between them had only been increasing, and some of their interchange at dinner had grown quite heated. More disconcerting was the thought that perhaps Eva was tiring of her, too. The heat had made her listless at night, and she had not responded to her lover's attentions with her usual enthusiasm.

Or was it she who was tiring of Evadne? One thing was certain, she was enjoying Emma's company far more than that of her lover.

Once Eva was installed in the *Pensione Buonarroti* Milly felt a sense of freedom envelope her. She sensed that Emma and Marco did too. They promptly invited her to accompany them into town in the evening since they had been invited to a 'Baby Party'.

'Everyone comes in baby clothes, with rattles and so forth,' Emma explained. 'It will be such fun! I have a frilly bonnet, lacy socks and a girl's flouncy dress that will do for you, my dear.'

The party was held in a rather grand mansion overlooking the river Arno. It was a glorious evening, and the guests were spilling out on to the vine-covered terrace when Milly arrived, feeling very self-conscious in her silly costume. She soon realised that everyone was in the same boat, some of the men looking utterly ridiculous in makeshift romper suits, nappies and short trousers.

The Italian equivalent of champagne was flowing freely, and soon Milly was joining in the most infantile of games. Their host strung baby's bottles filled with the sparkling stuff from the loggia beams and they had to compete in a version of apple-bobbing, vying in pairs to get the teat into their mouths with their hands behind their backs. Milly suddenly found herself face to face with a good-looking young man who introduced himself as Enzo, and her heart quickened its pace when she realised that they were to be partners in this absurd game.

'No cheating, now!' he grinned at her, dark eyes flashing.

Once they were under starter's orders Milly went for the teat with her mouth open and found herself clashing with Enzo's equally eager lips time and again. Lost in the frenzy of the game she hardly noticed when his mouth snatched kisses from hers. Eventually she got her lips around the elusive rubber before him, and sucked down the sweet wine of triumph.

'Oh you are a rapacious woman, Milly!' he laughed. 'So hungry for it, so greedy!'

'It's only a game!' she replied, smiling archly.

'I think you like playing games, yes?'

'Try me!' she giggled.

'I know a game for two players, but it must be performed in private. Shall we find a quiet corner to play it in, Milly?'

She looked around and saw Emma and Marco engrossed in talking to another couple. They would not miss her for half an hour or so. Milly felt a strong urge for some intimate male company. It was almost a month since she'd made love with a man, and her libido had been fuelled by all that sparkling wine. Nodding mischievously, she let Enzo take her by the hand and lead her through the merrymakers into the garden. His footsteps led unerringly to a small enclosed summer-house at the end of the garden, near the river.

'Let us hope it is not already occupied!' he whispered.

They were in luck, the place was empty. Enzo led her inside and turned the key of the door behind them. There was a collection of battered furniture inside and they were soon sitting on a sofa which had faded upholstery but was otherwise in order. Milly giggled.

'What is it?' Enzo asked.

'I was just thinking how ridiculous we looked, me showing my frilly knickers and you in that nappy!'

'Would you rather we removed our clothes? It is better for the game I had in mind.'

'I'll tell you what, why don't we play "Doctors and Nurses"? You may be doctor first, and examine me, then I shall be nurse and change your nappy.'

Enzo's handsome face broke into a smile of complicity. 'Excellent! I see you have a good imagination, Milly, as well as a healthy appetite. What a splendid young woman you are!'

She lay back compliantly and felt a shiver of anticipation pass through her as she looked up into his liquid brown eyes, that were glinting with wickedness. His hands pulled up her short skirt and began to pull down her knickers with a frown. 'Now let me see what kind of creature we have here ... Hm, a very furry one, I think.'

Milly giggled as his fingers probed into the hot, damp crevice of her sex. She squirmed against him, feeling her clitoris grow hard against his stiff digit. The stimulation was making her juices start to flow, flooding her vulva.

'Well now, we are quickly excited aren't we? I can see that someone has played this particular game before!' His finger slipped easily in through her entrance. 'Oh yes indeed!'

Her desire for satisfaction was growing urgent, and

she wriggled her hips in a bid to increase the friction. Enzo grinned, pulling her knickers right down over her knees so she could open her thighs wider and he could get his finger right inside her. Then he began to plunge it in and out with ever-increasing speed, making her thrash and moan with growing lust. It felt so good to have a man making love to her again, with all that aggressive fire and his cock no doubt rearing uncontrollably beneath that silly nappy.

Milly couldn't help wondering what his organ would look like, and the very thought of seeing it, playing with it, maybe even licking it, aroused her to fever pitch. She sighed with relief as her clitoris throbbed with rhythmic glee, taking her into the last, delicious stage before orgasm when she was all aglow with sexual heat and awash with lubricating fluids. She could feel her nipples sticking out like jujubes and the fact that it was impossible for Enzo to reach them beneath her tight-fitting dress paradoxically increased her arousal. She could feel them straining against the organza, which rubbed against their delicate skin whenever she moved her torso.

'What a sly little animal it is,' Enzo crooned in his seductive accent. 'So innocent to look at, and yet so experienced! This must be the rutting season for it is surely on heat!'

He was plunging into her with several fingers now, filling her vagina most satisfactorily. She clenched down hard on his invading hand and he gave a gasp of surprise. Then Milly felt the first thrills pass through her overheated flesh and gave out a whimper-like cry as they intensified into a pulsating welter of orgasmic bliss.

'Ah, definitely a randy little beast!' she heard Enzo say, somewhere on the dim margin of her awareness. He continued to stroke her labia gently and then, when she was almost back to normal, he bent his head and began to suck out her juices.

'Ah, yes that feels so good!' Milly said, to encourage him.

Not that he needed any encouragement. His licking of her grew more enthusiastic by the second, and soon she was well on the way to a second climax. Milly felt the hard tips of her breasts jutting through the thin material of her bodice. Taking the protruding nipples between her fingers and thumbs she proceeded to arouse herself more rapidly, and their combined efforts soon brought on the desired effect.

Enzo's tongue alternately probed inside her then flicked across her jutting clitoris, showing him to be well experienced in the art of pleasuring women. This time the first spasms came short and sharp, making her gasp first with surprise and then with satisfaction as they increased in strength and sensuality. At last, quite exhausted by such a surfeit of pleasure, Milly sank back against the padded upholstery.

'Now do not go to sleep on me!' Enzo warned, giving her a playful shake. 'You must play nursey next, remember?'

'Let me rest first!'

'Very well. But I really must remove this ridiculous baby cloth. It is making me itch, I am so hot. How a baby can bear it I don't know. Maybe that is why they are forever squalling.'

Milly sat up. 'Let me help with those pins.'

She struggled with the oversize nappy pins until they came undone and then she carefully unwrapped the folds of white cloth until he was free of them. His penis sprang up instantly, sturdily erect, from its curly mat of black hair. The organ was an attractive tawny colour, with a deep pink glans from which a few drops of pearly liquid were already seeping.

'Oh that is a fine one!' Milly smiled appreciatively, all her earlier weariness gone.

'You may inspect it closely,' Enzo invited, with a smile. 'My balls as well, if you wish. They are all quite open to you now Nurse. Do with them what you will.'

Tentatively she reached out with her right hand and began to fondle his sac, feeling the heavy testicles weigh against her palm. With her other hand she stroked the length of his cock and then encircled it with her thumb and forefinger, moving it slowly up and down. He groaned at the blood rushed to pump up his erection still further. Milly smiled at the weeping eye of his glans, and began to apply more friction until his prick was making impatient thrusts against her hand.

At last Enzo came in a series of fierce, hot spurts that flew half across the summer-house and landed on the dusty floor. He gasped and collapsed on to the sofa, breathing heavily.

'The organ seems to be working well,' she commented dryly. 'No need for further treatment, I think.'

She wiped him with the corner of his 'nappy' and then there came a fierce hammering on the door. A voice called in an upper class English accent, 'I say, who's in there? Let someone else have a turn, you rascals! I'll be damned if I'll let you hog this dinky little hideaway all night!'

Enzo grinned, pulling the corners of his nappy around him. 'Quick! The pins!' he whispered.

Not having had any experience at pinning napkins, Milly made a hash of it but at least it was enough to preserve his modesty as they made their exit. Pulling up her drawers, she followed him to the door. Outside she was surprised to see two men standing, one in a striped romper suit and the other in satin knickers. Both men had dummies strung around their necks.

'It's all yours!' said Enzo with a wink, not at all disconcerted by the fact that they were both male.

When they returned to the party, somewhat flushed, Milly was informed at once that her god-mother had been looking for her.

'Oh dear!' she thought, wondering if she was going to get into trouble. But then she caught sight of Emma coming towards her with a smile. 'Oh there you are, sweetheart! Marco and I thought we'd make our way back to the villa now, but if you prefer to make other arrangements . . .'

She glanced quizzically at Enzo. 'Alas, I do not live in Florence,' he said. 'I am here on a visit with my friends from Siena. I think I must go with them now.'

But Milly was not sorry that they must part like ships that pass in the night. She had enjoyed her little romp with him, but now she was ready to return to bed alone. After the hectic love-making she had experienced, first with Eva and now with Enzo, she was looking forward to a good night's rest all by herself for a change.

Chapter Four

*T*he day was nearing noon and Milly was lying in the olive grove outside the *Villa Donelli* with a flask of wine, a hunk of bread, cheese and some olives. Emma and Marco had set out very early for the market in Florence, but she had not felt like doing anything strenuous that day so she'd scrounged some lunch and was now reading *Three Weeks* by Elinor Glyn, which she had found in the Emma's library. It was about an affair of elicit passion in Venice and involved much rolling around on tiger skins.

Suddenly she became aware that she was being watched. A tousle-headed young man who she'd noticed before, working on the land, was standing half-hidden behind a gnarled trunk and clearly couldn't take his eyes off her. She smiled at him saying, in her halting Italian, '*Buon giorno.*'

The man came out slowly from behind the tree, moving in a slinking, foxy fashion that set Milly's pulse racing. He had a dark complexion and long, tousled black hair that fell around his face in appealing tendrils. There was the shadow of a beard around his chin, and his lips were full and sensual, very red.

His body was stocky and well-developed, and he looked at her with the melting brown eyes of a spaniel.

'Mees Meelly?'

'Oh, you know my name!' she laughed in surprise.

He came and stood just in front of her, making no attempt to shake hands. 'I hear them call you. My name is Enrico.'

'Oh, Henry! That's your name in English. Well, Henry, how do you do?'

Milly held out her hand to him and, reluctantly, he wiped his right hand on his grimy ragged trousers then took it. She could feel the hard calluses on his fingers, where he had worked with tools, but his palm was smooth and warm. Looking into those dark, absorbed eyes she felt a peculiarly exciting thrill, almost as if she were confronting a different species. This was a working man, a man of the soil. He really did seem to be a separate creature from the refined, sophisticated types she normally mixed with.

Milly saw him eyeing her impromptu lunch longingly. 'Would you like some?' she offered. He nodded circumspectly. 'It's all right, there's plenty here. Come and sit down.'

She patted the grass beside her and he squatted on his haunches. Taking up the flask he threw his head back and she watched him pour most of the remaining wine down his throat, the prominent Adam's apple moving up and down as he drank. He was fascinating to watch. Every movement seemed at once perfectly natural and strangely alien.

'Bread and cheese?' she offered, holding out the last hunk of each.

He grabbed them from her and crammed first the bread then the cheese into his mouth. 'Don't mind me!' she giggled. 'Just make yourself at home!'

'Co-*me*?'

He turned his naive, puzzled eyes towards her and

she felt ashamed for mocking him. She picked up the jar of olives and held it out, but he shook his head and made a throwing gesture. Puzzled she stared at him. He took one out of the jar and threw it into the air, then caught it in his mouth. Milly had a glimpse of his red tongue flashing out, and then he swallowed it. He pointed to her and made the throwing gesture again.

'Oh, you want me to throw them for you!'

She picked one of the black, sticky fruits out and held it delicately between her finger and thumb, then she tossed it up into the air. He opened his mouth wide, eyes concentrating hard on the olive, and bobbed his head as he caught it. His eyes gleamed mischievously at her as he made a great show of chewing it then spat the stone out.

Milly laughed and clapped her hands. Enrico took another olive and placed it between his teeth, baring his lips at her. He beckoned and pointed. Cautiously she drew near. What on earth did this wild man want her to do now? He made guttural noises, pointing urgently at the black fruit as it lodged between his teeth. Was she to take it out? She lifted her hand but he shook his head vigorously, and pointed to her mouth. His fingertip touched her lips briefly, tasting salty. At last she realised that he wanted her to take it from his mouth with hers.

Remembering the baby-bottle game at the party, and what that had led to, she hesitated. Did she want this dark, unruly man, who smelt of goats and hay and played with her like a daredevil child, to make love to her? Milly recognised the strong undercurrent of attraction that was linking them, like a catchy tune occupying both their minds, and knew that she did.

Gradually Milly's face drew nearer to his, near enough to smell the heady scent of wine on his breath and the crude, animal smells of his body. The heat of the sun was beginning to affect her and she felt her head swim as her lips approached his. The oily fruit sat there waiting to be plucked, making her feel like Eve being offered the apple, and a spicy thrill went through her. Putting her arms on his shoulders to steady herself, she opened her mouth and leant forward until her lips were touching his with the olive in between.

Carefully she levered the small fruit out with her tongue and flicked it into her mouth with a laugh of triumph. Before she could withdraw he was kissing her with crushing, urgent passion and she was moaning, collapsing against him, unable to help herself. They sank to the ground together, his rough hands pawing at her clothes. Oh God, he's going to rape me! Milly thought. This was not how she'd envisaged losing her virginity and she began to struggle.

But then his fingers were fumbling with the buttons of her blouse and in seconds he had freed the bounty within. His lips fastened hungrily on her nipples, sucking them as if his life depended on it and clawing them with cruel disregard. Milly moaned as the tingling bliss swept through her veins, evoking an equally strong response down below. While Enrico was fondling her pale breast with one hand his other hand was groping beneath her skirt, finding his way through the tangle of underwear, undoing buttons and opening her up to his exploring fingers.

Milly gasped as the callused hand swept up her naked thigh and found the hairy vee of her delta. He rubbed her briskly, making her wet and a little sore. Although her clitoris was swollen and throbbing she didn't feel ready for him inside, and she dreaded him forcing an entry. But then he suddenly withdrew his mouth from her breast and rolled her over, slapping playfully at her naked buttocks. Then his thick finger probed between them.

As Enrico continued to work his way into her arse Milly gasped and moaned, but she knew there was no use struggling or she would make matters worse. She felt uncomfortable, with the rough grass in her mouth and nose, and her breasts pressed against the hard ground beneath, but worse was the summary way in which her bottom was being invaded. He was stretching the delicate skin of her anus and, without any lubrication, she soon felt sore.

'You like thees?' he had the temerity to enquire.

'Not a lot,' she replied, with a grunt.

He must have misunderstood her, perhaps wilfully. Milly felt him pick up the discarded wine flask and start to insert it between her aching buttocks. She clenched her muscles to try and deter him and he stopped. 'You no like?' he asked, in genuine puzzlement.

'No, Enrico, I do not!'

His hand moved between her thighs and soon she felt his thick finger inside her pussy once more. She began to relax. 'Ah, that's better!'

But then his mouth started to bite at the flesh of her behind, and she yelped in surprised pain. 'Hey! Please don't do that!'

It was clear that Enrico had some strange ideas about love-making. A part of her was relishing it, loving the way he just acted out of blind instinct with none of the gentlemanly concern for her welfare that most of her other lovers had shown. But at least he was prepared to stop if she didn't like something. His mouth travelled down from her behind and she felt his tongue insinuate itself between her labia, but her clitoris was out of reach. She tried to turn over, but he pinned her down again. Relieved that he was leaving her sore behind alone now, Milly relaxed again.

Enrico seemed to sense that he was not hitting the mark, because he yanked her up by the hips until she was on all fours and began to finger her clitoris while he continued to lick her from behind. This was more like it! Milly waggled her bottom in delight as she felt herself being titillated towards a climax. Her juices were starting to flow under the stimulation, mingling with his saliva in the fleshy channel of her pussy. If he made her come she would return the compliment, she decided, although she might prefer to satisfy him with her hand rather than put his penis into her mouth. It would almost certainly be as dirty and foul-smelling as the rest of him.

When her rustic lover put two fingers inside her and began to grope towards her breast with his other hand, Milly felt her arousal increase to the point where she knew a climax was imminent. She was tingling and expectant all over, taut as a wire, concentrating entirely on the thrilling sensations that were leading her towards the melting bliss of an orgasm. So absorbed was she that she didn't hear the approaching footsteps until it was too late.

'Milly! What on earth do you think you're doing!'

The booming voice was all too familiar. Enrico jumped off her like a startled cat, and Milly twisted round to see Evadne's enraged face staring down at her. Beneath the brim of her boater her eyes were bulging with fury, her cheeks a fiery red. Milly scrambled to her feet, pulling up her drawers and smoothing down her skirt, and then noticed that someone else was there, a sly-faced young woman who was grinning in mockery at her.

Milly was dimly aware that Enrico had sidled off into the olive grove. As soon as he was away from the scene, he broke into a run and was soon out of sight. Evadne was still regarding her with scorn. 'I've never witnessed such a disgraceful spectacle in my life! I came here to introduce you to a new friend of mine, but you have shocked me to the core. I can never forgive you for this.'

'I'm sorry, Evie. But how was I to know you'd suddenly appear like that?'

'You think that excuses you? The maid told me you were in the olive grove reading. What if she, or another of the servants, had come upon you as I just did? I don't suppose that crossed your mind, caught up as you were in your filthy lust for that . . . for that *creature*!'

But Milly was astonished to see the young woman put a soothing hand on Eva's arm. 'Don't be too hard on her, Evadne dear. I'm sure we can think of some way for her to make amends.'

'You're too soft, Rita,' Eva snorted. 'And you don't know her. This woman is an incorrigible slut. She'll let any man she fancies take liberties with her.'

Despite the insulting tone of Evadne's voice, Milly's curiosity was aroused about her relationship with this strange woman. Just who was this 'Rita' and how did she come to be so familiar with her lover? There was a coarse, sensual look to her face that was not unattractive, and her figure was voluptuous with a large bosom and small waist. It didn't take Milly long to work out that they must be lovers, and a strange mixture of relief and jealousy seized her.

'We'll just have to teach her a lesson then, won't we?' Rita insisted with a knowing smile.

'I think you're right.'

The two women closed in on her and, before Milly realised what they were up to, they had her arms pinioned. 'Come on!' Eva grunted. 'Let's take her into the barn.'

They then frog-marched her towards the old barn that stood on the edge of the olive grove. Inside it was dark, with just a few rays of sunlight penetrating through cracks in the roof and walls. There was a pile of hay kept there for the animals and they threw her on to it, face down, quickly securing her wrists with a length of rope nearby.

'What are you doing?' Milly asked, scared but intrigued.

'Rita and I are going to punish you,' Evadne replied, severely.

'Then at least tell me who this Rita is!'

'We met in Florence. Unlike you, Milly, she shares my love of art and history so we have been spending quite a bit of time together.'

'Discussing the rival merits of Michelangelo and Donatello? I think not! You've been into her knickers, Evadne. Don't try to deny it.'

'Ah, so you're a jealous cat after all!' Eva sounded triumphant. 'Now you know how it feels, trollop, to have the one you adore making love to someone else. Not a pretty feeling either, is it?'

'I don't care! You could see how little I cared about you, Evadne, from the way you found me right now. Did you imagine I'd be moping for you, sighing for you?'

'How dare you!'

She felt a stinging blow across the back of her legs and realised that Eva had picked up a leather-thonged flail to assault her with.

'Come Eva, don't lose your temper. We must administer justice properly,' Rita said, in a soothing tone. 'Besides, I want my turn too. If she has insulted you, she has insulted me equally. I confess I was deeply shocked to see her engaged in such lewd behaviour.'

'Then let us secure her legs.'

Soon Milly lay in the hay trussed like a chicken, her heart beating wildly with fear and excitement. Just what did they intend to do to her?

'I think six lashes each, don't you?' Rita said,

62

answering her question. 'Shall we use an implement, or our bare hands?'

'She has a nice firm bottom. A good hand slapping would be very satisfactory, I feel. Or maybe a mixture of both?'

'Mm. The flail would be suitable. Or how about this winnowing fan? And do I see a harness hanging on the wall? Leather is perfect for flagellation. We might even find a whip lying around.'

Milly could hardly believe they would torment her so. What kind of a person was this Rita? She seemed even more zealous in exacting punishment than Evadne, who surely had more cause. Or was Rita jealous of her new lover's former attachment? Either way, it looked as if there was no way out of her predicament.

While she lay there with limbs tightly bound awaiting the inevitable chastisement, Milly's body was still burning and aching from Enrico's summary treatment of her tender parts. She was amazed to find that the more she pressed her mons into the warm hay the more she tingled with an excitement whose nature she could not deny. Her peasant lover had brought her to the very brink of orgasm before they were so rudely interrupted, and she still longed to be satisfied.

The two women stood behind her in the dark barn while Milly lay shaking with suspense. At last she heard Evadne say, 'You shall strike the first blow, my dear. But let me take down her drawers.'

Her lover had performed this same task dozens of times, yet now Milly shrank from the contact of her fingers as she eased the cotton garment over her rotund behind. She felt a brief, mocking caress and then Evadne rose to let Rita get at her. There were a few tense moments, during which Milly braced herself by clenching her *gluteus maximus* muscle as hard as she could, squeezing her buttocks tightly.

'Oh what lovely pert cheeks she has!' Rita said, her voice low and throaty. Then she gave them a sudden slap. The stinging blow made Milly's eyes smart, but before she could recover a second was delivered, and she gave an audible gasp.

'Ha! She is not quite so pert now!' Evadne chuckled. 'Why not try this, darling?'

Milly could not see what instrument Rita was using on her naked buttocks but she felt its sting keenly and her whole hindquarters began to throb and ache. Yet while the rear part of her was being sorely punished, she couldn't help noticing that the tingling in her groin was intensifying with each blow. She thrust her mons urgently into the hay, feeling its prickles mingle with her pubic hair, and just beneath she knew her clitoris was protruding stiffly from between her labia.

'My turn, I think!' she heard Evadne say, and braced herself for more flagellation. Yet even as she dreaded the excruciating sting of her hand or bite of the lash upon her exposed bottom, she knew that each savage stroke was bringing her nearer to ecstasy and her emotions were turned upside down. It seemed perverse to be enjoying such punishment, yet she could not deny that she was.

After three more slaps Milly was propelled helplessly into the dizzying sensuality of her climax, almost losing consciousness. She groaned aloud, hoping they would take her cries for agony rather than ecstasy. She was ashamed to admit that their intended punishment had turned into a reward. Scarcely aware of the remaining strokes she lay there immobile, heart beating loudly in her ears, until she heard Evadne say, 'I think we should just leave her here, to stew in her own juice. Come, Rita, time to return to Florence. We'll go back to that delightful restaurant we discovered last night, shall we? I'm dying to try their *osso buco*.'

.A swathe of sunlight fell across the hay when they opened the door. Milly lay prone and exhausted, listening to the distant cry of a cockerel and the nearer clucking of geese, until sleep overtook her. When she awoke it was dusk and the barn door was still open. Painfully Milly managed to roll over on to her back, but her limbs were still tied and ached where the ropes had chafed her wrists and ankles. She cried for help, and at last heard shouts and the sound of footsteps. Two male figures appeared at the door, one she recognised as Marco. When he saw she was all right he dismissed the servant and came to untie her bonds.

'My poor, dear girl. Who has done this to you? We returned an hour ago and have been searching for you ever since. Tell me who the villain was, and I will flog his hide!'

The irony made her giggle, but she sat up and rubbed her sore body with a wry grin. 'Actually it was Evadne.'

'Evadne? Your tutor? Why on earth would she do such a thing?'

'I think she was jealous.' Milly thought she had better not mention her dalliance with Enrico. 'She came with a new lover of hers, and they tied me up and beat me. It was to punish me for not being faithful to her in the past, I think.'

'What a vile woman! I disliked her on sight, Milly, I must admit. But I never thought her capable of such brutality. Tell me where she is staying and I will set the police on to her.'

'Oh no!' Milly seized his arm. 'Please don't. I expect I deserved it.'

Marco's face darkened. 'Do not say such a thing, Milly! You deserve nothing but kindness and affection. You are a sweet and lovely young woman, and . . .'

They were close, very close, and the atmosphere in the darkened barn was very intimate. Milly felt an overwhelming urge to make love with him, and she reached up and put her arm around his neck to draw him near. For a few seconds it looked as if he was going to give in to her. His eyes were gleaming with dark desire, and his mouth looked open and inviting as she gazed hungrily at it.

But when she began to move her lips towards his he leant back, holding her at arm's length. 'No, Milly!' he said, quietly. 'You have had a shock and you need to rest in your bed for a while. Let me carry you back to the house.'

Unresisting she let him take her in his arms. Leaning against his strong chest she closed her eyes and he carried her across the rough ground and in through the back door. Emma was surprised to see them, showing her concern by fussing round like a mother hen and insisting on helping her to bed. She tenderly washed her arms and legs, reminding her how she sometimes used to perform the same tasks when she lived with her as a little girl.

'Oh Aunt Em!' Milly said, falling into her open arms.

It was so comforting to snuggle up to Emma's ample bosom. Now she was glad that Marco had resisted her futile attempt at seduction, and she hoped that he would behave in the same way towards any woman who vamped him. The idea that he and Emma might be faithful to each other was appealingly romantic.

When she was safely tucked up in bed, Emma gently asked her what had happened that afternoon. Although Milly mentioned Enrico she said they had just been 'talking' when Evadne and her new lover had arrived and reacted in jealous fury. Emma shook her head, tut-tutting, and gave her god-daughter a hug.

'I'm sorry things have gone so wrong between you,' she sighed. 'But you know what they say about "a woman scorned". What you need, my dear, is a new diversion and I believe that may happen sooner than you think. But I'll tell you more in the morning, when you are not so weary. Now, shall I get Maria to bring you some supper on a tray, or do you wish to sleep?'

When Milly awoke next morning she remembered what Emma had said about a 'diversion' and at breakfast asked what it was about. She saw her godmother glance at Marco and he began to explain. 'I have a friend who is a photographer, Milly, and he is always looking for models. I thought you might like to meet him. We could go into Florence this afternoon.'

'Oh, I should like that!' she smiled, happily.

The humiliating events of the previous day were already fading, and as soon as Milly went out into the bright sunshine they had no more substance than a dream. She spent the morning reading in the vineyard, which was within sight of the house, as she didn't want to risk another encounter with Enrico. Although in some ways it had been exciting, his rough manner and unpredictable behaviour had taken her beyond the boundaries of what she expected from a man. Perhaps she needed to be rather more experienced in the ways of the world before she was able to handle someone like him.

After a brief siesta, Milly joined Emma and Marco for the trip to the city. When they arrived at the photographer's shop the window was full of staid portraits, wedding groups and First Communion pictures featuring little angels. Inside a pleasant young assistant greeted them warmly, and allowed them to go through into the back room which 'Signore' used

67

as a studio. Soon the man himself appeared and Milly was impressed by his dark, passionate eyes and shock of glossy black curls.

'Milly, this is my old friend Leo Venuti,' Marco smiled. 'He has seen the photograph you lent to Emma.'

'Oh!' Milly felt a slight flush in her cheeks. She hadn't realised how embarrassed she would be that her *risqué* photo had been seen by a total stranger.

He smiled at her very politely, however, and extended his hand. 'Miss Belfort – or may I call you Milly? I thought your photograph quite charming, and very witty too. Perhaps you would care to see some of my own more "artistic" work?'

Reassured, Milly allowed him to sit beside her on the sofa while he balanced a large album on his knee. With Emma and Marco looking over their shoulders, they leafed through the pages together. At first Milly was rather shocked to see the pictures of half-nude girls, often against backdrops of sylvan scenes, or lounging on the very sofa she was occupying. Sometimes there were several girls together, arranged in bathing scenes or engaged in their toilet. Evadne would love these, Milly thought with a pang of regret.

'I hope you find them tasteful,' Leo said, hesitantly.

'Oh yes, very!' Milly assured him.

'They are not unlike the photograph of yours that Marco showed me, I think.'

But Milly couldn't help thinking of those other, more explicitly sexual, photos that she also had in her bag. What would he think of them? The idea of making such pictures commercially, to be viewed by unknown men in secrecy, was very appealing in a wicked way.

'I should be very pleased if you'd consent to pose for me yourself, Milly,' he said at last. 'I am sure Emma will chaperone you if you feel the need. Give it some thought if you like. You do not have to decide at once.'

'Thank you, but I think my mind is already made up. I should be delighted to sit for you.' She looked round at her godmother, who was smiling her encouragement. 'And I think I shall be quite safe with you, Signor Venuti.'

'Splendid!' He closed the album and stood up. 'I confess I have been thinking about how I might arrange your sittings if you were to consent, and I've come up with some ideas that excite me. You will be remunerated, of course.'

He named a sum in lire. When Milly had it translated it into pounds, she was pleasantly surprised. 'What happens to these photographs?' she asked him.

'They are sold through various channels. Some go to gentlemen's clubs, some to individuals, some to the aristocracy for the men to peruse after dinner when the ladies are absent. You would be surprised at how large a market there is for erotica of various kinds.'

This set Milly's mind racing ahead. There could be a career for her in this, if she played her cards right. It would certainly be a lot more fun than school teaching!

She left the photographer's in high spirits, having made an appointment for the following afternoon. Later, when Emma asked if she were missing her 'friend' Milly realised that, on the contrary, she was feeling marvellously free. In a way she was glad that things had ended badly between them, since there was no possibility of Evadne trying to crawl back into her life again. Or, if she did, she would get very short shrift. Caroline had been right, she admitted to herself, their relationship had been an unhealthy one based on jealousy and possessiveness. She vowed never to get into such a destructive affair again, with man or woman.

When Milly next presented herself at the photographer's shop she was feeling excited at the prospect of posing in the nude. Marco had told her that Leo had connections with some film-makers and that they were always looking for new talent, so she had high hopes of being discovered some day. She was received courteously by Leo's assistant and asked to wait for him in the studio. On entering, she gave a gasp of surprise.

A corner of the room was arranged to look like a bathroom, with a tub and towel rail, bath mat and even a rubber duck! She heard a chuckle behind her and Leo entered, smiling.

'Milly! Good of you to get here so promptly. What do you think of my idea for a setting?'

'You want me to take a *bath*!'

'Not exactly. I want you to *look* as if you're taking a bath. There will be no water involved, I promise you, and you will be nude to the waist only. Now if you'd like to change behind that screen while I'm setting up the lights we can get on. I have an appointment at four.'

Stunned, Milly did as she was told, stripping to her knickers. She flung a robe around her shoulders as it was quite cool in the room, and emerged nervously to find Leo flooding the scene with two large lights on stands. He grinned at her, waving her towards the bath-tub which stood proudly on four lion's claws.

'Get in, my dear, make yourself comfortable. I will be a few minutes more yet.'

Milly spread the towelling robe in the bottom of the bath to give her something soft to lie on. She felt self-conscious at first, but Leo seemed so intent on getting his lighting right and his camera in focus that he obviously had no time to ogle her, so she soon relaxed.

'Now let me tell you what I'd like to do,' he began at last. 'First I shall take some views of you washing your arms. Let me see you pick up the sponge and . . . yes, that's the idea. Raise your arm high above your head and start to sponge your forearm . . . not too low, or you'll hide your breasts! Yes, that's better. Now, hold it!'

Milly held still with her arms above her head, showing the outline of her breasts to the camera. She knew the bath was hiding the lower part of her body, and only her torso was visible. Leo made her change position several times to get different angles on her breasts. Her nipples had hardened on exposure to the air and he seemed very pleased with the way they showed up in his viewfinder.

'Excellent!' he proclaimed at last. 'I can think of quite a few gentlemen who would enjoy such a sight, Milly. But now I would like you to change position entirely. Can you lean out of the bath towards the camera as if you were reaching for the rubber duck on the mat? I'd like a big smile, please, and your eyes looking up towards the camera.'

It took them a while to get the second pose right, since he wanted her breasts to bulge over the side of the bath, but if she knelt up then the top of her knickers became visible.

'Would you mind awfully rolling your underwear down a little?' Leo asked at last. 'Just until it's out of sight of the camera.'

'I'll take them right off if you like,' she offered, boldly. As the session progressed Milly was warming to Leo, and starting to regard him as a bit of a challenge. It didn't seem natural for a man to be taking pictures of semi-naked women without making any attempt to seduce them.

'That won't be necessary,' he commented dryly.

Eventually Leo had all the film he wanted and he waved her back behind the screen while he tidied up. Milly felt elated by what she had taken part in, and wanted to know how long she would have to wait to view the results.

'I should have the prints ready by tomorrow afternoon. Maybe you would like to do some more, if they are successful?'

'I should love it!'

'Very well,' he smiled, shaking her by the hand. 'It has been a pleasure to work with you, Milly. Please give my regards to Marco and your godmother.'

What a strange man he is, Milly thought as she waited in the front of the shop for Emma to arrive. The photographic session had been so business-like, not at all what she had expected. She had to admit to herself that she was a little disappointed that there hadn't been more opportunities for flirtation with the good-looking but aloof Leo Venuti.

A mother and her young son had gone through to the studio on the dot at four, and the shop assistant had given Milly a chair to sit on while she waited. He eyed her curiously while he pretended to sort through some packets, and she couldn't help responding to him with shy glances and little smiles. Does he know that I've been posing in the altogether, she wondered, and the thought sent a thrill through her. No matter how cool Leo might be about the matter, his handsome young assistant was behaving very differently.

Maybe he helps Leo develop the negatives, she thought, and her secret excitement increased. Next time she walked through the door of *Il Photografo Venuti* would that young man be looking at her with new eyes? She giggled at the thought.

Chapter Five

*L*eo told Marco that the photographs he had taken of Milly were the best he had ever done. There were three series, 'Bath time Beauty,' 'Intimate Moments', – which showed her primping at a dressing-table dressed only in her knickers – and 'Eve's Awakening', which had her wearing only a fig leaf. When Emma saw the pictures she beamed with delight.

'Milly, you have a real talent for modelling. Would you like to take it further?'

'How do you mean, Aunt Em?'

'Well, Leo is not the only photographer of Marco's acquaintance. He knows several others, specialising in various fields. Some of the work is very risqué, of course . . .'

She let her words trail away on an interrogative note, obviously unsure how her god-daughter would react. Milly decided it was time to show her the photographs she had secreted in her bag. She brought them out with a shy grin. 'Do you mean . . . more this sort of thing?'

When Emma glanced at the photos of Emma and

her friends in sexually provocative poses she gave a low chuckle. 'Well, I see you are several jumps ahead of me in this game, you little minx! My goodness, we know one or two gentlemen who would pay over the odds for photographs like this!'

'Really? I never gave it a second thought. We did it for our own amusement, that's all.'

'I can assure you that it would amuse many other people too. But this trade is obviously the very antithesis of respectable, so you must take care. I strongly advise you to use only those contacts which Marco can personally recommend. That is, if you really wish to pursue it.' Emma sighed. 'Your dear Mamma would heartily disapprove, of course.'

Milly frowned. 'She would disapprove of anything I did. Unless I became a staunch supporter of the Women's Movement, of course, and even then I am sure we would find things to disagree about.'

'Well you must make up your own mind, dear. I see no reason why you should not make some extra money at this while you are in Florence, at least. What you do after that is up to you.'

'You do not think it immoral, then?'

'Speaking personally, I do not find the idea of posing for such photographs in the least immoral. Men will always have a curiosity about such matters, and women too although they would die rather than admit it. My late husband had a collection of erotic drawings that was second to none, and photographs are merely the modern equivalent.'

Emma's words reminded Milly that she had once been married to Sir Henry Longmore, but when Milly was a girl her lover had been rakish Daniel Forbes, Lord Merton. She remembered how frosty they had sometimes been towards each other, and how she had once overheard them arguing. It was clear that her godmother was far happier with faithful, easy-going Marco.

The money she had earned from her work with Leo was deposited in her bank account, by arrangement with Marco's Florentine branch. Emma realised that she could build up her savings quite nicely. Her mother had instilled in her the virtue of being financially independent for as long as she possibly could. In Kitty's view, one became a 'Career Woman' or a 'Wife and Mother,' the first being infinitely preferable to the second. No other possibilities – such as 'Kept Woman' or, almost worse, 'Lady of Leisure' – were acceptable.

Once he heard that Milly was interested in doing some more work with photographers, Marco invited an old friend of his to dine at the villa. Georgie Barker was an ex-patriate Englishman who had emigrated to Italy to escape the 'Puritan Curse' as he called it. He was a florid-faced man in his fifties, who wore extravagant cravats and waistcoats and walked with a limp because he had been wounded in the war. When he heard that Milly had posed for Leo he gave a snort of a laugh. 'I thought that old bugger only took boys' arses – pun intended!'

Then Milly realised why Leo had not made a pass at her and she felt foolish for ever imagining that he might.

When Georgie produced his photograph album after dinner and invited Milly to leaf through it, she was intrigued at once. She soon realised how different they were from Leo's 'artistic' shots. For one thing they showed several models at once, not just in tableaux but touching each other intimately. There were couples of men and women, foursomes, girls with girls and boys with boys. It was obvious that *Saucy Snaps*, as Georgie's company was called, specialised in even more racy photographs.

Although none of the pictures showed outright intercourse taking place they were very titillating and Milly could see why they sold like hot cakes in the international market.

'They go down very well in America too,' Georgie said, proudly. 'And we're starting to sell to the Far East, although the market needs developing there.'

He talked about it as if it were any other business which to him, of course, it was. Milly couldn't help being impressed when she heard that he paid his models three times what she had been getting from Leo. When, at the end of the evening, she was asked if she wished to join his 'stable' of young models, she agreed at once.

'Excellent! I can tell that you are very photogenic, Milly. The camera will love you, and so will my customers!'

It turned out that Georgie used a room in his own house as a studio, and he suggested Milly might go along for her first session the following afternoon. She was delighted when he promised to invite his other young models to dine with them afterwards, giving her a chance to get to know them. The thought of posing in the nude with complete strangers, and even performing intimate acts with them, was daunting. Yet it was very alluring, too.

Georgie lived in a fine old house on the *Via del Corso*, part of which he rented from an illustrious family that had fallen on hard times. Inside the heavy oak door there was a charming courtyard with a stained glass roof and fountain. Marco and Emma went off on business of their own, promising to return at eleven, and a servant led Milly upstairs to Georgie's quarters, which were furnished with Renaissance antiques and Persian rugs. She was introduced to a young Italian called Bruno and a German girl called

Lotte, both very good-looking. They smiled and shook Milly's hand in a very welcoming manner.

'Bruno and Lotte are used to working together, and they will help you and Carlo to settle into the work,' Georgie told her. He looked at his watch. 'Where is the boy? I told him to be here at four on the dot.'

The distant jangle of the doorbell told them that the tardy Carlo had just arrived. Milly waited with bated breath to see what kind of partner she had been assigned. When he walked into the room she gave an involuntary gasp of recognition.

'Do you two know each other already?' Georgie asked with amusement.

'Yes, he's Leo's assistant!' Milly blurted out.

The young man gave a shy smile. 'Hullo, Milly. I thought you would be surprised to see me. I work for Georgie on my free afternoons and in the evenings.'

'Does Leo know?' she couldn't help asking.

'No. But what I do in my spare time is up to me, isn't it? It's no great secret. I would tell him if he asked. But so far he has never enquired.'

'Well, it's quite nice to see a familiar face anyway,' Milly declared. It was true, much of her earlier nervousness had been dissipated.

'Right, down to business lads and lassies!' Georgie said, briskly. 'Follow me, if you please.'

He led the way from the drawing-room into the adjacent studio, where all kinds of theatrical-looking props were stacked against the walls. Milly noticed at once that there were no screens to change behind, but then realised that there was no point since they would all be seeing each other in the nude. Her apprehension returned now she was on the brink of the action. What if her body were not considered attractive enough? What if she could not bear to be touched by the others, or developed scruples?

But soon the combination of Georgie's matter-of-fact instructions and the merry quips of the other models put her at her ease. They all stripped, leaving their clothes on some chairs, and stepped on to the dais where assorted chairs had been left in casual array. Milly felt very self-conscious standing there in the altogether, and clasped her hands in front of her in a vain attempt to hide her pubis from view.

'Now I want you all to warm each other up,' Georgie told them. 'Give your partner a nice big hug and rub their back and chest to get the circulation going.'

Milly allowed herself to be embraced by Carlo's brawny arms. He looked like he was of peasant stock, being heavily muscled even though he worked at a non-manual job. 'Don't worry, Milly,' he whispered in her ear. 'You need not be embarrassed. You are among friends.'

She giggled as he began to rub her back vigorously and was soon following suit. Then she attacked his hairy chest while he put one hand on the top of her chest and the other on her stomach, rubbing in opposite directions. 'You like this?' he grinned.

'It's very . . . invigorating!'

Strangely enough the mutual friction did seem to break the ice and by the time they drew apart Milly was glowing and relaxed. She sat down on a velvet-covered chair with bow legs and the others also took their seats to listen to Georgie's instructions.

'What I had in mind this time was a Roman orgy,' he began.

'Oh, *wunderbar*!' Lotte grinned at once. 'Do we drink lots of wine? Who will be ze eunuchs?'

'Lotte, you are so unromantic!' Bruno chuckled.

'Now children, don't squabble!' Georgie grinned. 'See what magnificent props I have for you.'

He held up some togas which, he assured them, would be worn for maximum exposure. There were fat bunches of grapes, laurel wreaths and magnificent gold and silver goblets.

'I borrowed these fancy cups from downstairs,' he admitted. 'So do take care of them. They're seventeenth-century, and worth a fortune.' He held up two of the wreaths. 'Now then, who wants to be crowned King or Queen of the May?'

When each of their heads was swathed in laurel they began to arrange their togas. Lotte showed Milly how to pull one shoulder right down so that her left breast was exposed.

'Such a nice bosom!' the German girl smiled, stroking it as softly as one might a kitten.

She had a magnificent bust herself, with breasts that rose steeply from her broad chest and were tipped with sturdy rose-coloured nipples. Lotte lay herself down on the long, low couch that the men had pulled into the centre of the dais and pulled her toga apart so that her golden bush was visible at the top of her long, shapely legs. 'Will that do?' she grinned, flapping her eyelashes at Georgie who was nevertheless completely unmoved by her vampishness.

'That's fine. Bruno, I want you sitting on the end with your dick showing, that's it. Now dangle that bunch of grapes over Lotte's mouth. Open your mouth Lotte, get into the spirit of the thing for heaven's sake or we're all wasting our time! Now Bruno, with your other hand I want you to touch her down below. That's right, perfect!'

'Where's the *vino*?' Lotte asked. 'I'll soon get into the spirit if you pour some of that down me!'

The atmosphere in Georgie's studio was so different from that in Leo's that it took some getting used to. Milly hung back, unsure how to behave, until Georgie's voice rang out in her direction. 'Come on, Milly, your turn now. I want you to lie on the floor in front of the couch. You're going to be looking up at the other two enviously. Raise your left knee and let your toga fall open, casual-like. Yes, that's the idea.'

Georgie took several shots of the scene. It was clear that he envisaged making some kind of story out of the photographs, like a series of movie stills. Milly was supposed to look like a gooseberry at the beginning but would gradually be allowed to join in the fun. The second shot had her looking up in surprise as Carlo straddled her, waving another bunch of grapes.

'All right, now squeeze those grapes over the girls' breasts!' Georgie told them.

Milly squirmed and giggled as the juice fell down her cleavage, but once Carlo was given the order to lick it off she threw her head back in sensual enjoyment and quite forgot about the camera as her partner licked and sucked at her burgeoning nipples.

'Wonderful! Now we are cooking. Time for some wine, I think.'

Georgie soon had them drinking from the magnificent cups and then bade the girls dip their breasts in them and offer their dripping nipples to the men once more. Milly began to wonder how far they would go, and she felt quite disappointed when Georgie called a halt to the proceedings. When she looked up at Carlo's flushed face, and saw the extent of his erection peeping from the folds of his toga, a shudder of desire passed through her and she wondered how she was going to last through the evening in her frustrated state.

The two women were shown to the bathroom at the end of the corridor where there was a steaming hot bath already drawn, sweet-scented soap and fluffy towels. Lotte seemed very friendly towards her as they got into the tub together, and was soon offering to soap her back.

'You turn around now, Milly,' she told her, once she had the soap in her hand.

Milly did so and was soon closing her eyes in bliss as her new friend massaged the creamy lather into her back. She seemed to take a long time over it. But then she felt those slick palms moving round to the front of her body and she moaned with delight as the German girl began to give her bosom equally thorough treatment, squeezing her breasts gently as she soaped them and stimulating her nipples between fingers and thumbs.

'You like?' she murmured just behind her ear, going on to nuzzle the skin at the back of Milly's neck which always increased her ardour.

'Mm, yes! I was feeling so frustrated after that session,' Milly sighed.

'Me too. Georgie never lets us go all the way with the men in front of the camera. Although sometimes we take it further by ourselves!'

Lotte's right hand was down below the waterline now, tangling with the seaweedy strands of Milly's pubic hair. 'Come,' she whispered, lifting up her bottom with strong hands. 'You get on to my lap, so.'

Soon Milly found herself lying over the other girl's thighs with her body half out of the water, like a stranded whale. Lotte replenished her supply of soapy foam and began to explore between the swollen lips of her pussy. Realising that she was going to be satisfied after all, Milly let out a long sigh and opened her thighs wide.

Keyed up as she was, it didn't take Milly long to obtain the gratification she craved. Almost as soon as Lotte's long fingers entered her hungry quim she felt a sudden intensification of the throbbing in her clitoris and a few strokes with a lubricated finger brought her to an overwhelming climax. She thrashed around in the throes of her ecstasy, making violent waves and spilling some of the bath water in the process, but Lotte only laughed. 'Oh, you are such a passionate creature, Milly!'

When she had recovered, Milly got out of the bath and rubbed herself dry then got back into her clothes, but Lotte still languished in the warm water. As Milly prepared to leave she called out, casually, 'Oh, send Bruno in now, would you? Tell him I want *my* back washed!'

Irrational though she was being, Milly resented the fact that Lotte was going to have a romp with her partner. She would have preferred to take a bath with Bruno or Carlo herself, being rather tired of making love with women. She was grateful to Lotte for relieving her frustration, of course. But she hadn't had a good taste of penis for a long while now – her brief interlude with Enrico hardly counted – and she longed to experience once again the pleasures of fellatio with a fine, meaty cock in her hand.

While Bruno obeyed the summons to the bathroom with alacrity, Milly was left in the company of Georgie and Carlo. They made polite conversation for a while, which seemed strange after the activities they'd been engaged in earlier, and when the other guests started to arrive Milly soon found herself surrounded by bright young things of both sexes and several nationalities. A cosmopolitan air prevailed as she was introduced to 'Jacques from France, Hilda from Holland, Nico from Greece' and so on, until her head was whirling.

Eventually she counted nine new guests, all very good-looking and with friendly dispositions. They were united by a secret bond, which made them all very familiar with each other. Milly noticed how readily they touched each other, kissed and hugged. She began to feel as if she were part of one big, happy family and it was a very nice feeling indeed.

Promptly at eight they all went into the large dining-room where the table was set for fourteen. They made a merry party, with jokes being told in one language and translated into other languages all down the table. At the head sat Georgie, very much in command, and when the meal was drawing to an end he stood up, glass in hand, and proposed a toast, 'To the newest member of our little company: Milly, from England!'

'Milly from England!' came the resounding response.

'We don't ask our novices to give speeches,' Georgie began. 'But we do require that you take part in a special ceremony of initiation. It's a kind of party game really. It helps you to get to know people . . .' At this there were sniggers all round the table, which he silenced with a frown. 'And I think you will enjoy it, too. Carlo, the blindfold!'

She was startled when a thick, black scarf was tied over her eyes. Was this to be a game of Blind Man's Buff? Somehow she didn't think so. There was a great deal of giggling going on as she was led away from her chair. She heard them clearing away the dishes and cutlery, then she was helped up on to the table top by willing hands.

'Now kneel down,' she heard Georgie say at her side. 'Don't worry, there are people all round you so you shan't fall. Good! Now then, you shall choose your first victim. Names into the hat, fellows.'

There was more giggling and scuffling, then Milly's hand was guided into a hat filled with folded scraps of paper. She took one out as instructed. There was a pregnant silence and then an outbreak of whispers and giggles. 'Lucky fellow!' she heard a girl's voice say nearby. 'He'll have the best of her tongue, before she gets tired!'

The words fired Milly's imagination and when she

83

heard someone climb up on to the table just in front of her she grew even more excited. Georgie began to explain what she had to do in his deep, authoritative voice. 'Now my dear, you are going to have to guess the identity of this young man, whose name you have just pulled out of the hat. But I'm afraid the only clue you will have is the taste of his member. If you still cannot guess his name after you have used your tongue on him, we may give you a clue. Oh, I nearly forgot: hands behind your back! We trust you not to use them and we shall not tie them unless you misbehave.'

A warm flush of excitement filled Milly from head to toe as she contemplated doing what she had been longing to do earlier. She did not flinch from performing fellatio in front of the others since she had done it before with her friends and, besides, she knew that she would probably be working with them all sooner or later. It seemed as good a way as any to break the ice. Obediently she interlaced her fingers behind her back and half opened her mouth, ready to receive the lucky man's organ.

The feel of it surprised her as it knocked awkwardly against her cheek with eager force, like a blow from a padded hammer. A small cheer went round the table as the man realigned it and she enveloped the glans with her lips. Her tongue flicked into the groove where a drop of salty liquid resided and she sighed with the pleasure of it. She opened wider and slowly the long, thick prick was fed into her willing mouth, the top of the hard shaft rubbing against the roof of her mouth while she licked the underside with her tongue.

A loud groan told her that the anonymous male was enjoying it just as much as she was and, encouraged, she moved her head rapidly back and forth so that she could tongue the length of him more vigorously. The spectators quickly receded from her mind so that all she was aware of was the lusty cock and the man it was attached to, building up her own picture of him that probably had nothing to do with reality. She had entirely forgotten the point of the 'game,' believing that she was simply engaged in bringing her partner to a climax by the fastest possible route. So it came as a shock suddenly to hear Georgie's voice in her ear saying, 'Have you guessed the name of the man you are so expertly pleasuring, my dear?'

With her mouth full of solid, virile flesh, Milly could not possibly reply.

Someone nearby began softly whistling. It was a tune Milly recognised, though she could not give a name to it at first. Then the penny dropped: of course, the *Marseillaise!* The penis was pulled from her mouth and she hazarded a guess. 'Could it be . . . Jacques?'

A roar went all round the table, accompanied by sporadic applause. Georgie congratulated her, but before she had time to bask in her glory another name was drawn from the hat and a second phallus submitted to the lip-test. This one was long, thin and sweetly scented with a slightly soapy taste. Milly began to ponder on its owner's identity straight away. She had a hunch that he might be Italian. Could it be Carlo? No, his dick was quite short and thick she remembered. There was only one other Italian man and that was Bruno. Yes, she fancied that his organ's dimensions were similar to this. And perhaps it had that distinctive flavour because it had recently been in the bath with Lotte.

Milly moved her head back quickly so that the penis fell from her lips and said, 'I think this is Bruno!'

The laughter that spread round the table this time was knowing, suggestive. Milly knew they all thought she was better acquainted with Bruno's member because she had encountered it before. She blushed, wishing she had waited longer before identifying it. And, judging from the disappointed groan that issued from Bruno's lips, he wished she had too!

Milly calculated that she had three more to identify, and as the third erect cock was placed against her lips she mentally reviewed the candidates. Did this one belong to Hans, Nico or Carlo? There was a certain familiarity about it, she decided. Something about the smell or feel of it against her. Yes, she was sure she had been close to this organ before, so that could only mean that it was attached to her partner in that afternoon's proceedings.

'Carlo!' she announced, when she had given it a thorough tasting on all sides.

'Three out of three correct,' she heard Georgie say. 'Remarkable!'

But her luck did not last, neither could her powers of deduction prevent her from guessing the last two wrongly. She attributed the sturdy, circumcised member to Hans but it turned out to be Nico's. Although the last to present himself could only have been Hans, by process of elimination, he was allowed to have his turn and she gave his small, thick penis a good, long sucking before triumphantly announcing his name to loud applause.

'Well done, Milly. Now we shall remove the blind-fold,' Georgie said.

She blinked when the scarf was removed from her eyes and the first person she saw was Georgie, standing beside the table with a camera on a tripod.

'Oh no!' she gasped. 'You weren't taking photographs all the time?'

Everyone fell around laughing as Milly understood the trick that had been played on her. But was glad enough to join in the joke as it was all very good-humoured. And, besides, how could she object to such photographs since they were the sole *raison d'être* to her being there?

By the time Marco and Emma arrived to take her home, Milly felt perfectly happy about being one of 'Georgie's Gorgeous Gals' as he affectionately called them. She was looking forward to doing more work with them, and planning to remain in Florence rather longer than the original two weeks that she had agreed with Evadne. After all she was a free agent now, and enjoying herself so much that there was no point in returning to dull old England just yet.

But as they drove back to the villa by moonlight, with owls hooting and bats swooping all around, Emma told her that she had received a telegram from Milly's mother that afternoon.

'She wants to come and stay for a few days, on her way to Rome,' Emma explained. 'Apparently there is to be some kind of international meeting of women and she has been sent as a delegate.'

'Oh.' Milly fell silent for a few seconds. The thought of her mother intruding into her new life was disconcerting. She tried to disguise her feelings by saying brightly, 'That will be nice. When is she arriving?'

'On Friday.' Emma's hand closed over hers. 'Don't worry, my dear. No-one will say anything about what you are doing here. And Georgie never asks people to work at the weekend, he's too busy going to parties himself. So there is no cause for alarm.'

Milly smiled wryly. It was no use trying to fool her Aunty Em. She could read her like a book! But for the next two days Milly remained at the villa, since Georgie had some other projects on and did not need her until the following week. She couldn't help feeling apprehensive about her mother's visit, and as she sat reading near the house or went for walks with Emma in the late afternoon her mind was often distracted.

The question worrying her was, what if Kitty asked

her how long she intended to stay in Italy? A vague reply would not satisfy her mother, she knew that, yet she could not possibly tell her what kind of work she was engaged in. Perhaps she should talk of becoming a governess, but then she would be involved in deception on a grand scale. Kitty would expect regular letters full of details about the family she worked for. And if she described her real work with her new 'family' the poor woman would be shocked to the core!

In the end she decided that would ask Emma's advice. Her godmother thought for a few moments as they rested in the shade beneath an aromatic pine tree. Then she said, 'I suppose we could pretend that I had found you temporary employment, giving English lessons. That might satisfy your mother for the time being.'

'Yes!' Milly's face brightened. 'I could call it "teaching practice" and then she would be well pleased, thinking I intended to apply for a permanent post in the autumn.'

Emma frowned. 'I would not normally condone such deception, Milly. But, like you, I can think of no alternative. In all the years I have lived here Kitty has never visited me. I suppose she is only coming now because you are here.'

She sounded sad. Milly asked, tentatively, 'Did things go wrong between you and Ma, Aunty Em? She was once your maid, wasn't she?'

'Oh yes, but that was long ago. After she married your father we didn't see a lot of each other. It was only when she left him that you both came to live with me. Do you remember the house in Brunswick Square?'

They fell to reminiscing, and Milly gathered that the rift between the two women had been over Kitty's Suffragette activities. Although Emma was careful not to criticise, it sounded as if the young Milly had been dumped on her godmother while her mother went off to her meetings and marches. No wonder there had been some resentment on Emma's part, and no doubt Kitty had responded with her usual fiery polemic. Perhaps Milly and Emma had even more in common, since they had both been tongue-lashed by her mother!

By the time that Kitty arrived in Florence Milly found she was actually looking forward to seeing her. Despite their disagreements she still loved her mother and was proud of her achievements. The moment she saw her stepping off the train she ran into her arms.

'Mother! It's so strange to see you outside England! Did you have a good journey?'

Kitty smiled wearily as she kissed Emma on the cheek. 'Not too bad, although it was very tedious. I had no idea Italy was so far away!'

Everyone laughed at that, so the ice was soon broken. They took the journey back to the villa in a horse-drawn cab and Kitty visibly began to relax and enjoy the sunshine. Milly chatted about the lovely countryside, the beautiful buildings of Florence and the excitable Italians, while Emma and Marco could hardly get a word in edgeways.

That evening was a jolly one, with them all exchanging news around the table. If there were any lingering hostility between Kitty and Emma it was not apparent, and any subject that was liable to cause offence was carefully avoided by all. When she came to say goodnight to her mother Milly began to feel that she had been worrying unnecessarily.

The following afternoon, however, the three women were taking tea on the terrace at the back of the villa when there was the sound of a horse-drawn carriage arriving. Maria came out of the house to announce, 'This lady left her card, Signora. Are you at home?'

Emma took the card and gave a frown. She took a quick look at Milly and then seemed to make up her mind. 'I think not, Maria. Not just now ...'

But soon there came the sound of raised voices from inside the house. Emma got to her feet and was about to see what all the noise was about when Maria came rushing out in distress. '*Mi dispiace, Signora* ... but she will not leave!'

'What? How dare she ...'

The woman in question suddenly appeared on the terrace and then Milly understood why Emma was being so circumspect. Her heart sank as she saw the familiar face of Evadne Parker, now contorted in fury. 'This girl said I might not see you, when I knew very well you were here!' she snapped, throwing Milly a look of disdain.

Emma intervened. 'I am the lady of the house, Miss Parker, and I'm afraid you are not welcome here. Please leave at once.'

'Not until you hear what I have to say! Oh, I see you have company. Good afternoon, Mrs Belfort. What I have to say will no doubt be of interest to you, too.'

'Milly's mother has just arrived from England. I really do not think your behaviour is appropriate, Miss Parker.'

'Ha! It is precisely of inappropriate behaviour that I wish to speak.'

Emma repeated coolly, 'If you will not leave of your own accord I'm afraid I must summon a servant.'

'I shall not leave until I have said what I came to say.'

Milly sat there feeling paralysed with fear. By now it was evident that Evadne had come on some sort of revenge mission, that she had some poison to spread. Emma seized her by the arm and tried to escort her back into the house, but she stood her ground.

'Maria, go and fetch Antonio please!' Emma said, calmly. She obviously intended to have the unwelcome visitor ejected, but before the servant appeared Evadne seized her chance. She plonked both fists on the table and leant on them, her eyes flashing dangerous fire, then said in a horrible, gloating voice, 'Since you are her godmother, Mrs Longmore, and therefore the moral guardian of this trollop, I thought you should know that she has been prostituting herself by posing in the nude for payment!'

'What?' Kitty gasped staring from Emma to Milly, and back to Evadne, in disbelief.

'Who have you been talking to?' Milly asked, aghast.

'Your new pal, Lotte. She told me everything when I met her at a party last night. I knew you were a slut, Milly, but I didn't think you would sink so low as to sell your body . . .'

'How dare you talk to my god-daughter like that!' Emma intervened, her eyes flashing with menace. 'Ah, Antonio! Would you escort this woman to the door, please? She is making rather a nuisance of herself.'

Milly was relieved when, having delivered her bombshell, the woman finally departed. Yet she dreaded having to face her mother. The nightmare scenario that she had been dreading was now upon her. There was an ominous silence. Then Kitty said, 'Is there any truth in what that dreadful woman said, Milly?'

'A little. I have been posing for a photographer friend of Emma's.'

Kitty turned to Emma in horror. 'How could you let her do this? Your own god-daughter! I knew I should have listened to Vincent when he said you might not be the best person to guide our Milly.'

'It was all quite proper, Ma. Please don't upset

yourself,' Milly pleaded, realising that all she could do now was try to limit the damage.

'But you were in the . . . without clothes?'

'Partially, yes. But the photographs were very artistic . . .'

'Artistic!' Kitty snorted. 'I have heard filth being called Art before, and believed none of it. By taking part in this disgusting trade you are contributing to the exploitation of women the world over, Milly. I cannot tell you how utterly I abhor such depravity. If this is what your expensive education at Cambridge has done for you, then your father's money has been utterly wasted. And if you have the temerity to continue with this disgraceful business then you needn't bother to come running to me when you are in trouble.'

She continued in the same vein for several minutes, then rose and went to her room. Emma and Milly faced each other wryly. Even in the midst of her distress Milly couldn't help admiring the way her godmother had never lost her dignity throughout the sorry episode.

'That was most unfortunate,' Emma sighed. 'I will do what I can to placate her, but I can't promise anything.'

Milly sighed, putting her head into her hands. 'I didn't want to hurt Ma. But I don't see why I should stop doing what I want to do just because she objects. After all, I am of age now. What do you think, Aunty Em?'

Emma gave her a hug. 'I confess I do not know how to guide you, dear. You are, as you say, an adult now and must make your own decisions. But I hope you will continue to turn to me for advice whatever happens.'

Kitty did not appear at dinner, and Emma had a tray sent to her room. She went off to the station first thing in the morning, driven by Antonio, but Emma found two letters in the hall, one addressed to her and one to Milly. Both messages dwelt upon her 'disappointment' and hoped that Milly would 'come to her senses' and find some respectable career.

'I'm sorry, mother,' Milly sighed, tearing hers up. 'But you and I never will see eye to eye.'

Chapter Six

When Milly next went to Georgie's house she did so with mixed feelings. Although she believed that Lotte had mentioned her quite innocently to Evadne, never dreaming what horrid capital she would make out of the information, she was still not quite happy about the prospect of being in her company again. So she was very relieved when she discovered that Georgie was alone.

After a few minutes, however, it was clear that something was wrong. He had an agitated manner, and when he poured two glasses of Marsala wine his hand was shaking.

'When we made this appointment, Milly, I had hoped that we might work together. But now I'm afraid things have taken a turn for the worse.'

Milly took the glass and gulped down some of the sweet wine. 'What do you mean?'

'This morning, at dawn, the police raided my premises and confiscated most of my equipment and a large number of photographs. I fear I am to be prosecuted, Milly. For your own good, I recommend that you have nothing more to do with me.'

'But that's terrible!' Suspicions crowded in on Milly as she remembered the furious rage with which Evadne had swept out of the villa. Could she possibly have tipped off the police about Georgie's business?

'I will admit to you that I have been paying the police a sweetener. Everyone does it, and usually there are no problems. But it seems a member of the public has complained, and then they are bound to take action.'

'But who complained, and of what? Do you know?'

He shrugged. 'I rely on the discretion of my models and someone has been indiscreet. I do not know who, and I do not wish to know. But the police have given me twenty-four hours to get out of town if I don't want to end up in jail.'

'Poor Georgie! Where will you go?'

'To Paris, I think. The laws are more lenient there, and the police more agreeable. The Parisians take a *laissez-faire* attitude towards everything. I do not think I shall have any trouble there.'

'But what about your models, your equipment? Will you have to start from scratch again?'

Georgie gave a cheeky grin, his eyes twinkling at her. 'Not quite, my dear. Fortunately my profits are safely stashed away in a Swiss bank account. It is a nuisance, but not the end of the world. I am only sorry that I have had to let so many people down. Yourself, for instance. I was looking forward to working with you.'

'Yes, I don't know what I shall do now.'

It seemed so ironic. After seeing her mother so upset about her new job, she was not now to be doing it after all! She finished her wine and rose to leave saying, 'Well you must have a lot to do, packing and so forth. I wish you well, Georgie.'

She held out her hand and he took it, but then said, 'You know, you could always come with me. Nico has already decided to come, and I think Hilda will too. It might be tough for a while, but there are all kinds of jobs that a pretty girl like you might find there.'

Milly's mind raced. She was being offered a unique opportunity, but she would not accept without first talking it over with Emma. 'Do I have to decide now?'

'By no means. But if you wish to come with us, make sure you're at the station at ten-thirty tomorrow morning, ready to catch the train to Paris.'

Milly wished him well as they parted, and went hurrying out into the street to find Emma and Marco. She knew they had been heading for the leather shops where Emma was hoping to purchase a new bag. It didn't take her long to find them, and her godmother stared in alarm as she entered the shop. 'Milly! What on earth . . . are you all right, dear?'

'Oh yes, Aunt Em. But I must speak to you. Can we go somewhere quiet?'

'Of course.' She told the shopkeeper with a charming smile that she would be back later to examine his goods more closely, then led the way out of the shop. Marco followed, looking bemused, and they ended up in a café just off the town hall square.

'Now, Milly, why didn't you stay at Georgie's?' she asked, sternly. Her manner plainly said, 'Woe betide him if he has tried to take advantage of my goddaughter!'

'The poor man has been raided by the police,' Milly divulged, in a whisper.

Emma looked shocked. 'How terrible!'

'But they have allowed him time to get out of Italy. He is going to Paris, Aunt Em, and he wants me to go with him, to work with him there. I said I would think about it.'

'I see.' She gave a nostalgic sigh, and Milly remembered how fond Emma was of that city. 'You must do as you think best, dear. Follow your star of destiny wherever it may lead. That was my guiding principle when I was your age, and it has never failed me.'

'Then you think I should go?'

'Perhaps. If I were not with Marco I would offer to go with you, but he hates the French. I used to know a few people in Paris, one in particular. But I heard she died . . .'

Milly squeezed her hand, sorry for upsetting her, but Emma pulled herself together. 'The question is, do you trust Georgie? Do you like him, and want to work for him? Only you can answer those questions, my dear. I believe the man to be trustworthy, but you never know.'

Marco, who had been trying to look as if he weren't listening, now joined in the conversation. 'Georgie is an English gentleman!' he declared, grandly.

Emma laughed. 'And so was Daniel, but I would not trust him with a sack of potatoes tied in the middle!'

They all giggled, and Milly felt better. It was good to have the offer of a job in Paris, but equally good to know she could stay with Emma and Marco for as long as she wished. Her fate was indeed in her own hands, and not even her mother had the power to stop her from living her life as she wanted.

Yet as Milly lay in bed that night, weighing up the pros and cons of Florence versus Paris, a deep melancholy overtook her. With freedom came responsibility, as her mother was forever pointing out, and if she went to Paris she would be entirely responsible for her own life. Although she could just about manage on the allowance her father had allotted her she could not imagine it going far in an expensive city like Paris, and she would not go cap in hand to either of her parents.

Marco had told her that he should be able to

introduce her to other photographers in Florence if she preferred to stay, but what if the police decided to make further raids? It was possible that what had happened to Georgie was not an isolated incident but a planned campaign, and soon the whole business would be under threat in that part of Italy.

By the following morning Milly had made up her mind. She would throw in her lot with Georgie. The very thought of it lifted her spirits. Paris was synonymous with gaiety and love, the city where the female form was venerated, just as the original 'Paris' had adored the beauty of Trojan Helen. Her heart told her that there she would find not only wealth, celebrity and liberation but also the one thing she had never really experienced: romantic love.

Milly made her farewells to Marco at the villa, but her godmother accompanied her to the railway station. Waiting for the train with Georgie were Nico and Hilda. They all welcomed her warmly, but just as the whistle blew and Milly turned to embrace Emma there was a loud cry and someone else came rushing up.

It was Carlo. Milly was so pleased to see him that she gave him a joyful hug. Then, as the others scrambled on board, she turned back to Emma. 'Thank you so much, dear Aunty Em, for putting me up – or should I say, for putting up with me?'

They laughed together, but their laughter was tinged with sadness. Milly wondered when she would be able to see her godmother again, and Emma was doubtless thinking of the life she was about to lead in Paris. 'I envy you, dear,' she murmured, with her last kiss. 'Paris was always good to me. I hope it may be as good for you.'

Seated in the puffing train, Milly smiled brightly at her fellow travellers and brushed away the last of her tears. They had a carriage to themselves and again she was struck by the feeling of belonging to a happy family, a smaller one than before, but very friendly all the same.

Georgie had managed to rent an artist's *atelier* near Montparnasse, which he planned to convert into a studio and they all had quarters on the floor below. It was a bit of a squash, and Milly was obliged to share a bedroom with Hilda while the two male models went in together, but nobody minded. Georgie had made it plain that it would take a while to get settled in and they were all prepared to put up with some hardship at the beginning. Only Milly had private means, so the other three were being subsidised by their boss until they were able to earn.

Meanwhile, there was the glorious City of Love to explore. Every morning they helped to sort out the studio and make their apartments habitable, but Georgie let them to go off in the afternoons to see the sights. Milly marvelled at the elegance of the buildings and bridges, statues and fountains. She was amazed by the height of the Eiffel Tower, dazzled by the splendour of the Arc de Triomphe. It was very different from Florence but equally impressive.

By night, however, the city really came into its own. Georgie accompanied them as they sampled the delights of the Folies Bergère and the Moulin Rouge. After they had wallowed in the glamour of the shows he would take them on to lesser-known night clubs where the entertainment was more saucy. Here the girls did not merely pose in the nude with haughty expressions, with feathers and tinsel hiding their private parts. Instead they danced with provocative movements, flirted with men in the audience and were prepared to strip down completely and waggle their bare arses with bravado.

'You see, anything goes here my dears!' Georgie declared with satisfaction, as if the decision to change location had been based on his sound judgement, not forced upon them.

Georgie put them to work as soon as he had the studio 'ship-shape.' While they had been settling in he had conceived several new ideas for photos which he was eager to try out. One afternoon he called all four of them up to the studio and told them what he had in mind.

'I thought we might stage an original version of the Can-Can. I managed to hire these flouncy skirts for you girls, and you can wear black stockings with garters and high-heeled shoes. But there will be one vital difference: you will dance topless and, when you perform your high kicks, you will be without underwear.'

'What, no knickers?' Hilda giggled, pretending to be shocked.

'And what about us?' Nico asked. 'Don't we get a look in?'

'That's exactly what you do get. I'll have the pair of you lying down front of stage and looking up the women's skirts. Let's try it out, shall we?'

The two girls got into their costumes and began practising while Georgie fixed his camera. The hard part was lifting their legs high and keeping them still in the air. They put their arms around each others' waists and giggled as they toppled on one leg, but at last they managed to stay put while the men ogled them below.

Georgie was very pleased with what he saw through the viewfinder, and Milly could imagine that it made quite an impact. He had rigged up a backdrop with the great phallic symbol of the Eiffel Tower painted on it, and against that the two dancers with their red skirts and white petticoats, black stockings with pink rosettes on the garters, would make a striking picture. Hilda, with her blonde bob and melting brown eyes, contrasted well with Milly's dark curls and striking blue eyes.

Their figures were different too, Milly having breasts that were round and full, sitting high on her chest, while Hilda's were more long and pointed with a tendency to droop. When they lifted their legs one pale and one dark bush were on display, fringing the fleshy lips beneath. The two men were mesmerised by the sight, gazing up with wide eyes and flushed faces with obvious erections beneath their loose-fitting trousers.

'Wonderful! Hold it there!' Georgie called.

'I hope he's going to find something equally acrobatic for the men to do!' Hilda murmured through stiff lips as they both strained to hold the pose.

They collapsed on to the small stage giggling when the business was done. 'I feel like a lady contortionist at the circus!' Hilda laughed.

But Georgie was pleased with their efforts, and then announced that he had a more ambitious scheme in mind, 'The Seven Stages of Courtship,' a kind of Rake's Progress.

'Sounds interesting,' Carlo grinned. 'What did you have in mind?'

'Something for you and Milly to perform, ' Georgie smiled back. 'Hilda is perhaps a little too experienced for this particular scenario. I think Milly can play the innocent more successfully.'

He made Milly put on some underwear and a demure, high-necked dress then sat her on a chair. Beside her he placed an aspidistra in a *jardinière*. Carlo dressed too, and Georgie asked him to kneel before her kissing her hand while he took some photographs. Then Carlo had to kiss her on the mouth, with his hand on her breast. For the third photo he had to undo her blouse and take out one breast, which he put between his lips. The next stage was to lift up her skirt and put his hand down her knickers. In the fifth scene he managed to divest her of her knickers and put his fingers inside her, while the next showed him performing cunnilingus.

'And finally,' Hilda chortled, watching the sequence unfold, 'he will give her a good rogering, no doubt.'

Milly blenched. She was quite happy to let any man kiss and fondle her in front of the camera, but she had no intention of losing her virginity as part of the spectacle. Georgie seemed to sense her apprehension. He came up and put his hand on her shoulder.

'Don't worry, my dear, I always insist on my models simulating the sex act.' He turned and gave Hilda a frown. 'My actors can do as they like outside the studio, but while I am in control there will be no actual intercourse. I am running a photographic studio, not a brothel. I have no wish to end up with pregnant women and pox-ridden men. Any girl who comes to work for me as a virgin will remain that way, as far as I am concerned.'

He had spoken like a stern father, and Hilda was duly chastened. But Milly was reassured. She would have found it embarrassing to refuse, but now she knew that the intercourse was to be only simulated she had no such scruples. Georgie had them both lying on the floor, with Carlo thrusting between her legs, but as she feigned a look of rapture he whispered in her ear,

'Maybe sometime we do this for real, eh Milly?'

She didn't know what to say, so she kept silent. Although she had grown fond of Carlo the idea of making love with him while they were away from Georgie's watchful eye made her nervous. For the first time since leaving Florence she really missed Emma. Without her godmother's guidance she might be in danger of getting into deep waters.

When the session was over, Milly excused herself

and went to her room. But even there she could not be alone, for Hilda followed soon after, flopping down on to her bed with a sigh.

'Whew! I don't know about you, Milly, but that Can-Can really wore me out. Did you like what you did with Carlo? He's very handsome, isn't he?'

'Yes,' Milly replied, non-committally.

Hilda turned her shrewd brown eyes towards her. 'He fancies you, you know. That's obvious. Are you going to give him what he wants, or are you just a little prick-tease?'

'Hilda, I'd rather not talk about it. He's just someone I work with, that's all.'

'But you can't pretend that what we do is normal work. Don't you want to know what that gorgeous prick of his feels like when it's inside you? I can't believe you're still a virgin. I lost my cherry when I was sixteen, and enjoyed every minute of it!'

'Well good for you!' Milly snapped, irritated by the conversation.

'Mm, sex *is* good for you. That's what I believe, anyway.' She lay back languorously with her arms behind her head. 'I've had Carlo myself, you know, and I can thoroughly recommend him. He's got a lovely thick dick and he knows how to use it. He's not too quick, either.'

'Hilda, please don't talk like that. I don't want to hear it.'

Milly felt awkward listening to such frank revelations about the man she worked with. Although she and Caroline had often laughed and joked about their boyfriends they had both been virgins and their conversations had been limited by their lack of experience. Between her and Hilda, on the other hand, there was a gulf that she did not wish to discuss.

'What's the matter?' Hilda asked, her tone slightly

mocking. 'You're not prudish, surely? If you are, you're in the wrong business!'

'No, it's not that. I don't mind talking about what we do for the camera. But as for going all the way, well I want to keep that as something special. I shall only give up my virginity when I fall in love, and I'm not in love with Carlo.'

Hilda was regarding her with scorn. 'Who put silly ideas like that into your head? If you wait for Prince Charming to come along you'll find it's not all a bed of roses. Better to get in some practice with the frogs, first!'

She gave a coarse laugh, making Milly wish the subject had never been raised. It was hard enough sticking to her ideals without having them ridiculed. Then she remembered what Georgie had said and felt comforted. If she were in any trouble he was sure to protect her.

But later that night Hilda's words returned to taunt her and Milly wondered if she were not rather prudish after all. In the stuffy world of Cambridge it had been easy to convince herself that she was a liberated woman, free to indulge her own sensuality however and with whomever she chose. The acts that she and Caroline had undertaken with their various partners had seemed daring enough, and her affair with Evadne had further developed her capacity for erotic pleasure.

Yet the way Hilda had spoken made her feel like a green schoolgirl, who fantasised about making love but had never experienced it. Of course she knew what an orgasm was like. She had learnt to pleasure herself in that way long before she had any physical contact with a man. The girls at school had whispered about such things, and there had been much activity beneath the sheets after lights-out.

But to feel those delicious sensations when a man's

body was closely joined to yours, when he was right inside your secret place, must be wonderful! And if it was that special, she didn't want to share it with just anyone, only with a man who was special to her in other ways too. Sighing, she turned over to sleep and resolved not to brood upon the subject.

The next day only Nico and Hilda were needed for work. It was a beautiful summer's day and Carlo invited Milly to walk with him in the Bois de Boulogne. At first she demurred, thinking that he might regard her acceptance as encouragement, but the lure of woods and lakes was too strong. She missed the countryside, both of Florence and of Cambridge. So they took a cab to the outskirts then joined the throng of ramblers, cyclists and horse-riders who were enjoying this little taste of rural seclusion on the outskirts of the city.

'Oh Carlo, this is so nice!' Milly smiled, slipping her arm through his as they wandered along the leafy paths. 'I was sad at leaving Florence, but now I don't mind so much. How about you?'

'It is all good for me,' Carlo said, in his lilting Italian accent, and Milly began to warm to him. He *was* handsome, as Hilda had said, and the doting way his brown eyes looked at her was very appealing. From the moment she had noticed him in Leo's shop she had felt attracted to him. Yet something told her she could never love him, not with all of her heart and soul. She hoped, nevertheless, that they could be good friends.

'You don't miss working for Leo then'

'No. I was only working there because I could not get enough of this type of work to live on. I dream of being a star one day, Milly. I wish to perform for the camera all over Europe, maybe even America. How I love the camera! It gives me immortality. I shall always remain as young as my photograph!'

Milly looked askance at him, thinking he must be joking. But no, he was deadly serious!

'You cannot go on doing this forever,' she told him.

'Why not? I have seen photographs of old men with young girls. It is no problem. For you, as a woman, perhaps. Forgive me, Milly, but when your looks start to fade you must find a husband, while I may go on and on. It is unfair, but life is so.'

They had reached an obscure corner of the woods, where they seemed to be the only people around. Suddenly he seized her and began to kiss her with violent passion. Milly struggled, but he pulled her further in amongst the trees and began to claw at her clothes.

'Oh Milly!' he breathed. 'I have wanted you from when I first saw you! I only came to Paris because I believed you were coming too!'

She pushed at his chest, forcing some distance between them. 'Carlo, wait! This is not right. I cannot make love with you here.'

He kissed her hand contritely. 'Of course, I understand. You want to be wooed, like a lady. Well let us take a room in a hotel. I know of one near here . . .'

'No, Carlo, you don't understand. I don't want us to make love at all. Not outside of work, anyway. I like you a great deal, but . . .'

'But I am not good enough for you!' he interjected, sulkily. 'I know you are a virgin – Hilda told me. But there is only one reason for a girl to remain so in this profession: to gain a rich husband. You are waiting to sell yourself to the highest bidder!'

Milly was shocked. Nothing could have been further from her mind, and his words made her feel cheap. 'You are quite wrong, Carlo.'

'Then prove it, by letting me take your maidenhead!' To her dismay he forced her down on the ground and began to lift up her skirt. 'Here will do as

106

well as anywhere. It is best to get it over with as soon as possible. Girls seldom enjoy it the first time, but I guarantee you will come to love it in the end, just like Hilda!'

Milly was horrified, and struggled hard but he pinned her down with his powerful thighs and pinioned her wrists above her head with one hand while he took out his penis with the other. She glanced down and saw his erection thrusting impatiently out of his trousers. To her it looked red and angry, more like a weapon than an object of desire.

'You will not rape me?' she wailed.

'I am doing you a favour,' he replied, his face set with determination as he found her knickers and began to tear them down.

Milly felt her heart race with fear. She knew she could not hope to shake him off, he was far too heavy. In desperation she spat into his face but he only slapped hers in response. Sobbing, she turned away from him. But then anger seized her. Why should she put up with this? He might be her colleague but he was not her lover and, even if he were, she would let no man treat her like this. Summoning up all her breath she screamed, 'Help! *Au secours!*' at the top of her voice.

This is useless, she thought, but continued to cry out feebly as Carlo positioned himself between her thighs. She felt his impatient hands opening her up, ready to thrust in with his hard tool and hopeless tears rolled down her cheeks. It was all her stupid fault for getting into this dubious business. She deserved all she got.

Then, to her utter relief, she heard the sound of running feet. 'Hullo!' a man's voice called. '*Qui est là?* Is anyone hurt?'

'Help, please help me!' Milly called.

A young man raced into view. He came straight up

and seized Carlo by the collar. 'Leave her, monsieur, or I shall call the police. *La Police, vous comprenez?*'

Carlo came out of his lustful frenzy with a snarl and tried to throw the stranger off his back, but he received a kick in the ankle that made him howl. The momentary diversion was enough to allow Milly to wriggle out from under him. Pulling up her drawers she began to thank her rescuer but he seized her hand saying, 'Run, run! Or that beast will be at us both.'

The pair of them raced off, leaving Carlo on the ground looking momentarily stupefied. When they reached the more public part of the woods they slowed down. Milly was gasping, with a stitch in her side, and her rescuer led her to a seat.

'Oh, how can I ever thank you?' she smiled at him, when she had recovered her breath.

It was her first chance to take a good look at him. Clear hazel eyes regarded her from beneath straight brows. His mouth was generously proportioned, perhaps a little too large, but with lips that looked soft and red. He had brown hair tinged with auburn, that went back in loose waves from a broad forehead. Even if he had not come to her rescue Milly knew that she would have liked the look of him.

'It is not necessary, any decent man would have done as much,' he replied, without the faintest trace of a French accent.

Milly's curiosity was roused. 'I cannot tell whether you are French or English,' she smiled.

'Then let me introduce myself. My name is Robin Dupont. Although my father is French my mother is English, and I was raised in Berkshire.'

'My name is Milly Belfort. I am very pleased to know you, Robin.'

They shook hands with awkward formality, then Robin said with a wry smile, 'I wish we could have met some other way, Milly. But let me give you a word of advice. Next time you go for a walk in the *Bois* make sure you keep to the public paths.'

'Of course, it was stupid of me to trust him. But . . .' she realised that she was about to give away the nature of their relationship, and hence of her work, so she stopped abruptly. The horror of what had almost happened to her came over her again and she began to tremble uncontrollably.

Strong arms enfolded her. 'Milly, you have had a great shock. Let me hail a cab to take you home. Where do you live?'

But she didn't want Robin to know her address in case he found out about the life she led there. He believed her to be pure and innocent and she could not bear to disillusion him. She made an effort to pull herself together. 'I shall be all right, you need not trouble yourself. But a cup of tea would be nice. I believe there is a café somewhere near here. We . . . I passed it earlier, near one of the lakes.'

They were soon sitting at an open-air table enjoying tea with lemon, and Milly felt herself relaxing completely in the company of this pleasant young man. She discovered that he was a post-graduate student at the Sorbonne, writing a thesis on the French symbolist poets. Milly had read some Verlaine and Rimbaud, and they were soon engaged in earnest discussion. He seemed delighted to have discovered an educated woman by accident.

When he asked what brought her to Paris, however, Milly felt obliged to lie. She told him she was visiting her godmother, which she thought was near enough to the truth to be sustainable. But she swiftly turned the conversation back to literary matters.

'We really must talk again soon,' he said when, after her third cup of tea, Milly reluctantly decided that they could prolong their conversation no longer. 'Let me give you my card. I am living in a student hostel, but there is a telephone and you could leave a message with the concierge if I am out. Please say you will see me again, Milly.'

She nodded. 'I will. But please hail me a cab now, Robin. I must get back.'

'Let me accompany you to your door,' he pleaded. 'You have had a terrible shock, and I want to make sure you get home safely.'

'There is no need, but thank you. I shall be in touch again soon, I promise.'

She waved at him from the rocking cab until he was out of sight, then settled back with a sigh. What an extraordinary afternoon! But now she must face the question of what to do about Carlo. Her spirits sank as she wondered whether to report him to Georgie or let matters rest. Well, she would see how he behaved when they met again. If he showed proper remorse she might forgive him. After all, if it hadn't been for him she would never have met Robin Dupont. As the memory of those thoughtful hazel eyes returned to her she had the odd feeling that their meeting had been more than mere chance.

When Milly returned to the apartment in Montparnasse she found that Carlo was already there, drinking tea with the others, and the cool stare he gave her made her heart sink. She tried to avoid being alone with him, but when she rose to go to her room he followed her, pinning her against the wall as she reached her door.

'I'm sorry about this afternoon,' he began, although his tone was anything but contrite. 'I should not have tried to force you in public like that, but I mean to have you all the same. Hilda and I have come to an agreement. She will swap beds with me tonight. She wants to sleep with Nico in any case.'

'No!' Milly protested, but he swiftly clapped his hand over her mouth.

110

'It's no use, my dear. I always get my own way in the end. You may as well come quietly!'

He laughed at her discomfiture then slunk off. Milly knew she couldn't put up with such cavalier disregard for her feelings. And if Hilda were involved too that made it even worse. Now was the time to test Georgie's promise to look after her.

Later, Milly found her boss alone in his office and, when she said she wished to talk with him, he urged her to come in and shut the door. She almost lost her nerve when he smiled at her so amiably, not wanting to tell tales out of school. Yet she knew she must.

Georgie listened gravely to her story then said without hesitation, 'The boy will be dismissed at once. I cannot believe he behaved so badly. He is lucky that you did not report him to the police.'

Miserably, Milly went to her room where Hilda sat reading in her armchair. She looked up with a sly grin. 'Hullo, Miss *demi-vierge*! I think that after tonight you will be *vierge* not at all! Did Carlo tell you what we planned?'

'Yes, and I went straight to Georgie. He is going to dismiss Carlo for attempting to rape me. I should not mention your part in this to anyone, if I were you.'

Hilda's face turned pink and she screwed up her mouth in ugly defiance. 'You little bitch! How dare you accuse him, when you know you were leading him on. I've a good mind to . . .'

'What, stand up for him? I wouldn't, if I were you.'

Hilda balled her fists, and looked as if she would like to sock Milly in the jaw. Sullenly she threw her book down on her bed and stalked out of the room. Milly lay down on her own bed and sighed, staring at the ceiling. Everything seemed to be going wrong for her now. Then she thought of Robin, and things didn't seem so bad. At least she had a new friend out there in the *Quartier Latin*.

111

Maybe she would arrange to see him again. A warm flush of pleasure went through her at the thought. Since leaving Cambridge she had missed the lectures, the hours of study, even the essay writing. Now that Evadne was no longer in her life she was ready for someone to take over her rôle as intellectual mentor.

But what about the other aspect of her relationship with her tutor – could Robin take that over too? Recalling his handsome face and tall, manly figure Milly found she could not rule out the possibility that they might become lovers. She had found the clasp of his hand reassuring, his embrace comforting. And then, when he had kissed her cheek on bidding her farewell, she had felt a brief flash of unmistakably sexual excitement.

Yet the thought of allowing him to take her home through this dubious neighbourhood, of him finding out what she did for a living, made her shudder. She decided, there and then, that she must move out into a place of her own. Relations with Hilda were likely to be strained from now on, and she no longer wished to share a room with her. Besides, hadn't Georgie said that the accommodation arrangements were temporary?

Milly alone of the 'Gorgeous Gals' had private means, and her father's allowance would pay the rent while she could live on what she earned. No sooner had she made up her mind than she was making her way back to Georgie's office to tell him of her decision.

'It is done,' he informed her solemnly as soon as she arrived. 'I have dismissed him and warned him that if he ever tries to contact you again he will have to answer to me.'

'Thank you, but where will you find a replacement? I'm afraid I've made things awkward for you.'

'Not at all!' Georgie laughed. 'I already have a French couple in mind, Gaston and Louise. They were recommended to me by a friend. At the moment they are working as artists' models but I'm sure they will be glad to work for me as I can offer them more money.'

Milly felt relieved. 'One more thing. Although I want to go on working for you, Georgie, I'd like to move into a place of my own as soon as possible. Do you know how I may find a flat, not too far away?'

By bedtime she felt calmer than she had all day. Hilda had haughtily announced her intention of spending the night with Nico so she had the bedroom to herself. Milly lay thinking about Robin Dupont, and her heart soon filled with a yearning desire for the man who had rescued her. Yet it was more of a soulful feeling than a physical one. She sensed that he was not like the men she had met at Cambridge, nor those she had known since. There had been a probity about him, not stuffy or strait-laced but upright and straightforward. Milly wanted him, above all, to think well of her.

Chapter Seven

Milly spent all next morning following up leads for apartments. Georgie put her on to a couple, but they were too expensive so she bought a newspaper and eventually found one near the Jardin du Luxembourg. It wasn't far from the Sorbonne, she was pleased to note. The student tenants who had inhabited the place before her had gone at the end of term, and the landlady was glad to allow her to have it as a summer let for a low rent. She gave a deposit and told her she would be back later on that day with her belongings.

First, though, Georgie had asked her to work for him once more. She hurried back to Montparnasse and found that she was required to pose with Hilda for some lesbian pictures. The other girl was looking daggers at her, and the thought of being intimate with her was daunting, but Milly told herself that she must play the trooper and maintain a professional attitude. It wasn't going to be easy, though.

Georgie wanted them together in the nude, on the big four-poster bed in the studio. While they waited for him to set up the camera Hilda said under her breath, 'I suppose you're pleased with yourself for getting Carlo kicked out. Selfish cow!'

Don't let her rile you, Milly told herself. But Hilda went on, 'You should see the couple of amateurs Georgie's taken on in his place. They don't know their arse from their elbow.'

'I'm sure they'll learn, same as I had to,' Milly said, tartly.

'Ready, girls?' Georgie called, and they fell automatically into a clinch for the camera.

'Now I want you to be fondling each others' breasts. That's right. And smile, both of you!'

Through gritted teeth Hilda said, 'You think you're above the rest of us just because you won't fuck. Stupid bitch!'

Then she spitefully pinched Milly's nipple making her eyes water, although she managed not to cry out. 'Do that again and I'll tell Georgie,' she mumbled.

'You would too, little tattle-tale! I think I'll suggest we do some shots with whips. And guess who'll be doing the whipping!'

'You dare!'

'Oh I dare, all right. You forget, Little Miss Prissy, that I was working for Georgie long before you came along. He listens to what I say.'

'Right, that's fine!' Georgie announced. 'Now I want you to go down on Milly, Hilda.'

'Better do as he says!' Milly grinned, triumphantly. But her triumph was short-lived. As soon as Hilda's mouth came near her pussy she began to use her teeth, nipping into the soft flesh of her labia. This time Milly couldn't help screeching in agony.

'What's the matter?' Georgie called.

'Hilda hurt me a bit, that's all.'

He came up to the bed, frowning. 'Hilda, be more careful pleased. I'm surprised at you.'

She lifted her head and looked up at Milly, her eyes

slits of pure malice. 'Sorry, Georgie, it was a mistake. I'll be more careful in future.'

Her tone was menacing, plainly implying that it was Milly, not her, who should be more careful. I've made a real enemy of her, she thought miserably. Yet she felt vindicated in reporting Carlo to their boss, and what had happened after that was not her fault. She was angry that Hilda blamed her, but then she thought of Robin. He at least understood the nature of her ordeal. The sooner she saw him again the better. She was beginning to feel he was the only one who could understand her in this big, alien city.

As soon as she was settled in her new digs, Milly wrote to Robin. She felt more comfortable doing that than using the telephone in a foreign country. It was really a thank you letter, but she suggested they might meet at a café on the *Boul' Mich* in a few days.

Before then, however, she had to work with Gaston and Louise for the first time and she was very nervous. The family atmosphere that had prevailed when they arrived in Paris had ceased abruptly since Carlo's dismissal. Hilda and Nico were now definitely a pair and Milly was made to feel left out. She had compounded that by moving out of course, but it was better than having to endure it all the time.

Georgie, at least, was still kind to her. He introduced her to the French couple and explained his latest idea for a series of six photographs. The format suited his customers since the pictures could be linked together, concertina style, to tell a story.

'It's going to be called "Not Tonight, I Have a Headache",' he said with a grin. 'Picture one will show Gaston in bed with Louise. He has a hand on her breast and she has a hand on her forehead, looking pained. The next picture shows him chatting to a girl in a bar with his hand on her knee – that's you, Milly. Photo number three has him bringing the girl back into his bedroom and undressing her while the wife looks on. Next we have the three of them in bed together, with Gaston caressing Milly and Louise watching enviously. Picture five shows the wife joining in and the last one has them all at it together.'

'Ç'est compliqué, ça!' Louise complained.

'Oh you can manage it, I'm sure. Now, shall we take up our positions for the first shot?'

Milly sensed a lack of confidence amongst the other two. Perhaps Hilda had been right when she accused them of being amateurs. Still, she would do her best to put them at their ease. Smiling cheerfully at Gaston she went to sit on the bar stool that Georgie had arranged for the second scene while they shot the first.

It took several goes before Georgie could get it right. Either the angle was wrong, or Gaston was obscuring Louise's breast with his arm, or she wasn't looking sufficiently pained. At last he was satisfied and Gaston came over to do the scene in the bar. Milly had to perch on the stool, with a great deal of leg showing, knocking back her drink, while Gaston had one arm around her and another on her knee, his lips brushing her ear suggestively.

It seemed straightforward enough but, once again, there were problems. Louise was visibly irritated by the wait. But somehow Gaston couldn't manage to make his courtship of Milly look convincing.

'Put more warmth into it! You really fancy this girl!' Georgie urged him.

But he didn't hear Gaston mutter, 'It would help if I really did!'

Milly was upset. The couple had been cold towards her from the start, but she remembered that Hilda had already worked with them and would doubtless have poisoned their minds against her. Then Milly knew it was going to be an uphill struggle all the way.

The bar scene was eventually finished to Georgie's

satisfaction and then came the undressing scene in the bedroom. Milly stripped to her knickers and stockings, which Gaston was to roll down her thigh. In the background, Louise had to pretend to be asleep while peeping at them through her fingers. This proved to be quite beyond her powers as an actress, however. Over and over again Milly had to pose with one leg crooked, and it wasn't easy to keep her balance. Several times she toppled forward only to be cursed by Gaston.

At last they progressed to the bed scene. Milly had to lie over the bedclothes while Gaston sucked at her breast with his fingers in her vulva and Louise looked on. It seemed simple enough, and she had done many similar scenes before, but this time there was a coldness about the procedure that revolted her. The old easy-going, comradely atmosphere had vanished and now, instead of giggles and jokes when things went wrong, there were snorts and curses.

Milly began to feel awkward. She kept remembering how rough Carlo had been with her and she hated the feel of Gaston's lips and hands upon the intimate parts of her body. Georgie told her to relax, but that only made her feel worse. It was hard to look as if you were enjoying yourself when you were feeling so bad inside.

'Keep smiling, Milly!' Georgie urged her. 'Remember, you're an actress!'

His words helped to improve her morale. Milly told herself that she was indeed a kind of actress and must put her personal feelings aside for the sake of the job. If she really wanted to make a go of this profession she must learn to work with all types and in all circumstances.

After that things went a lot better. Once Louise joined in the action, Milly found she could focus her attention on kissing and fondling her breasts while

Gaston licked her pussy. Georgie was very pleased with the final shots, but once he pronounced himself satisfied the French couple began talking to each other in scornful tones. Although Milly's French was not good she knew by instinct that they were complaining about her. She felt angry, not so much with them but with Hilda. Now she was convinced that they had been prejudiced against her even before they began working together.

Still, she was resolved not to comment or complain. She would retain her dignity and not sink to their level. While she was getting dressed, Georgie came up and took her to one side saying, 'You did well there, Milly. Those two are turning out to be very temperamental, I'm afraid. Never mind, we shall see how things progress. But I would like you to meet someone. Tomorrow afternoon, if you have the time? It could be good news for you, my dear.'

Milly was curious but Georgie would say no more, so she agreed to meet him and the mysterious stranger at a café on the Boulevard St. Germain. On the following afternoon, as she was walking towards their rendezvous, Milly was afraid that she might come across Robin by chance. He'd not yet replied to her letter, but although she hoped to meet him soon she dreaded the thought of running into him while she was with Georgie and this other man. How would she introduce her boss? Awkward questions would follow, and if Robin realised how she made her living he would certainly want to have nothing more to do with her.

So when she arrived at the *Café du Jour* and Georgie asked her if she would rather sit indoors or out, she opted to go inside. Soon after they were settled the other man arrived, and was introduced as Serge Latour. Milly looked him up and down. He was every inch the suave Frenchman, from his silvered dark hair

119

to his shiny black shoes. Brown eyes surveyed her with amusement from beneath heavy lids, and his mouth was curved into a slewed smile. When they shook hands he squeezed hers momentarily within his huge grasp.

'Miss Belfort, I find that you are every bit as pretty as your picture.'

Milly threw Georgie an interrogative look. 'Yes, Serge has seen some of my photos of you,' he explained hastily. 'He's always on the lookout out for girls who are not camera shy.'

Serge decided to do his own explaining. He came straight to the point. 'I make films, Milly. Mostly ten or twenty-minute features for private showing. They are very popular with those who like to give their guests a treat at country house parties, or for showing at gentlemen's clubs, and so on. But my clients are always hungry for new ... faces. And when I saw how the camera adores you I couldn't resist asking Georgie to introduce us. I do hope you don't mind.'

Milly was flabbergasted. She had never imagined acting in films, not in her wildest fantasies. 'I ... I don't know what to say.'

'You don't have to say anything yet.' Serge smiled at her. 'I shall only ask you to come along for a screen test tomorrow. If you prove suitable, I shall let you see my standard contract and then you can decide whether to say yes or no.'

She sat there sipping tea while the two men chatted, more or less ignoring her. But Milly was all ears. The talk was of business, and it appeared that Serge had been so successful making short films that he was able to use the profits to finance a longer film. It would be what he called *Ciné Félin* and aimed to show a cat's eye view of everyday life. He even planned to attach 'whiskers' to the camera. It sounded most peculiar, but it was obviously a project dear to his heart.

After Serge had gone, Georgie and Milly chatted for a while. 'You needn't worry about working for Serge,' Georgie told her. 'If he takes you on he will look after you like a father.'

'Just like you have.' Milly smiled. 'I felt so bad about Carlo having to leave, you know.'

'I know, but to try and force a woman is contemptible. I'm aware that Hilda and Nico sleep together sometimes, but that is by mutual consent. I'm also aware that Hilda is not being very friendly to you lately. Is it because of Carlo?'

Milly nodded. 'I think so. And I believe she's said something to Gaston and Louise, too.'

Georgie sighed. 'I don't know, why can't people be nice to each other? None of this is your fault, Milly, but I couldn't blame you for wanting to move out. And if Serge gives you a chance you must seize it with both hands and not worry about me. I'll find someone to take your place.' He touched her cheek with a sad smile. 'Although I shall miss you.'

'It's very kind of you.'

'I admire talent, wherever I find it, and you certainly have plenty. You deserve to be seen by a wider audience. Who knows, some day you might even get to Hollywood!'

Milly laughed, but it was not so far-fetched. Stranger things had happened, and if she really did have talent it would be a shame not to make the most of it. She wondered what Robin would think of her flaunting herself on the silver screen. Well, she would cross that bridge when she came to it. She wouldn't be altogether surprised if she never heard from that young man again.

But when she returned to her apartment the concierge handed her an envelope. 'From a young man, Mademoiselle,' she said, suspiciously. 'I hope you remember that I will not allow men in my young ladies' rooms.'

'Of course.' Smiling broadly, Milly took the letter up to her flat.

Robin had agreed to meet her at the café in two days' time. Milly was overjoyed.

But first she must undergo the ordeal of the screen test. Serge had given her his card and on the following afternoon she took the Métro to the Opéra. At the fashionable address nearby a maid answered the door and showed her into the reception room where Serge greeted her.

'My dear Milly, how prompt you are! That is a very good sign. I warn you now, I cannot tolerate prima donna behaviour, keeping the crew and cast waiting and so forth. But today we are alone, and I shall work the camera myself. Come this way, please.'

He opened some communicating doors and Milly found herself in a vast room whose walls were covered with black cloth. There were props and lights everywhere, like a grander version of Georgie's studio, but the camera looked bigger and more complicated. It was mounted on a trolley for ease of movement. A corner of the room was set up like a bedroom with a small double bed, chest of drawers, chair and curtains that looked as if they covered a window, although there was only a blank wall behind.

'Now I want you to pretend you are going to bed,' Serge began. 'But in two very different moods. First you will look really miserable, as if your world is coming to an end. Perhaps it is the ending of a love affair. I want you to remove your shoes and top clothes slowly, fold them carefully and put them on the chair. Do you understand?'

'Yes, that seems plain enough.'

'But when you are down to your underwear I want to see your mood change completely. Now you are

122

full of joy and high spirits. Perhaps a man has just proposed to you – perhaps two men! You hurry out of your last garments and toss them carelessly on the floor. Perhaps you dance naked around the room, exulting in your female power. I leave it to your imagination. But do not look directly at the camera. Pretend you are alone. All right?'

Milly nodded. It didn't seem too difficult. She went over to the chair and waited for the order to begin. At last Serge called, 'Action!' just like a real movie director in Hollywood! The word sent shivers of excitement down her spine but she quashed them at once. She had to be sad, wretched, utterly depressed. What was the most miserable thing she could think of? Her mother dying. And Aunty Em. They both died together, knocked down by an automobile as they were crossing the road . . .

Milly sat down listlessly on the chair, unbuttoned the straps of her shoes and removed them. She stood up and undid her skirt then lowered it over her hips. She folded it and hung it on the back of the chair. Then she removed her blouse and folded it carefully, placing it on the seat of the chair. All the while she could hear the camera whirring, but she kept her eyes downcast except for when she looked up at the ceiling and uttered an occasional sigh.

'Very good!' she heard Serge murmur.

He wants me to make things up, she thought. Emboldened, she sat on the edge of the bed for a few seconds with her head in her hands, as if she were crying. It seemed a good way to make the transition from one mood to the other. Suddenly she removed her hands to show a bright, smiling face. She leapt up and began to pull down her petticoat, which she whirled gaily around her head before tossing it to the ground. She did a little dance in her underwear, then quickly took off her stockings and threw them down too.

Unselfconsciously she removed her camisole and cupped her own breasts briefly, with a dreamy smile, as if imagining the hands of her lover caressing them. Serge gave a chortle of approval. She turned her back to the camera as she removed her knickers, thrusting out her naked buttocks before she turned around to reveal her equally naked mons. Again she cavorted beside the bed, filled with a deliciously heady excitement.

Milly was doing something her mother disapproved of, 'making an exhibition of herself,' and she felt wonderfully naughty. Her dance continued to the music in her head, drawing her into it so that she forgot all about where she was and why she was dancing. Enraptured, she entered a different dimension where she was free to enjoy her body, free to move this way and that in lithe abandon. It was only when Serge clapped his hands loudly and called, 'Cut!' that she came back to the present, blinking vaguely.

'That was very good!' he smiled. 'You have a natural talent, Milly. Even more than I hoped. Get dressed now, and I'll get Alice to bring you some tea in reception.'

'Will I be able to see the film?'

'Yes, if you come back tomorrow at the same time. I shall have it ready by then.'

Milly's heart sank. She had arranged to meet Robin tomorrow afternoon. But she couldn't afford to let this chance pass by. She would have to send him another note to postpone their meeting, but what excuse could she give? It seemed like an ill omen. How long could she go on deceiving him, putting him off? Perhaps she should look for a companion amongst her fellow actors rather than choose an innocent like him.

Yet, as Milly went home on the Métro, she had a strong instinct that fate had chosen him for her. She knew her feelings were not simply of gratitude for being rescued from Carlo's clutches. Never before had she felt so attracted to a young man, and she just had to see where the attraction led. So she decided to send him a note asking him to meet her at five instead of three, which should give her enough time to keep both appointments.

When she returned to Serge's studio-cum-apartment next day Milly was surprised to see three more people there. Serge greeted her with a broad smile. 'Since I've already decided to offer you work, Milly, I thought you might like to meet some of your fellow-actors.'

She was too excited to take in their names. All she noticed was that the three men and one woman, Chloe, were extremely good-looking. They went through to what Serge referred to as the 'viewing room' which was set up like a small cinema. They all sat down, Milly next to Serge who clapped his hands as a signal for the projectionist to start the film rolling.

When the short scene began Milly could hardly recognise herself. The camera moved in – she remembered him bringing it close on the trolley – and she began to perform. She hardly recognised herself as the shy, melancholy creature sitting alone in her bedroom, but as she stripped and the mood changed to one of joyous celebration, she could see how she sparkled in front of the camera, how gracefully she moved and how pretty she looked.

'Charming!' the man called Stefan murmured.

Soon the others were congratulating her warmly, and Milly began to feel at home amongst them. She had faith that it wouldn't take her long to recapture some of the family feeling that she'd known when she first joined Georgie's troupe, and which had been so cruelly destroyed by Hilda.

'Now we shall see our latest film,' Serge announced, and the lights went down again.

The short was called, simply, *Seduction*, starring Chloe and Stefan. Much to Milly's surprise, it began with Chloe embracing a long, slow-moving snake. She was wearing a white robe in some diaphanous material, belted with a gold chain, through which the dark points of her nipples were clearly visible. Stefan stood nearby, wearing only a kind of loincloth beneath which his erection could be seen as he watched her allow the creature to slither between her breasts, over her shoulder and around her waist, then down over her thighs. Milly shuddered. 'How could she?' she wondered aloud.

Chloe heard her. 'Oh Willy's quite tame. Perfectly harmless, in fact. And not cold and slimy as people think, but warm and smooth. Quite adorable, in fact!'

But Milly privately hoped she wouldn't be called upon to caress 'Willy' in the line of duty.

Chloe was next seen with an apple – a second obvious reference to Eve. She cut it into portions and then removed her garment and lay down on a grassy bank in the nude. She had a very good figure, with perfect small breasts and a very slim waist. With slow deliberation she inserted some of the apple into her pussy and beckoned Stefan to come and taste it. He seemed reluctant at first but eventually succumbed, to Chloe's histrionic satisfaction. After that she knelt before him in gratitude and pulled off his loincloth, then performed fellatio on his impressive member. The film ended with them skipping off into the sunset, hand in hand.

A round of applause greeted the ending, in which Milly joined. Yet she had her reservations about the quality of the film. There was a rather childlike amateurishness about it which was a far cry from the more sophisticated output of Hollywood.

'What did you think of it?' Serge asked, putting her on the spot.

'It was quite . . . charming. In an allegorical way, I mean.'

'You sound hesitant, Milly. Please tell us if you have a criticism. We are always looking to improve our work.'

Horrified, she realised that everyone was waiting for her reply. It was hardly her place, as a newcomer, to tell them how to do things, but she had to say something. 'I thought the bit with the snake was good, and the apple. But after that it wasn't so interesting. I mean, all we saw was the back of Chloe's head.'

Serge smiled, and one of the men murmured something under his breath. 'How do you think we might have improved it?' Serge persisted.

'By bringing the snake back in!' Milly said, suddenly inspired. 'Yes, that would have been a nice ending to have both the man and the woman petting the snake as it crawled over both their bodies, uniting them.'

'I think she's got a point!' Serge grinned round at the others. 'I've half a mind to re-shoot that last part. What do you reckon Chloe, Stefan?'

Stefan, being a man of few words, just nodded but Chloe was enthusiastic. 'Yes, I never liked that silly skipping bit at the end. And I'd be glad of any excuse to cuddle Willy again!'

'In that case we'll do it! And I can do a fade at the end, which will be more artistic. Swirling mists of time, and so forth. Hell, Milly, I think you've started something here. I'm starting to see the "Erotic History of the Bible" in twenty episodes. I think I must go and re-read the Old Testament for inspiration.'

'Really?'

Milly was pleased when they all crowded round to congratulate her. Chloe in particular gave her a big hug.

'Good to have you on board, Milly!' she smiled. Then she put her arm around Ella, the only other woman, kissing them both in a display of sisterly affection.

Suddenly Milly looked at her watch, 'Oh no, look at the time! I have to be at a café on the *Boul'Mich* by five!'

'Let me give you a lift,' Serge offered at once.

Milly couldn't prevent a look of horror from passing over her face. Chloe noticed, and came to her rescue. 'It's all right, Serge, I'm going that way myself. We can share a cab.'

Once Serge had asked Milly to attend the following morning at nine, Chloe linked arms with her and they marched out of the small cinema, waving good-bye to the others. Once outside the building Chloe hailed a cab by rushing into the flow of traffic without any inhibitions. One stopped instantly and they got in.

'Meeting your boyfriend?' Chloe enquired, raising one thinly arched brow. 'Oh, don't worry, I know the score. He has no idea what you do for a living, and you don't want him to see you drawing up in Serge's flash automobile. Right?'

Milly gave her a rueful smile. 'Not quite. He's not a boyfriend, just a friend. But you're right, I'd prefer him not to know what I do. He's a student at the Sorbonne, and I was at Cambridge, and . . .'

'And you miss the intellectual conversation, is that it? I could tell straight away you were smarter than average, Milly. But you won't find many bluestockings in this business so you'd better keep your trap shut about having been at college.'

'Why? I'm not ashamed of it.'

'Neither should you be. But men like their women

empty-headed in this game. Flash your gnashers, bat your eyelids, waggle your tits and arse and you'll get along fine. If you have an idea, like you did today, be careful how you express it. And don't get upset if he pretends it was all his idea. Don't try to outsmart him. Remember, he's in charge.'

But as the cab lumbered down the *Rue de Rivoli*, Milly sighed. If she were going to further her friendship with Robin, as well as her career with Serge, it looked as if she would have to get used to inhabiting two very different worlds.

Robin was still waiting at the *Café Maurice* even though it was nearly five-twenty by the time Milly arrived. She was cheered by his sunny smile as she hurried up full of apologies.

'I just couldn't get away,' she began as she sat down at his table in the cordoned off pavement area. 'My godmother had visitors and I was obliged to listen to their tedious stories and not rush off, or it would have seemed rude.'

'That's perfectly all right, Milly. I knew you would come.'

Milly was shocked at how easily the lie came to her, and even more disturbed by Robin's casual acceptance of it. A precedent seemed to have been set, and she felt vaguely guilty.

'Did you?' She smiled over-eagerly, saying she would like some tea as the waiter came up. While the order was being given she had time to study Robin's face without him noticing. It struck her just as before, open and pleasant without a trace of vice. She began to feel like a different woman when she was with him, wholesome and simple.

'I brought this for you.' Robin thrust a book into her hands. It was a book of Shakespeare's sonnets, illustrated in pen and ink. 'I found it in a second-hand bookstore and thought you might like it.' He smiled, rather nervously. 'I wrote in it. Here.'

Milly looked at where he had written a line from one of the sonnets: 'Thou art as fair in knowledge as in hue.' Then he had drawn a picture of a robin, colouring its breast. She was touched. No-one had given her a book as a present before, not even Evadne.

'Thank you, Robin. That's very kind.'

'I wanted to make up a little for what happened to you the other day.' He took her hand and squeezed it gently before letting it rest on the table again, and Milly felt a tremor of excitement pass through her body at his touch. 'It should never have happened to such a sweet girl as yourself. I do hope you've had nothing to do with that brute again.'

'Oh no! I've not seen him since.'

They soon began discussing poetry, with Robin describing the theme of his thesis in more detail, and they became so engrossed that two hours passed. When he realised how late it was Robin invited her to dine with him.

'There's a student brasserie just down the road. It's cheap and cheerful, but you get some lively conversation there.'

Milly agreed readily, and Robin steered her into the street with his arm around her waist. She could feel the warmth of the contact even through her clothes, and a deep current of desire was awakened in her. She wondered if he felt the same, but if so he gave no sign of it.

The brasserie was crowded and noisy, the food wholesome and the wine free-flowing. Milly soon relaxed and began to enjoy herself with the lively crowd, who all seemed to know her companion. Although her French was not fluent, Robin translated for her and she felt a part of it all. They discussed philosophy, art and literature with a refreshing frankness, refusing to take anything on trust and with a marked lack of reverence for the establishment. Recalling the stuffy lectures she had attended at Cambridge, Milly was both surprised and pleased by their iconoclastic attitudes.

Then the conversation moved on to the subject of 'Free Love.' Most of the students seemed to be in favour of following their instincts where romance was concerned, but Robin said he believed in commitment. 'If you love a girl enough to take her maidenhead, then you must love her enough to marry her,' he stated, unequivocally.

'Not necessarily,' replied a rakish-looking man with a beard and spectacles. 'There is sex and there is love No point in confusing the two.'

'But can a woman make love without being *in* love?' asked a woman called Sophie.

'I am sure she can,' Milly replied. 'If she is sensually awakened.'

She bit her lip, realising that she had spoken without considering the impact on Robin. So much for my pure reputation, she thought wryly.

'Sensually, or sexually?' Sophie asked. 'We should not confuse the two.'

'Poetry can be sensual,' Robin said. 'Particularly the Symbolists. The sounds as well as the images. Think of Baudelaire: "*Luxe, calme et volupté.*"'

Milly was relieved that he seemed not to want to take her up on the matter of a woman's sensual awakening. He seemed prepared to discuss anything intellectually, but his personal feelings were another matter. She suspected that he was a hopeless romantic where women were concerned. Did that mean he was getting romantic ideas about her?

That seemed more and more likely as he insisted on accompanying her home after their evening at the brasserie. He placed a proprietary arm around her waist as they skirted the railings around the Jardin du Luxembourg.

'Oh Milly!' he sighed, as they walked along under a lovers' moon. 'I've hardly stopped thinking about you since we met in such unfortunate circumstances. I've been worrying about you, wondering if you were all right.'

'I'm fine,' she answered brightly. 'There was no real harm done. Although I dread to think what might have happened to me if you'd not decided to take a walk in the *Bois* that day.'

His face clouded. 'Me too. But having rescued you, I feel somehow responsible.'

He drew her into the shelter of the park gates, pulling her into a shadowed corner, and gazed at her longingly. 'I should hate anything like that to happen to you again, Milly.'

They were very close, his breath warming her cheek. Milly wanted him to kiss her, and yet she was afraid. He obviously believed her to be completely virginal and inexperienced. How could she hope to hide the passion she felt for him once he made that first, intimate contact?

When it came, however, his kiss was gentle, undemanding. He pressed his closed lips to hers and they felt soft as butter. He held her gently, too, as if she were a fragile doll. It was all Milly could do to restrain herself from pressing closer to his body, or letting her tongue slip between those tantalising lips. She held her desire in check, bracing herself against the thudding insistence of her heart as it urged her on.

'I've wanted to kiss you all evening,' he confessed, as they drew apart. 'There's something so special about you, so alluring. You are a mystery to me, Milly, but I am content to let you remain so. I revel in your mysteriousness.'

She smiled, but wished that she didn't feel such an

132

imposter. Of course he found her a mystery, since she had something to hide! But if he ever discovered her secret she would be mortified – and he would be horrified! Still smiling, she took his hand and pulled him back on to the pavement. They walked on, hand in hand, until the apartment block where she had her temporary home loomed before them.

'That is where I am staying,' she told him.

'I should like to visit you there, and meet your godmother.'

Milly's pulse raced, but she remained outwardly calm. 'Perhaps, some day.'

'How much longer do you intend to remain in Paris?'

'At least until the autumn, I expect.'

'Then I hope we may meet again.'

Their footsteps slowed as they reached the huge front door behind which the concierge kept her vigil. Milly held out her hand and he raised it to his lips with tender devotion, his long lashes sweeping to a close as he did so. Then he lifted his head and his eyes met hers in the glow from a nearby street lamp.

'Goodnight, Milly dearest. I shall be in touch soon.'

She waved and rang the bell, still clutching the slim volume of Shakespearean verse to her bosom. Aware that Robin was watching her from the street corner, Milly felt a lightness in her being that she had never felt before, provoking a crazy urge to sing and dance. Other men had excited her, it was true, but none had ever moved her to this extent. Robin Dupont, with the intriguing mixture of his father's Gallic charm and his mother's English reserve, had touched her heart and soul.

Chapter Eight

*T*hat night Milly dreamed about making love with Robin, letting him take her virginity. No other man had ever inspired her to fantasise in this fashion, and she awoke next morning vaguely shocked by her own imaginings. Was she in love with him? Her feelings were so new and strange that she could not tell. All she knew was that something had dawned in her psyche, some tender yearning sympathy for another human being. But until she knew whether her feelings were reciprocated she would speak of it to no-one, not even her Aunt Emma.

For the next week she was kept busy by Serge, who wanted her to work for him practically every day. His Erotic History of the Bible was growing to epic proportions and Milly was called upon to play a number of dramatic rôles. First she played one of Lot's daughters with Chloe, acting out a drunken orgy. Then she played Delilah to Stefan's Samson, seducing him thoroughly and cutting his dark wig so that she could then bind him in chains and have her wicked way with him once again. The following day she became handmaiden to Chloe as the Queen of Sheba, helping to prepare her for a visit by King Solomon. Although she felt somewhat upstaged on that occasion, her chance to star came the following day when they moved swiftly on through Biblical history to Salomé's dance of the seven veils.

'Don't you think Chloe should play her?' Milly suggested to Serge, thinking the other actress would be disappointed not to get that part.

'No, no! I have seen you dance my dear, and I know that you are absolutely right for the part!' he insisted. 'Besides, I have another opportunity lined up for Chloe. She shall play Mary Magdalene – before she was redeemed, naturally.'

Since Chloe seemed content with that prospect Milly relaxed and set about planning how she would choreograph the titillating dance. There wasn't much time. Serge worked to a tight schedule, which was often frustrating. Milly knew he regarded his 'naughty shorts' as purely commercial ventures, and reserved most of his imaginative flair for his 'art' films. But she wished they had more opportunity to rehearse all the same.

The seven veils that she had to wear were just that: multi-coloured chiffon scarves that she had to wind around her naked body and take off one by one. Just before the camera began to roll Milly thought of Robin, and a way to get into the part came to her at once. She would pretend that she was dancing for him, and him alone. The thought of revealing her body to him for the first time was very exciting.

Stefan wound up the gramophone and a slow, seductive melody began. The music was ethereal, flutes and harp with some percussion. Franz, the German actor in the troupe, was playing Herod, and Chloe was Herodias. They sat on makeshift thrones while Milly began to make dainty, rocking movements to the music. She twirled around slowly, her

135

eyes fixed on Franz who was clearly already aroused by her erotic display. Yet it was not him she saw sitting there but Robin, and in her imagination they were not in the makeshift throne room that Serge had constructed but in some private bedchamber.

Gradually the dance took on the quality of a magical ritual. Milly's erotic imagination wove a spell around herself, so that her movements and expression became more and more compelling. She could see Robin's limpid hazel eyes regarding her with adoring warmth as she pirouetted and removed the first veil. Holding the gauzy strip above her head, she exulted in her own power over the man. He wanted her, she was sure of that. And his desire was her aphrodisiac.

As the dance continued, Milly imagined how she would caress and arouse Robin's naked body. She saw his pale phallus rising like a lily and her red lips enclosing it. Whisking off another scarf, she imagined taking the twin fruits of his testicles into her mouth and sucking them softly. She could hear his ecstatic moans as she twirled around, and her desire for him increased. Her quim had become an aching void, longing for fulfilment. Never before had she been aware of such sharply-focused lust and she began to moan softly, her voice a droning accompaniment to the flute and harp.

By the time she removed the third veil, Milly was completely immersed in a world of sensual bliss. Now Robin was eager to claim her as his own. His mouth was on her nipple and his hands were caressing her thighs and belly, stoking the already raging fires within. She felt her breasts tingle and the hidden cleft of her sex was dripping with moisture as she moved her hips and pelvis with increasing abandon. She clasped her bound breasts, feeling the hard nipples strain and tingle at her touch through the layers of thin gauze.

A fourth veil went floating up into the air and fell to the ground. There was a hypnotic quality to the dance now that held both dancer and audience enraptured. Milly was aware of the concentration of their gaze and her body seemed to feed upon it, revelling in the worship it was receiving. She knew that she was blossoming, her cheeks flushing pink, her skin softening and glowing, her eyes glistening like wet sapphires. She knew that she was beautiful, desirable.

Now, as she toyed with the fifth scarf, her flesh was straining to be free of its light covering, longing to be in open contact with the air and eager to display its charms in all their naked glory. Milly could see Robin's eyes worshipping her beauty as the great rod of his sex reared up between his thighs. She felt a current of irresistible force flowing between the red mouth of her womb and the red tip of his penis, and knew that they would have to meet soon, soon. A shuddering passed through her at the thought of it.

The scrap of chiffon floated away, leaving her with just two layers of covering. She caught the end of the top scarf between her finger and thumb and twirled around, unwinding as she went. It seemed to her as if she were removing the cerements of death or birth, a baby's swaddling clothes or a corpse's winding-sheet: either way she was preparing for her own re-birth. In a flash of precognition she knew for certain that on that very night she would lose her virginity to Robin, in a glorious rite of passage.

Catching the end of the last veil in her other hand she revolved with dizzying speed until the wisp of cloth fell away and she was revealed in total nudity. She held the two scarves up high, waving them as banners of her triumph, and heard Franz groan at the sight of her. Yet it was not the German who groaned in her imagination, but Robin. She felt him between her quivering thighs, sensed his face upon her heaving breasts, and knew a deep and utter peace.

He was her love, her destiny. She knew that now beyond any doubt. The dance had shown it to her. With slow steps she described a final figure of eight, twirling the scarves high in the air, and sank down in a ballerina bow to the floor.

'*Bravo! Magnifique!*' she heard Serge say, as the camera ceased to roll.

The others also congratulated her. 'Oh yes, indeed. *Wunderbar!*'

'Well done, Milly. That was a lovely dance.'

Still panting she smiled round at her colleagues, but her eyes were faraway and her smile was vague. Milly was still in another time, another place. She had known for the first time what it was to desire a man completely, to long for him to utterly possess her, and feeling such a strong emotion had been something of a shock for her. The sexual dalliance she had enjoyed with other men now paled by comparison with the complete union she had foreseen between herself and Robin.

When she got to her feet she was shivering, not with cold but as an after-effect of that powerful experience. She staggered across the room while Chloe raced up to put a blanket around her shoulders. 'Milly, dear, come and lie down,' she murmured, solicitously. 'That dance took it out of you, didn't it?'

'I knew I was right to have faith in you!' Serge beamed, as she sank on to a *chaise-longue*. 'You have real star quality, Milly. I can't wait to see how you have come out on film.'

It seemed no coincidence to her that when she returned to her apartment at six o'clock Robin had left a note. The concierge handed it to her with a grudging smile. Milly knew she didn't approve of young men leaving letters for young women. She thanked her with exaggerated courtesy and took it up to her room, where she could savour every word.

'Dearest Milly, A crowd of us will attend a showing of the film *'J'Accuse'* tonight. Will you join us? We meet at the *Café Auguste* at eight. I do hope you can come. Robin.'

The excitement that was still stirring Milly's veins now reached fever pitch. She performed her toilet at the small wash-stand with great care, dusting herself with violet-scented powder and spraying herself liberally with *Mitsouko*, an exquisite perfume that she had bought from *Maison Guerlain* on one of her shopping expeditions. When the assistant had sprayed it on to her wrist she had instantly adored its aromatic blend of 'chypre' and exotic fruits. Now, though, the subtle effect was heightened as she covered her naked body from head to toe in a light veil of perfume.

What to wear? That was the question that occupied her for most of the hour before her departure. Mindful of the solemnity of the occasion, Milly combed her small wardrobe for the ideal garment. What *did* a girl wear for her defloration? She giggled at the thought that something white and virginal, like a first communion dress, would be appropriate. It was not what she had in mind, however.

In the end she chose a pretty dress in rose silk with an embroidered yoke and drawn threadwork over the bust and sleeves. Over it she wore one of the long, fashionable cardigans she had bought from *Galeries LaFayette* in navy blue wool. Then she pulled on a navy cloche hat, trimmed with grosgrain ribbon, that she thought made her look a little like Mary Pickford when she peered out sideways from beneath the brim.

It was a fine evening when she set out, full of high expectation, for the *Café Auguste* on the *Boulevard St Germain*. It was not more than ten minutes' walk from where she was staying, and she arrived on the dot at eight to find the place overflowing with students. For a few anxious moments she scanned the crowd, unable to recognise Robin, but then she felt a tap on her shoulder and swung round to find herself looking straight into his laughing hazel eyes.

'You came! I am so happy.'

His adoring gaze was so similar to what she had imagined during her dance that Milly blushed. Robin offered to buy her a cocktail so she accepted a *Mata Hari* which she had heard was a popular drink in the smart cafés, although she had no idea what it contained.

'The film is being shown in the room upstairs,' he explained, as they wove their way through the tables. 'It's a special presentation by members of the Sorbonne Cinematograph Society. There's to be a discussion afterwards.'

The large upstairs room was already crowded, but Robin had got two of his friends to save them seats. A makeshift screen had been erected at one end of the room and the projector was at the other, with an aisle in between. There was an air of excited expectancy amongst the students which was infectious. Already keyed up just by being in Robin's company, Milly felt hot and took off her cardigan. She saw his eyes drop automatically to her bosom, where the écru lace of her camiknickers was visible through the bodice, and sensed the surge of his desire. She gave him a smile, saw his cheeks redden and was sure that he wanted her, just as she now wanted him.

The show was beginning, however. A student, the president of the society, opened the proceedings by announcing that the film they were about to see had been made 'against the abomination of war.' A mannish young woman sat at a piano, waiting to perform, and there were two other students at the side of the stage with scripts and torches. As soon as the lights went out the piano began playing Ravel's 'Gaspard de la Nuit.' As the titles and first images appeared on the screen the haunting music was overlaid by the voices of the students, chanting poetry by Rupert Brooke and Siegfried Sassoon.

Milly was riveted by the spectacle of soldiers in the Great War. She had seen many such pictures already, heard similar anti-war messages, but the combination of striking images and affecting sound made an impact on her very soul. The buoyant mood in which she had arrived soon evaporated, to be replaced by one of sorrow and despair. The film was quite long, a fourteen-reeler, and very different from the kind of superficial thriller, knockabout comedies or erotic entertainments she had seen before.

The soldiers rose up in their serried ranks to accuse those who had survived the war of desecrating their memory. What had she, Milly, and others of her generation done to justify such wholesale wastage of young male blood? Had she made society a better place? What had she done to stamp out greed and injustice and prejudice? The questions buzzed in her brain. As she stared at the faces on the screen they ceased to be anonymous but took on the features of young soldiers she had known: Jack Kent, the brother of her friend at Cheltenham who had been killed at the Somme; Bill Stokes, her mother's next-door neighbour, fallen at Ypres; Orlando Millward, an officer she had flirted with at a ball and who had died of trench fever.

Then, at the end of the film, an Irish student marched solemnly down the aisle playing a lament on his Uillean pipes while someone read an extract from a letter written in the trenches. The tears were rolling down Milly's cheeks and, when the lights went up, she saw that almost everyone else had been similarly affected, including Robin. He squeezed her hand, and she felt very close to him in that simple, poignant moment.

The evening proceeded with a discussion. The impact of the film had been purely visceral: it was the first time Milly had really understood the emotional power of the medium and its potential for propaganda. It made her half-ashamed of her own frivolous part in the industry, so that she was more determined than ever that Robin should not know about it. But neither Milly nor Robin were in the mood for analysing camera work.

'Shall we go?' he whispered, after the first couple of speeches.

She nodded, and they made their way out of the room and downstairs into the still-crowded bar. 'Would you care for another cocktail?' he asked her, but she shook her head.

'No, Robin, thank you. I'd prefer to go somewhere quiet, where we may talk by ourselves.'

'Will you come to my room?' he asked, tentatively, his greenish-brown eyes gleaming at her in the lamplight. 'My room-mate is away and ... of course, I understand if you would rather not be there without a chaperone.'

She slipped her arm through his. 'That would be wonderful, Robin!'

They walked down the crowded boulevard talking about the film. Robin had seen service as a dispatch rider during the last year of the war, and the experience had clearly affected him deeply. He had formed strong pacifist opinions and now he endorsed Abel Gance's message.

'They ask if the sacrifice was worth it,' he said, adding bitterly, 'I say it was not. Now it is all over people just want to enjoy themselves and forget all the death and suffering.'

'But that's natural, surely?'

'If we behaved according to what was "natural" there would be anarchy!'

'But some natural things are good.' Milly hugged his arm, nestling close to the reassuring warmth of his body. 'Love, for instance.'

He smiled at her, his eyes misty. 'Oh yes, Milly! Love is the only thing that compensates for the horrors of war. Love is . . . divine!'

Robin spoke with such heartfelt sincerity that she was sure he must be speaking from experience. But then he went on, 'I used to carry Shakespeare's sonnets with me everywhere on the battlefields. When there was a lull in the action and I could hear myself think, I would read one of those beautiful poems and remember that there was a better life, that other things were possible.'

'And did you have a sweetheart, during the war?'

'No-one in particular. I used to dream of girls in general, of their beauty and softness and kindness, but it was just that – dreams. I never loved a girl in the full sense of the word. I never felt those exalted emotions until . . .'

He stopped, looking at her with shy but sincere affection. Milly felt her heart fill with gratification. Although he had not said it in so many words, she knew he loved her. As, she believed, she loved him. Amidst all their melancholy talk of war the steady flame of their love still burned, feeding on their mutual sympathy.

Robin lived in a tall, dingy apartment block in one of the back streets near the Sorbonne. The porter was a Moroccan who smoked foul-smelling cigarettes and waved them on up the staircase without a second glance. How different from *Madame La Concierge* in my apartments, Milly thought with a smile. His room was small, with just a curtain hanging between the sleeping quarters. There was a chair each and a small

143

table, but most of the room was taken up with bookcases, groaning with serious-looking volumes. Robin soon had the smelly gas fire going and he also lit the reeking paraffin stove to make coffee.

'May I look at your books?' Milly asked, as he went to work.

'Of course!'

Amongst them she found some extraordinary drawings, twelve illustrations to Wilde's *Salome* in black and white. Robin looked over her shoulder. 'Oh, you've found the "Beastly Beardslies!" What do you think of them?'

'I find them quite extraordinary!'

'Decadent is surely the word. Yet I find they have a certain haunting charm.'

Milly could not help seeing the find as significant. There was Salomé in a flowing peacock skirt that seemed to catch the essence of her own dance. The blatant sensuality of the drawings reminded her of how she had felt when she performed for the camera, of how she had transmuted her desire for Robin into erotic movement. She looked up at him with a smile, and saw his face just inches above hers, his eyes meeting hers in a moment of mutual recognition.

Slowly his lips descended, not to her cheek or brow where they had sometimes grazed momentarily before, but towards the open invitation of her own mouth. All Milly's previous longing returned in full flood as his kiss swept her up into unadulterated bliss. She could feel his warm lips trembling with emotion beneath her own, and lifted her hand to his neck to give him a reassuring caress. He moaned softly, letting his sweet tongue slip into her mouth where he grew increasingly bold. Soon their tongues were engaged in a sensual dance, licking and sucking each other with passionate abandon.

'Oh Robin!' she sighed when, at last, they broke for air. 'I've dreamed of your kiss!'

'Have you, dear Milly? Have you really?'

His eyes were gleaming with adoration, just as she had imagined. 'Yes.' She dropped her gaze shyly. 'And that is not all I've dreamed of.'

'What do you mean?' He sounded eager, yet cautious. Milly knew he wouldn't dare hope that their desires coincided. What a wonderful surprise he had in store! But she must be careful not to play the harlot too openly, or she would frighten him off. He thought her pure and innocent and she had no wish to disillusion him.

'Since I met you I have had ... feelings. I don't quite know how to describe them, but they are very powerful. It is like a hunger, and yet there is such sweetness ... Whenever I think of you, I ...'

'Milly, Oh Milly!'

She found herself being swept into his arms. He kissed her again, this time with fierce and uncompromising passion, and his hands began to caress her breasts and buttocks through the silk of her gown. The almost desperate way in which he was handling her roused her desire for him even more. At last, embarrassed by his fit of ardour, he dropped at her feet and put his head in her lap, embracing her thighs.

'I love you my darling Milly. There I have said it! Never before have I felt this way about any woman, and I dream of you night and day. You are my sun and moon, Milly!'

He looked up at her with helpless, appealing eyes. She stroked the thick mat of his hair with a smile. 'I believe I love you too, Robin,' she said softly. 'All that talk of war and death just reminded me how important love is and how quickly life can change, for better or worse.'

'"Gather ye rosebuds while ye may,"' he smiled.

'"To the Virgins, to Make Much of Time," Robert Herrick,' she replied promptly.

He hugged her with a delighted laugh. 'Not just a pretty face, but an intelligent mind and a learned one to boot. I can't believe my luck, Milly!'

'Then ... should we gather rosebuds together?' she asked him, solemnly.

'I have begun already, dearest, sucking the honey from those dear rosy lip-buds of yours.'

His eyes fell to her bosom, and she read his mind. Slowly she unfastened the buttons of her dress and pulled her arms out of the sleeves so that the bodice fell to her waist, exposing the lacy top of her camisole. She slipped out of the ribbon straps which left the lace clinging precariously to her breasts.

'Oh Milly, may I?' he breathed, his voice hoarse with emotion.

She nodded, and his shaking fingers pulled down the scrap of lace that concealed her already tumid nipples from view. He stared at her naked bosom in wonder for a few seconds then, with a tortured gasp, held her left breast between his palms and put the red, excited nipple between his lips. His suckling was deliciously stimulating, sending ripples of pure joy throughout her body and soul. She had felt such sensations before, but not with such deep emotional satisfaction. This must be love, she decided, it feels so new and different.

Although she was eager to explore his body too, Milly restrained herself from being too forward. She knew she must let him take the lead, this first time at least, even though she suspected that she was far more experienced in the ways of love. What he lacked in expertise, however, he certainly made up for in enthusiasm.

Robin's lips were passing eagerly from one breast to the other now, and his hands were roving between her thighs, pulling up the skirt of her dress to feel the silk of her camiknickers. He was in the grip of unstoppable lust, and Milly knew that she must make some token protest if she were not to be thought of easy virtue.

'Please, love, your hands,' she began.

Robin withdrew them at once. 'I am so sorry, I became quite carried away.'

'It's just I don't know if we should. I'm afraid you'll not respect me if I let you go too far.'

He studied her face thoughtfully. 'But do you *want* me to go further, Milly?'

'More than anything – I love you so much! But I am afraid.'

She averted her eyes shyly, and he laid his head on her breast. 'So am I, dear love,' he admitted. I have never made love with a girl before, not properly. They say if you can pull out in time there is no danger.'

'I've heard that too. And if you wish to try, I shall not object. If I am to lose my virginity I would rather it were with you than any man alive.'

He looked up at her, flushed and tousled, his eyes full of tenderness. 'You don't know how happy that makes me feel, Milly.'

His lips returned to her breasts, and she stroked his head as he sucked on each throbbing nipple in turn. Her desire for him was intense now, and would not be thwarted. She murmured, 'Would you like to undress me, Robin? I shall not mind.'

Soon his fingers were everywhere, easing her out of her dress, unfastening her stockings, undoing the buttons of her camiknickers. When she finally lay naked before him he could not tear his eyes away from her, marvelling at every feature of her body as if he had just arrived in some new and promised land. Seeing herself through his eyes, Milly felt her pride and confidence increased which only served to make her want him more than ever.

'Dear girl, you are so beautiful!' he murmured. 'Can it be true that you will let me possess all this loveliness?'

He was caressing the curly hairs of her delta, and she guessed he had never been so close to a woman's sex before. She let her thighs fall open and he soon took the hint, lying down to peer into her crevice as he held her labia open with his fingers. Milly was longing for him to lick her there, but she could hardly suggest such a thing so she lay there in frustration wondering if the idea would occur to him.

At last he introduced a tentative finger. 'Does this give you pleasure, love?' he asked. She nodded enthusiastically and he delved a little deeper. 'And this?'

'Oh yes!' she sighed. 'It feels exquisite.'

'For me, too. Isn't that wonderful, Milly, that our pleasure should be mutual? I have often discussed these matters with my friends, and some say that a woman's delight in sex can be even greater than a man's. They say women particularly enjoy having their private parts licked and sucked. Does that seem strange to you?'

Oh thank you, thank you, anonymous friend! Milly breathed silently.

'Not really,' she said aloud. 'I mean, no stranger than the sex act itself. After all, if I enjoyed you kissing my lips, then my tender parts should be even more sensitive to your lips.'

'Then you would not mind if I . . . oh!'

He had already started kissing around her labia but suddenly his tongue slipped between them and Milly groaned aloud at the sudden increase in her stimulation. She wriggled against his mouth, trying to get him into contact with her clitoris as unobtrusively as

148

possible, and soon he was licking the little shaft with rapid movements of his tongue, quite unknowingly sending her to the brink of an orgasm right away.

But before she could reach that state of ecstasy Robin was on his knees, hastily unbuttoning his fly. Milly sat up to help him, and was soon able to view his prominent member. She was pleased to find it a good thick one, aesthetically pleasing in shape and colour. It was all she could do to refrain from lowering her mouth on to it. Instead she reached out and touched it gently, pretending it was the very first male member she had ever seen.

'But it's so big!' she breathed. 'I had no idea that a man's organ was this size!'

Robin gave a soft chuckle. 'I suppose you cannot imagine that it will fit inside you, my love. But I can assure you it will, with a little patience. I shall try not to hurt you. We must take it slowly.'

He knelt between her thighs and soon his cock was lodged in her vulva, just at the entrance to her quim. Milly felt him nudge a little and then, encountering no significant barrier, the sturdy member pushed further in. She winced and moaned, pretending the penetration was painful, because she knew this would be expected of her. Although she was technically a virgin, in effect her hymen had long been ruptured by probing fingers.

Milly did feel a bit tight and strained inside when Robin first entered her. The moment he pushed in with his full length, however, and she felt herself filled up completely, she was in heaven. All her former feelings of love and desire had returned in force, and as he began his first thrusting movements she synchronised her hips quite naturally to his and was soon lost in the bliss of rhythmic accord.

Now her dream began to unfold. The beautiful sensations of love that she had longed to share with

Robin were uniting them at last, and she could tell from the waves of powerful, sensual energy which engulfed them both that he was feeling the same rapture. Gaining in confidence, her lover experimented with fast and slow thrusting, gauging his movements to her reactions, letting his hands and lips stimulate her in other places while his hard phallus kept up the steady pace of love, as strong and regular as a heartbeat.

'Oh, this is so wonderful!' Milly breathed as she hovered close to the edge of tumultuous abandon. 'I love you, Robin, truly I do!'

His kiss propelled her into a long and tender climax, more sweetly satisfying than any she had received from the superficial fondlings of her other lovers. Milly felt she was yielding utterly to him, giving up her very essence as she sighed her way through the undulating bliss of her first vaginal orgasm. But just as the tremulous sensations reached their peak she felt Robin curse and abruptly pull out of her, shattering the mood of joyous fulfilment.

Milly felt bitterly disappointed. She heard him groan as he spilled his seed into the sheets and tried not to think of how she had wanted to hold him inside her, to embrace his manhood within her and hold him there until he was quiescent again. Of course she knew it could not be – they could not risk the consequences. Yet now she felt she understood the loving urge that made women want to belong completely to their lovers, at whatever cost to themselves. The urge was powerful, vital, irresistible. It was the spirit of Life itself.

To compensate for her disappointment, Milly took her exhausted lover into her arms and he lay with his head on her breast while his breathing slowly returned to normal. At length Robin turned his head and looked up at her with a vague smile.

'Are you all right, Milly? Not in pain, or anything?'

'Oh no! It was hardly painful at all. Now I am truly yours, Robin. I want you to always remember this moment, dearest.'

She felt her eyes fill with tears and, with a sudden terrible burst of recognition, she realised why. They were going to have to part. The inevitability struck her with the force of a prophecy, and although she tried to banish it from her mind the idea remained there, as irrevocable as a solemn oath.

Chapter Nine

Milly was sitting in the *Café Maurice* with Chloe the following afternoon, discussing Serge's rumoured plans to move his business to London. Franz had told Chloe there was too much competition from other film-makers in Paris, and since most of Serge's films were sold in England he thought he should set up a studio there.

'I suppose it would be all right for you,' Chloe was saying. 'Being English, I mean. It would not be hard for you to live in London. But I, being French, would find it most strange. I am not at all sure that I should like to live amongst the prissy English – oh, pardon! I do not mean to offend you, *ma chère*.'

'No offence taken!' Milly laughed. But as she glanced at the doorway she saw Robin suddenly appear and, once the thrill of seeing him again had passed, was thrown into a terrible panic. What if he should come to their table and join in their conversation? What indiscretions might Chloe commit, not knowing that their work had been kept secret from him?

Milly shrank away, hoping he wouldn't recognise her, but he made a beeline for their table.

'Milly!' he said, his eyes shining like beacons of hope. 'How wonderful to see you here. How are you?'

She was well aware of the silent second half of that question: *after last night?* Robin had walked her home and they'd exchanged a passionate goodnight kiss at her door. *Madame La Concierge* had been none too pleased to let her in at midnight, but Milly had been in too exalted a mood to care.

Now, though, she was in a state of trepidation as she introduced him to Chloe, her 'friend.'

'*Enchantée, Monsieur!*' Chloe smiled, archly. But then, to Milly's relief, she rose to her feet. 'I'm afraid I have a pressing appointment, so I must leave you both now. But I'm sure your gentleman friend will look after you, Milly.'

Smiling sweetly, she sashayed gracefully out between the crowded tables and was soon gone. Milly braced herself for questions, but Robin had something else on his mind. A group of his wealthier student friends had decided to hire a villa at Deauville for the whole of August and he wanted her to join them.

'It would be wonderful, dearest, think of it! A whole month to ourselves.'

'But how would we live, Robin?'

'Oh, we could give English lessons or something,' he replied airily. 'Once the rent is paid we should not need much to live on. I'm sure we could manage.'

'Well, I'm not sure . . .'

'Milly, do say you'll come!' he begged.

'I cannot make any promises. I told you I'm staying with my godmother, and I am sure she would not approve of me going away to live with students.'

'Then maybe I can call on her some time, and assure her of my honourable intentions?'

Milly laughed. 'Robin! How could you possibly assure her of any such thing, after last night?'

But to her amazement he raised her fingers to his

153

lips and kissed them fervently. 'Milly, my intentions *are* honourable. I know I am just a student now, and in no position to make an honest woman of you. But as soon as my studies are over and I can find a job I hope we . . .'

'Please, say no more!' she pleaded, only too aware of his drift. 'You have at least another year of study ahead of you. Anything may happen in that time. Situations change . . .'

'But not feelings, Milly. Not mine, at any rate. "Love is not love that alters where it alteration finds." I believe that most sincerely, my dearest.'

Suddenly she felt a great weight of guilt about her heart. What had she done in encouraging this naive young man, in making love with him? He was already thinking of her as his unofficial fiancée and yet he knew very little about her adventurous past, her present risqué occupation or her future plans. She averted her gaze, not wanting him to read the guilt and regret that was lurking in her heart. Not that she would have missed their love-making for the world! Oh, why was she feeling so wretchedly confused about it all?

She left the café soon afterwards on the pretext of having to do some shopping. Once outside, she hurried along to Serge's place. Although she was not scheduled to work that afternoon she was anxious to know if there was any truth in the rumour that he would be moving to London. Everything seemed to be happening so fast that she could scarcely work out how she felt about things.

When she arrived they were in the middle of filming the Mary Magdalene sequence, but she waited in the kitchenette and made them all coffee as soon as the camera stopped rolling. They sat around in the studio drinking, and then Serge suddenly came out with the news they'd all been so anxious to hear.

'Well, my friends, I have come to a decision,' he began, portentously. 'I know this will please some of you and displease others, but I have to make my business work one way or another, and it is clear that if I stay in Paris I shall be just another '*Marchand de Porno*' and never another Gance or Feyder or Delluc.'

Mentioning the other directors reminded Milly that he had pretensions as a director of the 'Poetic Realist' school. It was easy to forget that when he was not capturing their erotic scenarios on film he was working on projects nearer to his own heart.

'So,' he went on, 'I have finally made the difficult decision to move to London. A friend of mine has found me a large disused warehouse in West London that I can turn into a wonderful studio. And these little entertainments of ours are in great demand at the country house parties of the wealthy, as well as in the gentlemen's clubs. I believe we could all do well there.'

'What if we do not want to move to England?' Michel asked, sullenly.

'Then I shall give you one month's wages and my blessing.'

'Well I'll come!' Franz said, eagerly. 'I've always wanted to see London.'

Several others followed his lead, including Chloe. When Serge turned to Milly she felt all eyes were upon her, as the only Englishwoman. 'So, Milly, will you return to the land of your birth?' Serge asked, quietly.

She felt she was being torn this way and that. Everything was happening at the wrong time, or in the wrong place. Her heart seemed split painfully into three: one part was with Emma in Florence, another with her mother in London, and a third there in Paris with Robin. At every turn her longing to be with each of them was tinged with pain. If she went back to

155

Emma she would feel ashamed of her inability to make a success of her film career; if she returned to her mother she would be made to feel like a moral outcast, and if she stayed with Robin, masquerading as pure and innocent, she would feel a fraud. So what was she to do?

'Must I decide now?' she asked, desperately.

'No, by all means take your time. But I shall need to know by the end of the week. I plan to finish this Biblical epic in two days and then my equipment will be packed for the voyage. We shall be embarking for England next Tuesday.'

'So soon!'

The others were surprised too, but Serge had been contemplating the move for a while. The lease on his apartment was almost expired, so rather than renew it he'd decided to leave.

For several days after that Milly was in torment. Her mind and heart were at odds, and her soul caught somewhere in between. The prospect of a summer of love with Robin was delightful, and in some moods she would gladly give in to the idea of gathering rosebuds. But her conscience warned her that she would only compound her deception that way. If she stayed in Paris sooner or later he was bound to find out what her occupation was, and then she dreaded to think how utterly shocked and disgusted he would be.

If she went to London, time and distance would put their love to the test. If they still wanted each other in a year or two's time everything might be different. Robin seemed so sure of his feelings for her, but she knew that his experience of women had been virtually nil. Whereas she ... Sighing, Milly faced the unpleasant reality once again. Although her tender feelings for Robin were overwhelming right now, she didn't know how she would feel in the future. A part of her longed to be footloose and fancy free, but she dreaded hurting him.

The circular arguments continued to whirl in her head as the deadline for her decision approached. Milly had said nothing to anyone else about her dilemma: the decision must be hers alone. Robin was busy studying for an examination so she had not seen him since their chance meeting in the *Café Maurice*, a circumstance that was both convenient and frustrating.

By Friday morning, however, she knew her own mind. When she told Serge she was prepared to go to England with him, he was overjoyed.

'I will make you a star!' he promised, kissing her cheek. 'Let us think up a sobriquet for you. How about . . . "The English Rosebud"?'

At once Milly thought of Robin, and blushed. 'Yes, that will do well.'

'And I'm sure *you* will do well too, my dear.' He kissed her again, this time on the forehead, but her heart was heavy. Now that it was accomplished she was wondering if she had made the right decision.

Robin sent her a note saying he would meet her at the *Café Maurice* on Saturday night. Milly decided not to go. She was so afraid that seeing him would weaken her resolve. Besides, she had a superstitious desire to retain the memory of their love intact. The idea of a painful scene, with Robin begging her to stay and she forced to refuse, was anathema to her. She sent him a note saying that her godmother had made other arrangements and she would be in touch. She didn't let him know that next time she wrote it would be from London.

Even so she shed a few tears as she lay alone in her bed on Saturday night. She wondered what perverse urge in her was making her give up the prospect of true love for an uncertain future. Did she love Robin?

It certainly felt like it. But she was afraid that if she stayed with him now she would be both a distraction and a burden to him.

Besides, there was something else in her, something Robin couldn't satisfy. Her wicked, sensual side was driving her out into the erotic underworld, a world where she could discover the darker side of her own desires and perhaps gain a certain dubious fame and fortune in the process. The prospect of becoming a naughty movie star was exhilarating, and she couldn't wait for her films to be launched upon an unsuspecting world.

The boat train steamed into Victoria Station late on Tuesday evening. Milly said good-bye to the rest of the party since she was going straight to her father's house in Chiswick. Although she had not seen a great deal of him while she was growing up he had always made it plain that she was welcome to visit him at any time. Since his house was quite close to where Serge was setting up his studio Milly had decided to stay there for a few days at least, and had sent a telegram to that effect. She was also wary of contacting her mother before she had ascertained how she might be received.

As a young girl Milly had felt guilty because she enjoyed his company more than her mother's. Vincent Belfort was charming, urbane and still handsome. Milly had seen him mellowing over the years and now she could admire him objectively, in the same way as she admired her mother. But she could quite understand why he had separated from his militant feminist wife. Besides, his predilections ran in another direction. Vincent Belfort was 'guardian' to a pretty youth called Philip who was articled with his law firm. She had gleaned this information from Emma.

The housekeeper, Mrs Godwin, opened the door of

the Chiswick mansion and at once her face brightened. 'Miss Milly, how lovely to see you! And looking so smart, too.'

She was ushered in and the bell rung for Godwin to take her luggage up to the pretty bedroom that had always been reserved for 'Miss Milly.' Suddenly Vincent appeared from his study, pipe in mouth. Milly threw herself into his arms, relishing the comfortingly familiar smell of tobacco and Guerlain's *Mouchoir de Monsieur* that her father exuded.

'I hope you had a good journey, my dear,' he said, leading her into the drawing room. 'What shall we ask Mrs Godwin to bring you?'

'Oh some good old English tea, please!'

The conversation that she had been expecting began as soon as the tea-tray arrived.

'Well, my dear, your education is now completed. Theoretically, at least. Have you given a thought to the future?'

Milly sighed at the recurrence of the old refrain, but at least she could be franker with her father. 'I had a chat with Emma about it while I was in Florence,' she began, testing the water.

He gave a hearty chuckle. 'I can just imagine the sort of career that woman would sort out for you! Talk to her by all means, Milly, but take everything she says with a large grain of salt. She hasn't exactly led the most conventional of lives, nor the most respectable.'

'But you wouldn't want me to end up teaching in some ghastly school, would you Pa?'

'Not if you didn't wish it. I only want you to be happy, child.' His expression softened, the brown eyes growing sentimental. 'Of course, if no other avenues opened up I could always find a governess post for you, or something of the kind. I've plenty of contacts.

It's only what I should have done if I'd had a son, of course.'

'Actually, father, I have a temporary job with a man who makes films. He is setting up a studio not far from here, and . . .'

'A film star!' Vincent stared at her in astonishment.

'Not star, exactly. Just a modest actress. But I enjoy the work, it pays well, and it will tide me over until I can find something more permanent.'

'Well I confess, Milly, you never cease to amaze me. Of course I know you are a very pretty girl, and an intelligent one too. But I should never have thought . . . oh well, you know your own mind. Always have. Just let me know if you need any assistance at any time, won't you? And if you ever get into trouble, please don't ever hesitate to contact me. I know your mother isn't always the most sympathetic or helpful of women.'

'Thank you, Pa!'

Milly kissed his rough cheek, but then there came a knock at the door and soon young Philip had joined them. After the greetings Milly decided to withdraw to her room. She sensed the two men wanted to be alone.

Vincent Belfort was content to allow his daughter to stay with him as long as she liked, which was a great relief to her. He didn't enquire too closely into her work either, since he regarded the cinema as idle entertainment for the working classes and he apparently had no notion of it being used for erotic purposes. All of which suited Milly fine.

Over the next month the Latour Studio at Hammersmith leapt into active life. Every day Milly was there helping out. If she wasn't acting she was making tea, painting scenery or sewing costumes. It was a case of 'all hands to the pump' and a camaraderie sprang up amongst the small company that was even stronger than it had been in Paris. A couple of English actors had been taken on and although one of them, Richard, was quite prepared to act out erotic scenes with women, in his private life he preferred sex with men. Off-screen he was rather studious and well-read, only doing the work because he wanted to amass some savings for a projected trip to Greece. Milly found she could enjoy his company more than that of the other men, whose humour was a bit too crude for her taste.

About two weeks after her return to England Milly received a stiff note from her mother. It seemed she'd offended her by not getting in touch sooner. She wrote back at once, explaining that she was 'working all hours' and promising to visit soon, but she couldn't face it. The rift between them seemed to have grown to almost unbreachable proportions.

Putting all thoughts of her mother aside, Milly threw herself into the production of a new film called *House Party* in which she played the star part of 'Lydia, Lady Belgravia,' a society hostess who prided herself on providing exactly the right sort of entertainment for each of her house guests. It was a long film by Serge's standards, running a full forty-five minutes, and it was aimed, appropriately enough, at the County Set whose lives were reputed to be one long round of self-indulgent pleasure.

'I have wonderful news for you,' Serge announced one morning, when they had almost completed the film. 'We have been invited to première the film at a real country house party! Lord Sanderford, the shipping magnate, was very impressed when he saw my 'Erotic History of the Bible' at the house of a friend. He contacted me to see if he could have exclusive rights to any of my films. I had to refuse, of course, but I did offer him the chance to show *House Party* before anyone else and he jumped at the chance. Naturally he's paying handsomely for the privilege, and he's invited me and the principals to attend in a fortnight's time.'

There were groans from the one or two actors who had not been included in the production, but the rest of them were very excited. To mix with the aristocracy and the bright young things of the 'Flapper Set' on their own ground was more than they had dreamed of.

On the appointed morning Milly waited in high excitement for her friends to pick her up in the motor car they had hired for the occasion. She was allowed just one small suitcase, but into it she had packed a pretty chiffon dress and some new strappy shoes, with various accessories and her toilet things. They were only staying overnight on the Saturday, but it would be enough to give them a taste of the 'high life'.

Dressed in her travelling outfit of tweed skirt and jacket, Milly joined the bubbling crowd in the open-topped automobile and they set out, laughing and joking, for Lord Sanderford's seat in Berkshire. On the way they stopped at one of the new wayside filling stations for the novelty of having their engine filled at one of the hand pumps. Fritz, who had driven German tanks during the war, managed to deliver them all safely to the imposing portal of 'Maplefield,' which was set in fifteen acres of park land, with its own golf course and tennis courts.

They were welcomed warmly by Lord Sanderford's butler and shown to their rooms. Milly had to share with Chloe, but she exclaimed in wonder at the size of the twin-bedded room with its splendid view over water meadows to the banks of the Thames. There was to be a picnic lunch in half an hour, so there was little time to waste.

The scene when they emerged from the house was one of varied activity. In the distance gunfire could be heard from Lord Sanderford's shooting party, while other elderly men could be glimpsed fishing on the riverbank. The matrons were either sitting on the terrace or admiring the roses, all carrying parasols for it was a hot day. But the bright young things were always on the move, dashing here and there with cries of 'anyone for tennis?' or 'who'll make up a four-some?' The distant sound of a wind-up gramophone could be heard coming from the library where the carpet had been rolled back for impromptu dancing, and another small party could be seen punting on the river.

'It's all very informal and jolly, I must say,' Milly remarked. She had been afraid that the weekend would be rather stuffy and she might be nervous about breaking some rule of etiquette, but everything seemed far more casual than she had imagined.

A young man with a monocle approached them and Chloe stifled a giggle. He did look rather a caricature of a 'toff', Milly had to admit, but she was disposed to be polite to everyone and returned his nervous smile with a beaming one.

'Er . . . how d'ye do ladies? May I introduce myself? The name's Teddy Sanderford. Father said I was to look after the theatricals when they arrived. Could that possibly be you, ladies?'

'Yes, indeed!' Milly said loudly, to hide Chloe's hysterics. 'I am Miss Milly Belfort and this is Madem-oiselle Chloe Duvoisier.'

'Oh, a real French *demoiselle* – capital!' Teddy exclaimed, his pale grey eyes gleaming with interest. Then he said, in an execrable accent, '*Enchanté, Mademoiselle.*'

Chloe took his proffered hand, just managing to control her facial muscles but quite incapable of uttering a word. Milly quickly broke in. 'We were wondering which party to join, Sir. There are so many diversions here.'

'Call me Teddy, do! Well, ladies, I think the picnic will be starting soon. That's down in Peart's meadow, I shall escort you there. After that, dancing in the library – although there'll be bags of that tonight – or bridge, a bit tedious for you I'd have thought. There's always tennis of course. Oh, and the Wipers are holding their races I believe.'

'The Wipers?' Milly repeated, bemused.

'Sorry, bit of an in joke round here. They're the poor blighters who got whipped a cripple at Ypres. About a dozen of them, mostly officers, all from around here. They have wheelchair races and relays on crutches, all that sort of thing. Proceeds to the Red Cross.'

His tone was casual, but his words cast a chill over the two women. Milly shuddered, and Chloe's covert giggles ceased abruptly. Sensing their change of mood, Teddy said brightly, 'Fancy a preliminary noggin before lunch? Have whatever you fancy. It's Liberty Hall here.'

Soon they were sipping gin fizz on the terrace in the company of most of the *jeunesse dorée* who were assembling for the picnic. Looking at their tennis dresses and casually elegant jersey gowns or divided flannel skirts, Milly wished she had worn something more fashionable than her silk blouse, tweeds and sensible shoes. The talk was fast and flippant, and Milly found herself eavesdropping as she and Chloe were half bored to death by the idle chatter of Teddy and his equally tedious friend 'Algers'.

A large girl called 'Bunty' was saying, 'Jacky Ponders has invited me to fly over to Paris with him next weekend.'

'*Fly*?' her petite companion exclaimed. She had a shiny black bob and very blue eyes, which made her look quite striking. 'How divine! Where do you hop off from?'

'Hounslow. We'll spend a couple of nights in Gay Paree then take the cattle truck to Nice.'

'The *cattle* truck?'

Bunty laughed. 'Not a real one, silly ass! That's what they call the Riviera Express. It's always so dashed crowded. Still, if the honourable parents won't take the plunge into the twentieth century and allow one to drive, what else can one do?'

'Fly down, I suppose.'

'Don't say that to Ponders, whatever you do! Betwixt me and thee, the poor chump has got himself into debt. We're only catching the crate to Paris because Matty Harrison is piloting the thing.'

'Matty? A pilot?'

'Yes. Got his wings last September, I believe.'

'How awfully topping! Will you be setting foot on the Maudsleys' yacht in Nice, do you suppose?'

'That depends . . .'

Milly forced her attention back to the two young men before her as Teddy asked her a direct question. 'Do you play golf, Miss Belfort?'

'Er . . . no. I'm afraid I don't.'

He gave his friend a wink. 'Then perhaps you'd care to practise a few swings after lunch?'

Milly wasn't quick enough to think up a reason for refusing, but later kicked herself for getting saddled with such a boring companion. They were soon following across the grass towards the area designated for the picnic. It turned out to be a lavish, though informal affair, taking place on tartan rugs spread out near the river.

The food was delicious, the weather perfect and the company dazzling, but Milly felt an emptiness inside as she surveyed the scene. She had scarcely thought of Robin since she returned from Paris, pushing all thoughts of him out of her mind as she threw herself into her work, but now she couldn't help noticing that every young man present seemed to have at least one adoring young woman hanging on his every word.

There weren't enough young men to go round, of course. That much was obvious. There never were these days, Milly thought with a sigh, not after the flower of Europe's youth had been so cruelly decimated by the war. Perhaps she had been foolish to throw up what might have been her one chance of happiness. What if Robin found a new sweetheart and forgot all about her? Would she ever feel the same way about any man again?

Well, she had burnt her boats now. Apart from sending Robin a postcard of Shakespeare's monument with a brief message, she had not written to him. It was so hard to know what to say to him when she could not talk about work.

'Miss Belfort, would you care to join me for a spot of fore play?' Milly looked up, startled, into the faded eyes of Teddy Sanderford. 'The golf practice, remember?'

'Oh . . . yes. Of course!'

She started to rise awkwardly and he helped her to her feet then shepherded her back across the grass to the house, chattering all the way. 'So fortunate to have this fine weather, what? Jolly gathering. Life so boring in the country without good company. Good to have some outsiders to swell the ranks. Always a few artistic types to raise the tone. Dashed fine way to spend a weekend, spot of sport, spot of booze, spot of feminine company, by Jove yes! Capital way to pass the time.'

By the time they got to the house Milly was thoroughly bored and longing for some more entertaining company but she didn't know how to get away from him. He led the way boldly up to the Long Gallery where a set of golf clubs was conveniently situated in

an umbrella stand inside the door. 'We always practise up here when it's wet,' he explained.

Milly didn't like to point out that it wasn't raining
that afternoon. She felt oddly resigned to being alone
with Teddy. It was obvious that Lord Sanderford's
younger son was well plastered, and Milly feared for
the antique plates and vases that were displayed here
and there around the gallery, but it was hardly her
place to make objections.

'This, my dear, is a number three iron,' he told her,
his voice thick and slow.

She took the golf club and weighed it experimen-
tally in her hand. 'Let me show you how to use it,'
Teddy said.

He stood just behind her and, grasping her wrist,
put his hand over hers on the pretext of guiding the
club as she swung it. Milly was very aware of his hot
breath on her neck and wished he would not stand
quite so close, but the lethargy that had possessed her
since lunch still had her in its grip.

'Now, my dear,' Teddy went on, his voice low and
guttural. 'You must swing it back and forth, so, until
you make contact with the ball.'

'Where is the ball?'

'Ah!'

To her astonishment he came right in front of her
and bent down, presenting her with his fat behind
clad in Harris tweed. 'You may pretend this is the
ball, my dear!' he said, pointing to his arse.

'Don't be ridiculous!'

He surveyed her earnestly through his monocle. 'It
is only to practise your swing, you see. And this way
I can gauge the strength of your arm. One needs a
strong arm for golf.'

Suddenly she found the idea rather appealing. The
man was an insufferable bore. To give him a good

clout on the behind might be just what was needed to give vent to her frustration and teach him a lesson.

He took up his position once again, lifting his jacket up to reveal the seat of his trousers. Milly stood astride, imagining the ball on its tee, and then raised her iron to shoulder height. She whisked it forward vigorously and it met the broad bottom with a resounding thwack. Teddy yelped. But it was not the yelp of an outraged man in insufferable pain. It was more like the excited yelp of a young pup at play.

'And again, Miss Belfort!' He turned and grinned at her. 'Strike me harder this time. I'm sure you can do better.'

Milly obliged, and continued for several more strokes until Teddy was very red in the face. He was soon sweating and grunting like a pig, while she felt rather exhilarated. There was, after all, something very satisfying about a good golf swing.

'Oh, that was champion my dear!' he said at last. 'Though I don't know what would happen if you were let loose on a golf course. The imagination boggles!'

A party of bright young things suddenly appeared, wanting to use the Long Gallery for fox-trotting. Teddy said he was off for a 'bit of a lie down' so Milly joined in with the dancing crowd and was soon brushing up her footwork as she was whisked up and down the hall by one dashing partner after another. They were so caught up in the music that few of them went even so far as to ask her name, and Milly was happy to remain incognito for the time being. She was beginning to feel apprehensive about how the film would be received. It was scheduled for after dinner, but she couldn't help wondering how she would be regarded after they'd seen it.

After tea Milly went to her room and had a rest until it was time to prepare for the evening meal. She and Chloe did each other's hair and make-up, as they

168

were used to doing for filming. Again Milly felt nervous about the effect that their appearance might have on the other guests. With their bright lips and nails, eyelashes black with mascara and cheeks pale with powder, they might be mistaken for prostitutes. And the film would certainly reinforce that impression. What if things got out of hand, and the men began treating them as such?

They each wore dresses of pale chiffon. Chloe's was peachy pink, with a low flounced neckline and a skirt that ended in points like rose petals, with a tiny marcasite attached to each tip like a dewdrop. Milly's dress was a pretty sky blue, that complimented her dark hair and matched her eyes. It was virtually backless, and she wore a string of pearls knotted at her nape so that the heavy marcasite clasp hung down like a pendant between her shoulder blades. It was a style she had seen portrayed in *Vogue* magazine. Feeling rather self-conscious, she picked up her beaded clutch purse then followed Chloe down the wide staircase to the hall, floating on a cloud of *Mitsouko*.

Chapter Ten

The Long Gallery had been set up as a cinema, with rows of seats packed in and the portable screen that Serge had brought erected at one end. Milly, Chloe, Franz and Richard sat at the back behind Serge's projector, nervously awaiting the reaction of the audience as a Jerome Kern medley came from the wind-up gramophone and the first titles went up: '*House Party*, starring Emily Floret, the English Rosebud, as Lady Lydia of Belgravia'. The pseudonym had been Serge's inspiration, being almost an anagram of her real surname and suggestive of flowers as well.

When the first shot of Milly arranging long-stemmed roses in a vase appeared, she felt Chloe squeeze her hand. 'You look adorable, dear!' she whispered.

The scene proceeded, with Richard playing an abject type who crawled in on his hands and knees wearing only a stiff collar and bow tie. Everyone laughed at the caption, which read: 'Sir Ben Dover comes to fulfil Her Ladyship's Pleasure'.

Milly pretended to be angry with him over some misdemeanour. Taking one rose from the vase she struck him several times on his bare behind and 'Sir Dover' prostrated himself on the ground before her. Then she quickly stripped to her step-ins and undid the buttons at her crotch. With a blissful smile on her face she sat down on his back and proceeded to rub her exposed fanny up and down until she feigned an orgasm with much eye-rolling and sighing.

The delighted audience gave her performance a round of applause. Some of the bolder men stole a glance at Milly, but she tried not to notice. It was the first time she had attended a public screening of one of her films and she was finding it rather embarrassing. Remembering what came later in the film, her cheeks caught fire and she was glad of the semidarkness to hide her blushes.

Another caption appeared on the screen: 'Two Lesbian Love-Birds are spied upon by Sir Thomas Pepys, descendent of the notorious diarist'. The scene changed to a garden bower, convincingly created in the Hammersmith studio by means of ivy and other plants trailing around a wrought-iron seat. Milly and Chloe were seen approaching the seat, hand in hand, while the beady, monocled eye of Franz peered out through the foliage.

Milly watched as she and Chloe sat down and embraced, kissing passionately. It was strange to see herself so engaged, and when hands began to rove and garments were undone she felt decidedly uneasy, squirming in her seat. Seeing her breasts, and Chloe's, exposed for the camera was very arousing, but how could she be titillated by seeing herself in that way? Disturbed by her auto-eroticism, she wondered how she would dare look her fellow-actress in the eye again.

Her discomfort increased as she watched herself take Chloe's large, firm nipple between her lips. Milly was fondling the other girl's breasts while her own skirt was being hoisted up to reveal her naked pussy. An excited gasp went round the hall: evidently the audience had not expected the film to go that far. Some of the women were giggling nervously as they saw Chloe's fingers part the swollen labia and delve into the wet softness beyond. The camera panned to Fritz, who now had his fly undone and was rubbing his erect member vigorously while he spied on the women.

Milly watched herself moan and tremble as Chloe began to rub her clitoris. She remembered that the friction had actually brought her to a climax on that occasion, that her thrashings and shudderings were not feigned. Not that anyone but she would know that. Even so, her embarrassment grew acute as the remembered orgasm approached. She was clutching Chloe's breast and sucking hard as the other woman made her come in a series of sharp spasms, thrusting her fingers right inside her pulsating vagina.

In the film, Franz was triggered off by the spectacle. She had an inkling that was not feigned either. Afterwards, Milly knelt before Chloe and licked at her pussy, but she knew the other woman's supposed climax had been a fake. It had made her feel a bit weird at the time, but now she couldn't help wondering if anyone in the audience had been able to tell the difference between her real orgasm and Chloe's feigned one.

After the lesbian scene, a bedroom appeared with the caption: 'Two into One WILL go!' Milly saw herself lounging on a bed, dressed in a Victorian-style night-dress with the drawstrings loose about her bosom. She was dishevelled, her cheeks flushed as if she had been pleasuring herself. Suddenly the door to the room burst open and Richard and Franz entered.

A dialogue caption appeared: 'Have pity on us, Lady Lydia! We are dying of love for you!'

She gathered them into her arms on the bed and soon had a man at each breast, eagerly licking away while their hands were busy beneath the long skirt of her night-dress. Milly rolled her eyes exaggeratedly and soon the men began to unbutton themselves. Each took out his ready tool and began to stroke it, but Milly's dialogue caption said, 'Wait, Gentlemen! I have a better idea!'

After ordering the two men to remove their lower garments, Milly stripped off her night-gown and then beckoned Fritz towards her. She took his penis in her hand and placed her lips to the glans, giving it a kiss. At the same time Richard stationed himself between her thighs and pointed his erection at her hairy delta. As soon as she took the whole of Fritz's long cock into her mouth, Richard began to simulate intercourse and a synchronised rhythm ensued as the camera panned back and forth between the two activities while Milly gave every indication of enjoying the experience. When her two lovers exploded in an apparently simultaneous climax, she lay back on the pillow with a satisfied smile and her caption read: 'So you see, Gentlemen, it is possible to make two go into one after all!'

There was uproarious laughter at this, echoing all round the gallery. Some men stood up and faced the back of the room where the actors were, applauding heartily, but Milly averted her gaze. Even in the dim light she was afraid of catching their eye, although she was secretly becoming rather proud of the film's instant success.

The action proceeded to a 'Blind Man's Buff' scene, where blindfold men were stripped and bound by the two women, then flogged. Next came an erotic dance sequence, in which the quartet changed partners six times until everyone had had a chance to perform some intimate act with everyone else. Finally there was the grand 'Drunken Orgy,' where they indulged themselves in one mass, undifferentiated groping, licking, sucking and fucking session.

Unfortunately, instead of being the Bacchanalian Hymn to Excess that Serge had intended, this last scene came over as a writhing mass that resembled a rugby scrum rather than an erotic masterpiece. No-one seemed to mind, however. The film ended in a riot of whooping and applause from the men, screams and laughter from the women. People jumped excitedly to their feet and chairs were knocked over in the melée as they scrambled to congratulate the actors and director.

Soon Milly found herself revelling in all the attention. It was hard not to, with so many of the young 'smart set' paying homage to her 'beauty', her 'talent' and her 'extraordinary charm and sex appeal'. Someone even went so far as to call her a 'Goddess of the Silver Screen', a title which she'd thought Mary Pickford monopolised. It was all very gratifying, and Serge's prediction that he would 'make her a star' no longer seemed an idle promise.

While the guests paid court to the actors, servants bustled about unobtrusively clearing the room for dancing. A jazz band appeared from nowhere and set up around the small dais that they had brought with them, and soon the room was filled with the sound of raucous brass and catchy rhythms.

'Dance with me, Milly, I beg of you!' she heard Richard say in her ear. 'Otherwise I fear we shall both be mobbed by others wanting to partner us!'

His logic seemed sound, for as soon as they drifted into the centre of the room they were surrounded by admirers offering, in leering tones, to 'swap partners' in the manner of the film. Milly knew how nervous Richard must be feeling. It was one thing to pretend to like girls on film, but if they came on too strong to him now they would end up being very disappointed, and he would be equally embarrassed.

She decided to put an end to his silent discomfiture. 'I'm not sure I can stand much more of this,' Milly confessed. 'Shall we go somewhere quiet?'

He agreed readily so they slipped away between tunes, going back downstairs where the older generation were enjoying quiet pursuits such as bridge and backgammon or conversation over the port and cigars.

'I reckon I'd better lock the door of my room tonight,' he said, wryly. 'Unless I can find some pretty young boy for myself, of course.'

He gave her a wicked grin and she smiled back. 'Perhaps I could procure one for you!'

'Naughty girl! You wouldn't, would you?'

'I might. If you'd do something for me in return.'

'Depends what it is.'

She smiled. 'Earlier on I saw you talking to Lord Sanderford's elder son, Jamie.'

'What of it?'

'He invited you on board his Mediterranean yacht, didn't he?'

'Yes. I wondered if he might fancy me, to tell the truth. I'll have to make a few discreet enquiries.'

'You plan to take up his invitation, then?'

'Good Lord, yes!'

'In that case, can you try to get me included in the party?'

He looked shocked. 'Hey, steady on Milly! I hardly know the chap.'

'And I don't know anyone here either. But we were striking a bargain, remember? I said I'd get you a pretty boy in exchange for a favour . . .'

'Milly, you drive a dashed hard bargain, you know that? Well, I can but try. Give me an hour to see what I can do.'

'Ditto. Good luck!'

They parted, Richard heading for the games room where he thought Jamie and his cronies might be lurking since he knew they disliked dancing, and Milly making for the dining room. She hoped the staff might still be clearing away in there, and she was right. Earlier in the evening she had noticed a young footman amongst the servants whom she thought might be only too pleased to oblige Richard according to his predilections. She had heard him called 'Andrew' by Lord Sanderford.

There were only two maidservants left in the dining room. Milly asked one of them, in her most command-ing tone, to 'ring for Andrew' saying she wished to have a private word with him. Although the woman regarded her strangely at first, she curtseyed obedi-ently and did as she asked. After a few minutes Andrew came up from the kitchen and the maids discreetly withdrew, giggling behind their hands. Milly smiled, imagining what they might be thinking.

'You sent for me, Miss?' Andrew said, a faint sneer in his voice.

'Yes. I have a message from one of the guests. He wishes to have a particular service performed for him.'

His face showed slight interest. 'Yes, Miss? What manner of service might that be, then?'

'I am not sure, but it is something rather intimate I believe. The gentleman in question has a small medi-cal problem. He is too shy to mention it himself, but he thinks you might be the best person to help him with it.'

There followed a few seconds of silence, during which Milly guessed that the innuendo was not lost on the lad. She prided herself that she could spot one of his persuasion a mile off. It was a talent she had honed at Cambridge where, with so few eligible young men available, she'd learnt not to waste precious seduction time on public schoolboys who had never grown out of their sodomitic habits.

If asked how she recognised the signs, however, she would have been hard pressed to explain in detail. Something about their stance, perhaps, or a hooded quality to the eyes. Or maybe the way their mouths sometimes twitched suggestively in the company of other young men. At any rate, she had seldom been wrong in her instincts and she was prepared to bet that this time she would turn out to be right too.

'This ... um, medical problem. Would it perhaps be a matter of excess fluid in need of ... er, draining?'

Milly stifled a giggle. 'Bravo!' she thought, not knowing whether it was Andrew she was congratulating or herself. She nodded, sagely. 'Quite possibly. I only know how he described it to me. Some kind of sinus problem, perhaps. But if you think you can handle it ...'

'Oh yes, I can handle it all right!'

'I'm sure you would be well rewarded for your services.'

'Thanks, Miss. What time would the gentleman require this ... service?'

'Oh, I should say around midnight. His room is on the second floor, number twenty-two. Shall I tell him you'll be along, then?'

'Please Miss. Tell the gentleman I shall be happy to be of service to him. I am quite experienced in these matters and I am sure I shall be able to relieve his discomfort.'

Milly smiled. 'Of course. Thank you, Andrew. You may go now.'

When she was alone in the dining-room again, Milly gave a little dance of joy all around the long table. If only Richard had been as successful as she her hoped-for jaunt aboard a yacht in the Med was assured!

When she and Richard met up again an hour later

one look at his smiling face told her she was, indeed, in luck.

'Well?' they both said at once, then collapsed into giggles.

'Andrew the footman will be in your room at midnight, to help you with your little medical problem,' Milly said, triumphantly. 'Now, speak!'

'Milly, you're a gem! I said as much to Jamie, actually. Told him an English Rosebud was essential tackle for any Mediterranean voyage. No yacht should set sail without one.'

'And he fell for it?'

'Hook, line and sinker! No, actually he put up a bit of a fight. Said there were too many barmy women in the party already. But I said you were a raving lesbian with an insatiable appetite for female flesh who would keep them all out of his hair for the entire voyage.'

'You didn't!'

'Oh yes I did! And your name is now on the guest list, as Miss Emily Floret. Better not forget, Miss Floret!'

Milly gave him a hug then wandered back upstairs. As soon as she entered the hall Chloe gave her a discreet wave, the sort that meant she wanted a chinwag as soon as possible. Milly nodded towards the door and went back out, hoping her friend would follow. In a few seconds she did.

'What-ho, Chloe!' Milly began. She'd picked up quite a few choice phrases from the gay young things. Their jargon was very catching. 'You'll never guess what I . . .'

Chloe grabbed her wrist. 'Quick, let's go to our room where we can talk in private.'

As soon as they were alone, Chloe burst into excited chatter. 'Guess what? Oh you never would, how could you possibly? Anyway, not to put too fine a point on it, my dear, we've been propositioned!'

'What? By whom?'

'By two frightfully handsome, wealthy and silly aristocrats called Giles and Squiffy, would you believe? They want to come to our room at midnight and have their wicked way with us.'

Milly laughed, thinking what a hotbed of vice 'Maplefield' would become that night. 'And they say they'll make it worth our while,' Chloe added, her eyes gleaming.

Suddenly Milly sobered up. 'That makes me feel like a society whore.'

Chloe gripped her hand. 'But that's exactly what we *are* Milly. In this situation, at least. We're here to provide the sex, on screen and off. Didn't you realise?'

Now that she thought about it Milly had to admit that it was so. Seduced by Serge's flattery she had preferred to think of herself as an 'actress,' but now she knew that she could equally well be thought of as a prostitute. How naive she'd been!

'You don't mind too much, do you Milly?' Chloe asked anxiously. 'They want the pair of us, you see. If you don't want to join us, the deal's off.'

'Of course I don't mind!' Milly said, brightly. 'Tell the chaps we'll give them the time of their lives!'

But deep inside a nagging voice was reminding her that once she'd had higher aspirations. What on earth was she doing, being a plaything for these spoilt and immature young men? She thought of Robin, and her heart ached. He'd put a higher value on her, loved her mind and soul as well as her body. Did he deserve to be betrayed like this?

But you turned your back on him and everything he stands for, she reminded herself, a mood of heart-less realism taking hold. She was not going to fall in love with anyone else, only go to bed with them. And what harm was there in that? This house party was a lark, a bit of fun, that was all.

Suddenly she found herself drawing comfort from something her godmother had said to her, years ago. Emma had said there was no shame in making love outside wedlock, even if money or gifts changed hands, so long as both parties enjoyed it. What was truly sinful, in her opinion, was to make love without both parties deriving pleasure from the act. And joyless sex, as she pointed out, was something that took place more often within marriage than outside of it.

The two young men presented themselves at the girls' door soon after midnight, evidently tight as owls. Chloe and Milly were arrayed in their night-dresses and had allowed their hair to tumble loose, but they had re-applied their make-up and sprayed themselves with perfume.

'Erm ... we're frightfully grateful to you, ladies,' the lanky chap called Squiffy said. He had a decided list to starboard and Milly was afraid he would keel over at any moment.

'Yesh, fwightfully good of you!' Giles echoed.

'I don't think either of them will be able to get it up tonight!' Chloe whispered.

Milly rose from her bed. 'Come here, gentlemen, and make yourselves comfortable,' she invited, patting the eiderdown.

Soon the men were stretched out, one on each bed, while the two girls removed their shoes. 'I don't know, what are we going to do with them?' Milly asked aloud.

'We'll do anything for you, ladies! Splendid ladies!' Squiffy said, his tone maudlin. Sweeping his arm through the air in an expansive gesture he added, 'Your wish is our command!'

Milly suddenly knew exactly what to do and say. Drawing herself up to her full height, she said in an imperious tone, 'In that case get off the beds you miserable wretches, and prepare to do whatever I tell you.'

Chloe threw her a look of disbelief, but Milly frowned, putting finger to her lips. As she'd expected, Squiffy rolled off her bed and sat in a crumpled heap on the floor, looking up at her adoringly. After a few seconds the message sank in with Giles, too. He slowly vacated the bed and knelt down on the carpet beside his friend.

Milly knew she had to take control. The other girl was mystified, but she'd soon know the score. Milly addressed her in the same commanding tone. 'Chloe, lie down on the bed!'

'What . . .? Milly . . .?'

'Do as I say, don't argue!

Chloe raised her brows but lay down all the same, looking quizzically at her. Milly told the two men to kneel on either side of the bed. They shuffled round on their knees half falling over themselves in the process.

'Now, each of you take one of your mistress's feet and caress it with loving care.'

Both men obeyed implicitly, without so much as a raised brow, and Milly knew she had found the key to their satisfaction. Used to being bossed around by their nurses and governesses at an early age, they were only too pleased to knuckle under. A slow smile spread across Chloe's features as she realised that they were wholly devoted to her pleasure. She lay back on the pillow with her arms behind her head and gave a deep sigh.

'Now, kiss her toes,' Milly said. The men obeyed, tenderly taking each of her toes into their mouths in turn. She soon had them stroking Chloe's legs too, working their way up to her thighs. She lifted her night-gown above her waist to allow them access to her private parts and before long she had Squiffy mouthing her labia while Giles was stroking and kissing her stomach.

'Kiss her breasts, Giles!' Milly ordered, and soon Chloe was moaning and writhing with accelerating pleasure. The men were growing excited too, stoking and licking her with greater fervour as she responded.

Milly picked up the slipper that Chloe had discarded and began to whack each of the men on the behind, urging them to lick and stroke 'Faster, faster!' They wagged their tongues like demented automata, looking so comical that she had to stifle a giggle.

But her exhortation had the desired effect. Chloe gave a series of staccato gasps as her climax shuddered through her, causing a rosy flush to spread over her chest and face. The men slumped against the bed, equally exhausted, and Milly shared in the deep satisfaction that everyone was feeling. She ordered the men to put their shoes on and depart, sensing that they needed to return to their room and recover.

Before they went, however, Squiffy handed her an envelope with a wink. 'Dashed fine time had by all, what?' he murmured. 'Just the ticket!'

When they were alone, Chloe sat up with a grin. 'Good heavens, Milly, how on earth did you know that was what those chaps wanted?'

'Call it an inspired guess,' she grinned back.

'What have they left us?' Chloe asked, eagerly. Milly opened the envelope and two crisp five-pound notes slipped out. 'Mon Dieu! That's more than Serge pays us for a week's work!'

'They've more money than sense, if you ask me. Still, who are we to argue?'

Chloe looked thoughtful. 'You know, I reckon a girl could make a good living out of this lark. And no danger of getting knocked up, either.'

'Nor of catching the clap.' Milly laughed. 'Aren't

men pathetic creatures, Chloe? Like pigs, you can lead them by the nose to the trough!'

'Well, I heard a wonderful English expression,' Chloe giggled. 'It says, "where there's muck, there's brass". It looks like that is true of our little piggies, yes?'

The pair of them collapsed in laughter on their beds, which made Milly feel less guilty about taking money off the two men. She thought about the yacht in the Med, and began to wish she'd asked Richard to get Chloe an invitation too, but perhaps that would have been pushing her luck too far. What she would do, though, was ask Serge if she could take along a couple of his films to show to the yachting set. It would be free advertising for him, and was certain to lead to more orders.

As she lay in the dark that night, too excited to sleep, Milly found her mind racing ahead, thinking about what the future might hold for her. If she could make enough contacts in the smart society she'd glimpsed tonight who knew where she might end up? The world would be her oyster. Filled with excitement, she absently caressed her breasts beneath the cotton night-gown. They began to throb and swell, setting up a corresponding urge below. She lifted up her skirt and put her hand between her thighs, squeezing hard, while her other hand continued to pinch her nipple. What did it matter if a man satisfied her or not, she thought. She could always do this.

What she wanted out of life was fun, excitement, and you couldn't get that without money, or at least wealthy companions. Milly tickled her clitoris with the tip of her finger, sending exquisitely delicate thrills all around her abdomen. She had some idea of how the upper crust lived: skiing in St Moritz in spring, commuting between England and the Riviera in summer, migrating to warmer climes like Egypt and

Morocco in the winter. She knew their lives were one long round of pleasure, from harmless fun like tennis and boating, to silly parties of all kinds and on into the murkier waters of sexual perversions.

Slowly Milly introduced her forefinger into her wet pussy, pushing it up as far as it would go and feeling her clitoris harden against her thumb. She stirred it around and waves of sharp ecstasy swept through her, making her gasp. Tonight she had felt powerful, exultant, as she saw those two silly asses doing whatever they were told. It had aroused her, subtly.

Now she wanted a swift conclusion to that slow build-up, a fiery explosion at the end of the long fuse. The thought of living the sybaritic life, mixing with the idle rich and sharing their decadent amusements, was stimulating Milly towards a climax. She moved her finger in and out, drenching her vulva in her own juices, making the stiff bud of her clitoris throb and harden until it juddered into a long, satisfying orgasm that left her weak and breathless.

But at the high point of her ecstasy Milly's thoughts flew, like winged cupids, to the man who had taken her virginity and tears began to flow, turning her sighs of pleasure into groans and her gasps of rapture into sobs. She bit hard into the pillow, not wanting to waken Chloe, and did her best to banish his memory from her mind.

It was impossible. No matter how hard she screwed up her eyes, Robin's adoring face was there to taunt her. Worst of all, she could hear his gentle voice intoning lines from a Shakespearean sonnet, words which turned the sweet pangs of her self-consummated desire into the bitter pangs of guilt.

> *For thy sweet love remembered such wealth brings*
> *That then I scorn to change my state with kings.*

Chapter Eleven

'Shall we go to Lulu's beach party tonight? They say her last one was *très amusant*!'

'Oh, not another boring party! Chuffy wants me to motor into Monte with him, in his new two-seater.'

'But darling, you know he'll only spend all night at the Tables. Talk about *ennuyant*! You'll have much more fun here. It's to be a Troubadour party, everyone has to sing a song. And there's to be a treasure hunt, too.'

'I'll think about it. Are you invited to cocktails on the Van Holland yacht this afternoon? They say the *très chic* Marilyn Dubarry will be there.'

'And the *très riche* Pieter Van Holland and the rest of that notorious crowd, I dare say.' (Yawn). 'Really, Daphne, you are so transparent sometimes.'

'Are you suggesting I'm a gold-digger, *ma chère*?'

Milly lay on her deck-chair in her new beach pyjamas, a parasol shielding her from the sun, pretending to read a book. She could hardly help overhearing the conversation of the two girls on her left, but the affected triviality of their chatter depressed her. She had already begun to think she had made a dreadful mistake in giving up her job with Serge to come to the Riviera.

It hadn't gone at all as she'd hoped. He had been most put out that two of his best actors were deserting him, and the idea of using the opportunity as a marketing exercise for Latour Films had fallen on deaf ears. Although she had never signed any formal contract to work for Serge, he had made her feel that she had let him down by asking for two weeks off and he'd made it clear that she couldn't expect to find her old job waiting for her when she returned.

Richard had tried to reassure her, saying she was too good an actress to play in cheap porno movies and that if she went to the Côte D'Azur her luck would be bound to change. He'd led her to believe there were French, Italian and American film producers hanging around in every bar and hotel lounge just itching to sign up new talent. But so far the only types she'd met were the idle rich and their *coterie* of friends, whores, spongers and poor relations.

Jamie Sanderford's twelve-berth yacht, the *Lucky Lady*, was moored at Nice for five days then due to set sail for Corfu, calling at various ports on the way. Richard intended to stay in Greece for the rest of the summer, but Milly had no intention of leaving France. If no other opportunities presented themselves she would return to London by train.

So far, it didn't look promising. Milly had been on the yacht for three days and there hadn't even been a berth for her. Sleeping on deck under the stars was no great hardship in the warm Mediterranean night, but she had expected to be courted by at least one of the bronzed, pleasure-loving types that haunted the ship night and day. A few of them had chatted briefly with her, but without the *cachet* of starring in Serge's films Milly was considered a nobody. She knew no-one, she didn't speak the right lingo, she just wasn't part of the

186

'in' crowd. Not even the purchase of a pair of beach pyjamas, some yachting pants and a Jantzen elasticised bathing-suit (the sum total of which had almost bankrupted her) could alter her image as an outsider and a hanger-on.

Suddenly she heard someone call her name. Turning in surprise she found herself face to face with one of the women from the yacht, a tall and very handsome female called Emerald. She was holding out a gold Cartier cigarette case. 'Want a gasper, dear?'

'Oh, no thanks! They make me wheeze.'

'Dear oh dear, we are at a social disadvantage aren't we?' she smiled, lighting one up at the end of a long jade holder. 'You're like a fish out of water here amongst the yachting set, aren't you Milly? I've been watching you over the past few days and I would hazard a guess that you aren't exactly having the time of your life.'

'It's my own fault,' she admitted. 'I sort of invited myself. I should have realised that I wouldn't fit in.'

'Yes, Richard told me about your little wager. Care to earn yourself some spondulicks? I imagine that's one of the things you came here for.' Milly looked at her blankly, so she continued, *sotto voce*, 'I had a little chat with Squiffy too, back in Blighty.'

Milly felt her cheeks flush beneath her developing tan. 'He told you . . .?'

'Everything!' Emerald smiled, closing her green eyes against the smoke she was making.

'Well he'd no right to! That was private business, and . . .'

'Don't worry, darling, I'm the last person in the world to pass judgement. What goes on in the bedroom, whether it's one's own or someone else's, is sacrosanct as far as I'm concerned. But I do make it my business to know what people's tastes are. It makes life so much simpler if one can match like with like, if you know what I mean.'

Milly stared, not wanting to believe what her instincts were telling her. Was this woman some kind of society go-between, a procuress?

Emerald took off her towelling beach wrap and revealed her striped bathing suit. Her figure was fashionably slim and boyish, with long legs and an almost flat chest. She rolled over on to her outspread towel with a sigh and lay there with her face to the sun, her eyes shielded by dark glasses.

'You don't have to decide now,' she said, as if to the empty air. 'But I know at least one gentleman who would gladly pay five guineas for the kind of service you provided for Squiffy.'

Milly was silent but her brain was very active. This trip had been a fiasco so far: was this her chance to make good? If she was only expected to order this man around, make him do things, it would be money for old rope. Her curiosity grew. ''This man, is he English?'

Emerald shrugged, leaning over on her side and inhaling more smoke. 'Some are, some aren't. Furthermore, you can take your pick. I have an entrée into an exclusive club here in Nice where the dominant sex, that is to say women, are always welcome. You wouldn't have to go alone, I'd accompany you.'

'I see.'

'Interested? If you are, I'll meet you at Rafi's Bar, eight o'clock tonight. No need to say yea or nay right now. I'm going anyway. But if you're not there on the dot of eight I'll be going alone. *Compris?*'

'Mm.'

Milly closed her eyes, reflecting. She could do with some extra cash, after being so extravagant in the beachwear shop. Besides, there was precious little else to amuse her. The endless empty conversations bored her rigid, even when she was only eavesdropping. It was far worse to be expected to take part in them. She found herself dreaming more and more of Robin or even, on occasion, of Evadne. At least they knew how to have a civilised discussion.

Consequently when eight o'clock cast long shadows over the harbour wall and lights could be seen igniting all around the Bay of Angels, Milly was there in Rafi's Bar on the quayside, nervously quaffing a *Perroquet*. Suddenly a beaded curtain was drawn aside and Emerald appeared. She looked very stunning, clad in a black velvet cloak with a lime green feather boa around her neck and her dark hair slicked into a shiny bob. Her lips were very red, and when she smiled her teeth were pearly white by contrast. She seemed delighted to see Milly.

'You came, my dear!' she exclaimed, making a little *moue* in the air over her cheeks. 'I knew you would, you're such a sport. Wasted on that yacht, in that company. Just wasted! *Tout à fait*. Shall we go?'

To Milly's surprise she offered her her arm, and they set out walking through the cobbled streets. There were many other people promenading at that time in the evening, and few gave them a second glance. Milly had dressed in her black cocktail dress with the beaded fringe and over it she wore an embroidered Chinese jacket. It was her smartest outfit and she hoped it was appropriate for whatever lay ahead.

'Here we are!' Emerald said at last. They had reached a back street hotel called '*La Coupole*' and Milly followed her new friend through the swing doors to the desk. A man greeted them cordially and waved them towards the lift. Evidently Emerald had been there before. Faint dance music floated down the lift-shaft towards them but it didn't sound live. More likely a radio or gramophone.

When they got to the fourth floor the lift stopped, but Emerald didn't get out. She turned to Milly and said, 'Now listen, before we go in. I shall be taking you into a *salon* where all the men you will see are like Squiffy and Giles. Do you understand? They like nothing more than to be commanded by women, especially beautiful, intelligent ones like you and me.'

Milly giggled. 'I can't think why!'

'Ours not to reason why, Milly. But since this is your first time – at an establishment like this, I mean – I'm prepared to make it easy for you. If you like we can work together. I'll do the ordering about and, when necessary, the chastisement. All you have to do is act haughty and distant while the men do as I tell them. If they give you pleasure you mustn't show it. Not under any circumstances. It will require great self-control. Do you think you can do it?'

'I think so. At any rate, I'm willing to try.'

'Good.' Emerald smiled. 'I'm sure you'll do splendidly. Shall we proceed?'

They entered an imposingly large room with a high ceiling that was covered in gilded plaster. On the walls were mirrors, and small Louis Quinze chairs were dotted around dainty tables. Huge red velvet drapes were at the tall windows, held back by gold ropes with tassels. When she had become used to the grand scale of the room, Milly noticed that there were about twenty men in there and about half that number of women. Some stood in small groups, others sat round tables talking quietly, and there was a gramophone playing Mozart in one corner.

Soon after they entered, a large woman dressed in eighteenth-century style with an elaborate grey wig came bustling up. 'Emerald! *Que je suis contente de te voir ce soir . . .*'

They embraced, then Emerald introduced her to Milly. The woman, whose name was Jeanne-Marie,

190

looked her up and down with sharp, appraising black eyes. She spoke rapidly to Emerald in some French *patois* but after a few minutes held out her hand to Milly and said, in her thick accent, 'Come along, *chérie*, I have a gentleman who will love to meet you. Emerald, you know who I mean?'

'Oh yes!'

Full of apprehension, Milly followed the two women across the room to where two young men were standing, deep in conversation. Jeanne-Marie did not hesitate to interrupt them. As soon as she said, '*Attention, Messieurs*!' they instantly stopped their chat and bowed, continuing to stare at the ground with lowered gaze as she turned to Milly with a smile.

'Mademoiselle, may I present to you Monsieur Donald,' she said, touching one of the men on the shoulder.

Milly held out her hand, but Emerald discreetly pushed it down to her side again with a cautionary shake of her head. The young man dropped to his knees instantly and, much to Milly's surprise, kissed the toe of her shoe. Then he scrambled to his feet, still with his head bowed so she could not see his face.

Emerald said, 'Shall we ask this Donald to serve us, Milly? Do you think he is fit to lick our boots?'

He gave a fleeting upward glance and she saw the look in his brown eye. It was that of a spaniel who, although in disgrace, still wishes to please his master. Stifling a smile she said,

'Oh yes, I think so.'

'Then let us proceed. Do you have the key to our room, Jeanne-Marie?'

Emerald led the way to the door, with Milly following and Donald crawling on his hands and knees after them. She found it embarrassing at first but no-one seemed to take the slightest notice. Clearly the rules of etiquette here were not those of normal society!

191

Now that she was tuned into the general atmosphere of the place Milly realised that wherever the men and women were interacting there was no direct eye contact. The men were hanging their heads, sometimes kneeling, sometimes prostrating themselves. Only the women stood fully upright, subduing the spirit of their willing accomplices by virtue of their commanding presence alone.

They entered a room at the end of the corridor. It was small and intimate, with a large four-poster bed in the middle, a wardrobe, wash-stand and some chairs against a wall. As soon as they were inside Emerald locked the door behind them and threw her cloak and boa on to the floor. 'Pick them up!' she rasped. 'Hang them in the wardrobe.'

Eagerly Donald did as he was told. Beneath the cloak Emerald had been wearing a scarlet and black gown in an old-fashioned style with a cinched-in waist and low neck. Her breasts, which had seemed so flat in the bathing-suit, had been pushed up with a corset to give her some cleavage, and the overall effect was of a powerful *grande-dame* of some bygone era.

Milly's eyes turned to the man, who was hanging her clothes up on silk padded hangers. He had a handsome face with long, sweeping lashes, melting brown eyes and a long, straight nose. His black hair was quite long and curled about his ears. But there was something creepy, almost sinister, about the way he handled things, about the way he moved. She found him strangely toad-like, yet there was an attraction too. She thought of the legend of the frog prince, and smiled.

Suddenly Donald dropped the feather boa on the carpet. Emerald rasped, 'Pick it up, you clumsy oaf!' and caught him a stinging blow on the cheek. 'That will teach you to take better care of my things!'

Milly winced, wondering what part she had to play

in this charade. The stinging tone of her friend's voice was frightening even to her, yet the man seemed almost to be revelling in it. She saw his hand tremble as he picked up the boa and caressed it lovingly with his other hand.

'That's enough! Put it in the wardrobe! Then come and do obeisance to my companion.'

Emerald motioned Milly on to the bed, where she sat on the edge of the eiderdown feeling apprehensive. Donald came to kneel before her, awaiting orders. He was told to take off Milly's shoes, which he did with reverential care. As his soft fingers brushed her feet through her stockings she felt a tickling sensation pass right up her calves and buttocks to the base of her spine where it spread up to her head. She was so keyed up with the atmosphere of suspense in the room that she could hardly bear it.

'Now, remove her stockings!' Emerald ordered.

Again those careful, tentative hands moved up beneath her skirt and in seconds her silky stockings were slipping down her legs, being slowly rolled by Donald's fingers. He worked with such precision, as if he were engaged on some sacred task in a place of worship. Yet there was something despicable about him, unmanly. Milly looked down at the crown of his dark head and wanted to seize him by the ears, to shake his skull vigorously and startle him out of his languid, dreamy servitude.

'You may kiss her shins,' Emerald continued, sternly. 'But do not dare go above the knee without permission. Do you understand?'

He nodded, dumbly. His cool lips pressed against the front of Milly's foot and she felt another shiver of desire, this time more localised in her groin and belly. She could imagine that mouth travelling right up beyond her knees to the soft, sensitive skin of her thighs and then on to the even more sensitive flesh between them. She stared down at his abject body, revelling in her own supremacy. Power surged through her body, making her feel supremely in control, and a wave of dark eroticism possessed her. 'He shall become the instrument of my pleasure,' she thought. The phrase delighted her.

Milly drew back, her arms stretched out behind her on the bed, and felt her breasts expand in voluptuous abandon to the sensations coursing through her. She squeezed her thighs together and felt her clitoris stiffen, nestling in the warm pouch of her vulva. A low moan escaped her lips, earning her an instant frown from Emerald, so she turned it into a throat-clearing noise. She had momentarily forgotten that she was supposed to show no sign of the pleasure this young man was affording her.

His lips were travelling slowly up the front of her left leg. They reached her knee then began again at her right foot. Milly felt full to bursting with unsatisfied longing. Her whole body was crying out for attention and she began to feel as she used to feel in chapel, at boarding school. The girls sometimes attended Sunday services at a church where choirboys sang, and Milly used to while away the tedium by fantasising about those of the older boys she found most attractive. Now she felt that same straining, unconsummated desire that was more akin to torture than delight.

Suddenly she felt those tantalising lips stray above her knee. It was shock to feel them on the softer skin of her thigh and she wondered at once if Emerald had noticed. She had.

'Impudent creature!' the woman screeched. 'I saw you stray above the knee, although I expressly forbade it. Come here!'

The man turned and crawled like a serpent on his belly towards his mistress. Milly felt shocked. Did the man have no pride, no self-respect at all? He lay prostrate, and to Milly's astonishment Emerald placed her high-heeled shoe in the small of his back and ground it hard. There was a gasp from the man as the air was rapidly expelled from his lungs, but no more.

'Worm!' Emerald said contemptuously. 'Did you think you were worthy to kiss the silken thighs of my lovely companion?'

Donald shook his head. Emerald knelt by his side and hissed in his ear. 'Shall I thrash you then? Shall I tan your miserable hide?'

She seized a clump of his hair and pulled his head up, forcing it back until the man was half choking, his eyes staring wildly. Milly was afraid he would come to real harm. She sat on the edge of the bed, her hands clasped tightly between her thighs to ease the throbbing ache in her groin.

'No, I have a better idea!' Emerald declared. 'The lady you have wronged shall punish you herself. Six strokes of her fair hand upon your naked buttocks. And do not dare to flinch or I shall administer another six myself, with the strap next time!'

Emerald told the man to loosen his belt so she could roll down his trousers and underpants. Soon the plump white mounds of his behind were showing as he lay face down on the floor, and Emerald beckoned Milly from the bed. 'Kneel down, my dear, and give it every ounce of strength you have. The wretch deserves all he gets for taking such a liberty.'

Milly took her place on the floor beside the man's prone body. His pale buttocks fascinated her, so provocatively round and smooth, like two vanilla blancmanges. She lifted her arm and brought her hand down with a smack on the left-hand sphere. She could feel the flesh tremble beneath her palm, and when she drew her hand away she saw it flushing slightly. Exhilaration filled her veins. She slapped him again, on the other buttock, and saw him flex his muscles against the pain. His jaw was clenched, his mouth hard against the pile of the carpet.

'Harder!' Emerald snapped. 'Give it everything you've got. He deserves it.'

Milly did as she was told and completed the punishment. Soon Donald's pallid skin was reddening, showing the stripes of her fingers. The exercise left her breathless but Emerald seemed satisfied and told her to go and lie on the bed. She made Donald get right on to the bed at her feet and resume his kissing of her feet and legs.

Now the aching emptiness was growing once again, filling Milly's belly with a hunger for something other than food. She lay with legs outstretched and slightly apart, watching the man's craven lips crawl up towards her knees, praying that this time Emerald would allow him to go a little higher.

Her prayers were answered. When he reached her knees Emerald said, 'You may now kiss the lovely thighs of Mademoiselle, but make sure you do so delicately, with all due reverence.'

The result was tiny, whispering kisses that sent currents of exquisite delight spiralling upward into Milly's private parts. The moist tissues of her vulva swelled and throbbed with longing, and she began to imagine how it would feel to have him kiss her there. She knew she was only tormenting herself, but she couldn't help it. Her need was extreme, and if she didn't gain satisfaction soon she believed she would have to do something about it herself. But she feared Emerald. The dominatrix had them both under her control, and Milly believed she was quite capable of exacting punishment from her, as well as Donald, if she overstepped the mark. So she lay in frozen suspense, blindly hoping for better things.

When the man's lips had reached the inner planes

of her upper thighs, and his nose was almost touching her camiknickers, Emerald came to sit on the bed beside them. Her expression was stern, but there was a gleam in her eye and Milly wondered what was going on beneath that stony exterior. Was she deriving some secret pleasure from watching all this?

'You hate a woman's scent, don't you Donald?' Emerald said in a gloating tone. She went on in a low, sinister voice that took on a mesmerising, sing-song quality. 'Well I'm going to make you stay there, with your nose practically in her pussy, sniffing it in. Go on, undo those buttons and take a deep breath.'

Milly felt tentative hands undo her crotch buttons, exposing the overheated flesh within. Emerald continued in the same vein. 'That's right, sniff it again. You hate this don't you? You hate how slippery and wet it feels and the musky smell of a real woman, don't you?' But you're going to wallow in it. Oh yes you are! And, by Jove, you're going to taste it too. Think of that, Donald.'

He stayed between her thighs, cowed and immobile, his lips pressed close to Milly's wet labia while she silently screamed for some relief. Emerald's hand reached for her hair and began to stroke the dark, silken strands. Tingling anticipation raced up and down Milly's spine as she was touched above and below, and the hollow swirling inside her became a raging tumult.

Then, at long last, came the command she had been dying to hear. 'Lick her!'

Donald's tongue insinuated itself slowly between her tumid folds and Milly opened her mouth to give vent to her feelings but found a hand immediately clapped over it. She glanced at Emerald with frightened eyes. The woman's face was calm, unmoved as she watched the slow progress of the man's tongue into her pussy. Milly held herself in check, although

197

with great difficulty, as the thick and sensual organ probed between her inner lips and made a brief inroad into her open quim. Then the tip flicked upward and found the jewel in the lotus. Sudden flurries of exquisite rapture burst through Milly like wildfire as her rampant clitoris finally obtained the stimulation it so desperately needed.

He began licking her with the broad flat of his tongue, taking in most of her folds and crevices in repeated sweeps, but every so often the mobile tip would concentrate on her ever-throbbing nub and new spasms of delight would shudder through her. The thoroughness of his performance belied Emerald's claim that he detested the female pudendum. It was all just a game, she realised, a ploy to give him what he wanted while freeing his conscience.

Keeping a lid on her excitement grew increasingly hard and Milly was afraid she would soon boil over, like a saucepan, emitting loud gasps. She managed to restrain herself, however, and after a while began to find the experience gratifying. It forced her attention inward, enabling her to concentrate on her feelings without distraction, and the intense sensations soon escalated towards orgasm. When she reached the brink she felt literally about to explode.

Instead, when the release came she felt amazingly light-headed and floaty, her body delicately vibrating like a fine-tuned instrument dedicated to expressing the sweet throes of sex. Her skin felt ethereal and glowing, as if it were made of pure light, and for a few timeless seconds she was immersed in pure bliss, totally unaware of her surroundings, back in some womb-like state of mindless contentment.

'Enough!' she heard Emerald's sharp voice interject, bringing her back to reality. 'Make yourself decent. Over there, in that corner!'

When the room fell silent again, Milly drifted off.

She opened her eyes to find Emerald still sitting beside her on the bed but Donald had gone. She stretched languidly, her body utterly relaxed and fulfilled.

'Well done!' Emerald smiled down at her. 'You behaved impeccably, Milly.'

'Did I?' she sat up, rubbing her eyes. An envelope was put into her hand and she stared down at it, then opened it. There were five crisp pound notes and five shillings inside.

'Five guineas!' she exclaimed. 'Oh, I cannot take all the money Emerald. You did most of the work, after all.'

The other woman laughed. 'Don't be silly, that's your share. I split it fifty-fifty.'

'*Ten* guineas? You mean he paid ten guineas?' Emerald nodded, plainly enjoying her amazement. 'But that's more than a schoolteacher earns in a fortnight!'

'He can afford it. His father is the Earl of Dunbride. Don't look so astonished, Milly. There aren't many women who would be prepared to do what you and I have done tonight, and poor fish like Donald really appreciate it. Their lives would be utter misery without it.'

'Milly shook her head. 'I can't pretend to understand it.'

'You don't have to. But now you see how it's done, you could do it yourself if you so wished. As you see, there's a good living to be had from this sort of work and you can take it just as far as you like.'

She opened the black leather clutch purse and drew out a card case. 'I'm going to give you this, Milly. It's my card. When you return to London this will give you an entrée into any of the establishments similar to this. I shall write one address on the back. I can highly recommend this lady, who has been in this business for years. She's always looking for new recruits. Here.'

Milly read both addresses then put it in her bag. 'Thanks, Emerald. I appreciate this.'

'I know you've lost your acting job, Richard told me. You might be glad of the chance to earn some extra income until you can get back on your feet again.'

'I don't know how to thank you!'

Although Milly wasn't sure she would take up this opportunity, she was glad to have it up her sleeve. Emerald left the yacht next day, going on by train to Rome, and Milly felt *de trop* again amongst the other guests. She did her best to flirt with the men and chat with the girls, but inside she was longing for the week to end. It was only out of consideration for Richard that she was staying on, afraid she would let him down if she left early.

But on the last evening he found her alone on deck. 'Milly, are you sure you want to return to London tomorrow?' he asked her.

She nodded. 'I must. I have to find digs for myself, since I can't impose on my father's hospitality any more. And I've not seen my mother for months. We parted on bad terms. It's been preying on my conscience.'

It was only partly true. Her thoughts had been more occupied with Robin lately. A part of her longed to see him again, but he would be in Deauville by now and it would be hard to discover his address. Once she was settled in her own digs in London, however, she was determined to write him a long letter and re-establish proper contact.

'But what will you do, how will you live? Do you think Serge will take you back?'

She shook her head. 'I would not want to go back. I believe it's almost always a mistake to try and retrace one's steps. Better to go on to fresh fields and pastures new!'

She spoke gaily, in a flippant tone. Yet before she'd even finished the sentence she realised, with a sharp pang of insight, that her words could equally apply to her brief affair with Robin.

Uncannily, Richard seemed to voice her secret fears when he said, 'You know you're getting quite a reputation as a vamp, Milly. You flirt with everyone but sleep with no-one. Are you waiting for some great director to come along and sweep you on to his casting couch?'

'I don't know what I'm waiting for,' she sighed. 'Once I dreamed of being a great actress, but now I'm not so sure. If I have to sleep my way into the movies I'm not sure the game is worth the candle. Would they ever take you seriously if they knew about your shady past?'

Richard shrugged. 'I've no such ambitions, as you know. When this summer is over I shall have to return to London and take my place in father's firm.' His eyes dimmed as he gazed towards the horizon, no doubt seeing the isles of Greece where beautiful naked boys wreathed with garlands were beckoning him. 'This will be my last summer of perfect freedom, and I intend to make the most of it.'

Somehow Milly had a feeling that the same might apply to her.

Chapter Twelve

*M*illy returned to London in a strange state, half apprehension and half regret. She didn't even bother getting in touch with Serge or her parents, but found herself some miserable lodgings near Vauxhall. Although she had money in the bank she felt far from secure, and as the first hints of autumn arrived and she saw crocodiles of schoolchildren appearing in the London streets she wondered whether she should take up a post as governess or even try to find work in a school.

But the thought of it depressed her. She would not mind teaching older students, who really wanted to learn, but she could not abide the thought of teaching children. Then, as she was turning out her collection of handbags, she came across the card that Emerald had given her. Those Mediterranean days seemed long gone, here in chilly England, and she hadn't given another thought to the introduction she'd been given, but now it seemed like a godsend.

The address of 'Madame Vavasour' was in Kensington and Milly decided to take a taxi there immediately. She found a typical West End mansion with four floors of white stucco and a square, imposing porch with pillars. A man ushered her inside, his obsequious manner only too familiar, so Milly knew she had come to the right place. He took the card on his silver tray and invited her to wait in the drawing-room on the right.

Within a few minutes a large, effusive woman came sailing into the room dressed in a long negligée of black chiffon with flounced neck and sleeves. Her silver hair was done up in an elaborate chignon and Milly smelt the spicy bouquet of Guerlain's *L'Heure Bleue.*

'Please excuse my *déshabillé,*' she smiled, as Milly got to her feet. 'I was in the middle of dressing for a dinner engagement. But I simply couldn't let you go away again without making your acquaintance. How do you do? I am Tamara Vavasour, but you may call me Tammy. Everyone does.'

'And I'm Emily Floret,' Milly smiled, deciding to use her 'stage' name. 'But you may call me Milly.'

'Emerald wrote to me about you,' Tammy said when they were seated. 'And your turning up here now could be to our mutual benefit. In fact,' she leant forward and took Milly's hand in her smooth, white one, 'I think you could just be heaven sent!'

'Really?'

'Yes. Oh, here's Tarquin with some tea. I trust you would like a cup, Milly?'

The man moved like a ghost between them, setting down the tray and pouring the tea, his hands clad in pristine white gloves, then glided off without a sound. Milly found him spooky.

When he had gone Tammy gave her a conspiratorial smile. 'Tarquin is just one of my many willing slaves. I'm sure you understand perfectly.' She gave a sudden peal of laughter. 'I see by your blushes that you do, my dear! Well, shall we get down to business? I take it this is not just a social call.'

'I don't exactly know. I just thought, seeing as Emerald had given me your address . . .'

The woman started asking all kinds of questions: Had she enjoyed being on the Riviera? How long had she known Emerald? Where was she living in London? Did she have private means? Was she looking for employment? Surprisingly the interrogation didn't seem intrusive. Milly had the feeling it was a mere formality and Tammy knew exactly why she was there.

At last she came to the point. 'Well, Milly, something has cropped up which makes your appearance very opportune. My sister has been taken ill in Edinburgh and I wish to go and stay with her for a month or so, but I need someone to look after this house. Of course, my gentlemen could manage perfectly well on their own. They do everything for me – shopping, cooking, cleaning – but they do need controlling, if you know what I mean.'

'You mean, you want me to take over here?'

'I'm sure if Emerald recommends you there will be no problem. I have another house down the road but that is run by my girls. Of course, if you needed any help they would be only too pleased to assist you, but my impression is that you could manage my gentlemen very well. What do you say?'

'I confess I don't know what to say. What would I have to do, exactly?'

'Simply live here, and treat my gentlemen as your servants. You'll find them very obliging. They all come from good homes and work on a rota basis. Hand me that book on the table beside you and I will show you.'

Milly's eyes were like saucers when Tammy showed her the entries in her 'Household Agenda' all written in a neat hand. The men's particular predilections were documented in detail. She read the whole of one entry:

Charles Ponsonby-Smythe, younger son of Sir Broderick and Lady Anne. Eton and Oxford. Particularly enjoys the slipper. Excellent at oral training. Makes a fine Welsh Rarebit. Likes to wear an apron for dusting. Responds well to The Look, and will take a taste of the whip on occasion but mustn't overdo. A boot-licker. Best kept apart from others, tendency to gossip. Will manicure one's nails beautifully. Likes handling underwear. Has a thing about 'stains.' Good all-rounder when short-staffed.'

Milly looked up to see Tammy smiling wryly at her. 'I like to get the best out of my gentlemen. I shall place this book at your disposal, so you may refer to it whenever you like.'

'But I haven't said I will take this on yet,' Milly reminded her.

'Oh, I think you will.' Tammy's voice and expression held just a hint of the iron fist in the velvet glove. 'I shall pay you fifty guineas for the month. There will be tips from the gentlemen too, of course, which should at least double that. Not bad for one month of idleness, eh?'

Milly grinned. 'Since you put it like that . . .'

'Good. Can you start tomorrow? I should like to go to Scotland on the noon train.'

So it was all arranged, much to Milly's delight. Fifty guineas was an extraordinary fee for what sounded like a very pleasant month's 'work'. She decided to ask Tammy for Emerald's address so she could write and thank her for this most fortunate introduction.

By the following afternoon Milly was installed as Mistress of Number Seven, Holland Mansions. Quentin greeted her at the door and introduced her to the other 'staff' of that day: a tall, lugubrious character called Edward, a chubby fellow called Sam and a very good-looking young man called Julian, to whom she took an instant fancy. I can have some fun with him tonight, she thought, and a tremor went through her.

Waited on hand and foot by Quentin, and with the others at her beck and call, Milly sat in the drawing-room where Tammy had reigned supreme only twenty-four hours ago, and felt a wonderful peace come over her. To think she was being paid for living like a queen! Sipping her tea and nibbling on a madeleine, Milly leafed through the 'Household Agenda' to acquaint herself more closely with the quirky ways of Julian Davenport.

'Loves to be treated like a lap dog. Obedient nature, very versatile. Sweet tooth, will sit up and beg for chockies. Fetches and carries. Prefers to be on all fours. Likes to wear dog collar and chain. Carries own everlasting sheath around in collar for performing "tricks." Very obliging in all departments, loves to be of service.'

'This puts a very different slant on things,' Milly thought. From browsing through Tammy's notes she gleaned that the woman had a gentler, more caring style than Emerald, and that her 'gentlemen' were more like friends than clients. The notes about Julian intrigued her greatly. The reference to the sheath was promising, although she knew from what Chloe had told her that the thing was hard and uncomfortable for men to wear even if it did enable them to have full intercourse in relative safety.

For a few nostalgic seconds she thought of Robin, and the old ache returned to her heart. Blissful though their last encounter had been, for a while Milly had dreamed of making love with him completely, without the necessity of withdrawal. She had known at the time it was a foolish dream, and now it seemed more unlikely than ever. Several times she had picked up her pen meaning to write to him in Paris, but then her nerve had failed her. She was terribly afraid that if she wrote to him after all this time he would not reply.

Her longing for complete sexual fulfilment was acute, however, and she began to think that perhaps Julian might fit the bill. After the delicious supper that Sam and Edward cooked for her, she rang the bell and summoned all four men to the drawing room.

'I wish to assign your evening duties,' she began, almost breaking into laughter as she saw them standing in line, all looking at their feet. 'Sam, please step forward.'

She put a finger beneath his chin and lifted it up so she could look into his clear grey eyes. 'You provided me with an excellent meal tonight.'

'Thank you, mistress,' he murmured, his face flushing.

'You will prepare my bath at ten o'clock this evening.'

His grey eyes flickered but he said nothing, only bowed and stepped back in line. She ordered Edward to come forward next. After congratulating him also, Milly asked him to attend to her laundry. She told Quentin to clean her shoes and prepare her breakfast tray then bring it to her room at nine o'clock next morning. Finally she turned to Julian.

'You shall bring me my night-cap. I require a glass of brandy at eleven o'clock tonight. You are to bring it to my room in your usual uniform. Is that understood?'

His beautiful green eyes glinted at her momentarily. 'Yes, Mistress. Thank you, Mistress.'

She dismissed them with a clap of her hands and then settled back in her chair with her feet on the footstool and took out her book of Shakespeare's sonnets to read by the light of the lamp, but no sooner had she begun than her eyes filled with tears.

'Damned oil lamp!' she exclaimed, although she knew the lack of light had little to do with it. Her earlier regretful mood had not quite left her and she needed diverting. 'What the heck am I supposed to do here in the evenings? I know, I'll ring for Quentin.'

When he arrived she asked, 'What does your Mistress do here after dinner?'

'If she has no guests she plays cards with her gentlemen. Sometimes cribbage or backgammon.'

'Very well, send for the others. We shall do likewise for an hour or so.'

But it was a frustrating evening since none of the others could bring themselves to beat her. By dint of some ingenious 'cheating' Milly found that they made her win every time!

It didn't take her long to discover an alternative form of entertainment however. She had only to look and smile at the bashful Julian to make him blush crimson, and she pursued him relentlessly with her eyes and lips to that end. Although he tried hard to stare at the cards in his hand, or the table or floor, she would fix him with such a relentless stare or say, 'Your turn, Julian!' in such a commanding voice that he couldn't resist glancing at her, and every time he did his cheeks were set on fire.

At last Sam was dismissed so that he could prepare the mistress's bath. Milly was looking forward to that. When it was ready she asked Julian and Edward to accompany her upstairs. She commanded them to help her undress, which they did with carefully averted eyes, then she bade Edward take her clothes away and told Julian he was to scrub her back.

The water was just the right temperature, and scented with lavender. Milly sank into it with a sigh and asked Julian to pass her the soap. His gorgeous green eyes were shuttered against the sight of her but she ordered him to wash her feet, lifting one leg high out of the water. How she enjoyed embarrassing him! He took the cake of soap and carefully washed first one foot, then the other while she lay back in languid ease. Later, she thought, I shall have you naked except for your dog collar and chain. The thought excited her greatly.

'That will do, Julian. Now my back.'

Milly leant forward and hugged her knees. Soon his slow, careful hands were sliding all over her back and massaging the soap in gently. She relaxed under his touch, all her troubled thoughts disappearing as the mood of sensual indulgence took hold. How long was it since she'd really made love with a man? Too long. She had been lost in a nostalgic dream of love instead of exploring the possibilities in reality. Well all that would change tonight!

Julian held the warm bath towel for her as she stepped out, pink and sweet-smelling, then she told him to rub her dry. He did so with the utmost decorum, never touching her skin directly. After she had got into her dressing-gown Milly dismissed him with a reminder about the night-cap, then went to her room. She lit the bedside lamp then lay down on the half-tester bed looking up at the embroidered silk canopy.

The agenda had informed her that Madame kept a box of chocolates in the bedside cabinet for rewarding her gentlemen. Milly opened the door and found the Charbonnier casket which she placed beside the lamp. Then she lay down again, still in the pretty cotton and lace gown that Sam had found for her. The clock on the mantelpiece told her it was ten minutes to eleven. Her stomach felt queasy with desire: she would need that brandy to settle it.

As the little clock began its tinkling chimes, there was a quiet rap on the door.

'Come in!' Milly called, trying to sound authoritarian, although her voice was quaking.

There was a brief fumbling at the handle and the door was pushed open to reveal Julian on all fours, naked except for a dog collar, to which was attached a long chain and a black bow. On his straight back was a silver tray with a decanter half full of brandy and a glass.

Milly couldn't help laughing at the sight. As he entered, carefully shutting the door behind him, she gave him some applause. 'Julian, how splendid!'

She saw him blush, and knew that she must behave more correctly if she wasn't to embarrass him thoroughly. She had no wish to make the man feel more ridiculous than he looked. If he felt humiliated in a negative way he would not perform well for her, in all senses.

As he shuffled forward with his offering Milly realised that there was more to this business than she had at first thought. There was a fine line between wielding her power and abusing it. Although these men loved to be treated harshly, spoken to angrily and even whipped, they had to believe their mistress was sincere and not making fun of them. It was a game with unspoken rules, but each side must keep to them or the charade simply wouldn't work.

'That will do, Julian!' she said, as he came to a halt by her bed. She lifted off the tray and poured herself a brandy. He remained stock still on all fours. Reaching over to the chocolate box she took out one with a crystallised violet on top. 'I want to see you sit up and beg!'

Obediently he got into a kneeling position with his hands held up limply in front of his chest. His green eyes looked up at her pleadingly, and the tip of his tongue protruded from his mouth. If he had a tail he'd be wagging it, Milly thought.

What he did have, however, was a sturdy cock that was already standing to attention. She surveyed it briefly, feeling a sudden rush of lust deep within her. She held out the chocolate saying, 'You may have three licks. You haven't earned any more yet.'

Julian closed his eyes and waggled his tongue. When she put the chocolate to his nose he sniffed it rapidly then tasted it. After three licks she took it away and placed it on the lid of the box. 'So, you like licking do you?' she said, thoughtfully. 'Let's see what else we can find for you to taste.'

She opened the front of her robe to reveal her breasts. The nipples were already taut and eager for some physical contact after all the mental stimulation. Milly moved to the edge of the bed and lifted her bosom towards him. His eyes widened a little but he remained immobile, his cock stiff and upright. His attitude reminded Milly of a pointer dog in sight of the prey.

'Lick my nipples!' she ordered him.

Julian moved his face forward at once, and his red tongue appeared. Soon he was applying it thoroughly, making first one nipple wet then the other, increasing her arousal. She told him to suck her too, and he went on mechanically licking and sucking, on and on. Milly realised that he would go on doing the same thing until she told him to stop. Well, she might as well make herself more comfortable. She moved back on to the bed and lay down, telling him to kneel beside her and continue his work.

The eager lips and tongue were bringing her to a state of orgiastic bliss with their regular caresses. Milly could feel a tremulous longing in her lower region that clamoured to be satisfied. 'Now, lick me down below!' she snarled as the hunger became unbearable.

At once he shifted his position and kissed the open lips of her pussy. Milly soon discovered that he was an expert at this job, and his rapid tonguing of her clitoris soon brought her to the summit of ecstasy. She shuddered and moaned her way through a long series of climactic thrills that left her breathless and spent.

Yet Julian seemed quite unruffled. He slid down from the bed and resumed his former doggy posture, staying perfectly still with downcast eyes while Milly slowly recovered her wits. Eventually she reached for the chocolate. 'Here boy! Take your reward.'

He took the remains of the chocolate slowly into his mouth, savouring it. Then, remembering what the notes about him had indicated, Milly grew curious about what was hidden in his collar. She ordered him to take out his 'everlasting sheath' and let her examine it. Julian unclipped his bow and she saw that there was a small packet behind. He took out the sheath and handed it to her. It was thick and rigid. Not very comfortable to wear, she suspected, but it certainly looked efficacious.

Milly knew that in the cupboard by the bed there was a box of soluble 'check pessaries'. She reached over and took one out. 'Now be a good little doggy and put this inside me,' she said, handing him the tablet. Julian did so, pushing it as far inside her as he could and incidentally rekindling her desire. But there was something that must be done first. She sent him over to the wash-stand to pour some water into the bowl then bring it over to her. He held it while she filled the rubber sheath and held it up, to make sure there were no leaks.

'Good. Now you can put this on!' she told him.

His erection was still strong, miraculously maintained by sheer will-power she presumed. Julian winced a little as he crammed his penis into the device, but his green eyes had a hint of cunning greed in them, like a spoilt lap-dog that recognises an opportunity for a tit-bit. When his cock was encased in its protective shield Milly got up on all fours on the bed.

'There, now you can take me from behind, like a randy dog! But first you must lick me, to make sure I'm ready. All dogs do that to their bitches.'

Milly braced herself on her arms and sighed with pleasure as his mouth insinuated itself below her buttocks and found her still-wet labia. Her libido revived quickly, encouraged by the prospect of full penetration. When she felt good and ready, Milly spread her thighs wide and tilted her pelvis to allow him ease of access. The hard tip of the sheath nudged at her entrance and then he was ramming it home, painfully at first but then, as his slow movements loosened her up, giving her increasing pleasure. The liquefying pessary, together with her own hot juices, was making it easier for him to slide in and out and soon the pace was fast and furious, just as Milly desired.

She was soon clenching her arse and waggling her hips in an attempt to increase her satisfaction. Then she called to Julian, 'Lean over my back and grab my tits!' He obeyed instantly, and his rough handling of her full, pendant breasts was immensely gratifying. Realising that he would do anything she liked, for as long as she liked, Milly told him to use his right hand to rub her clitoris and soon she was being propelled into another fierce climax, this time even stronger than the last.

'Oh! Oh!' she called aloud as the rigid organ teased wave after wave of gut-wrenching pleasure from her. Julian slowed down as her orgasm faded, but did not stop altogether. Although her legs were aching, Milly was floating on a plane of sensual bliss and unwilling for the rapture to cease. She sank on to her side with the man's prick still inside her and rocked her hips back and forth, matching her rhythm to his.

It wasn't long before she was coming again, this time with excited little flurries of erotic spasms that rippled up and down her spine and down to her knees. Yet though she was thoroughly satiated physically, Milly began to feel an emptiness in her soul. The wild urges that had led her on, unthinking, into the realm of pure sensuality were beginning to wane and she was left feeling vaguely disgusted.

'That will do, Julian!' she said, sharply. He pulled out of her at once, and got off the bed. She told him to take the sheath off and wash it in the bowl. It was starting to irritate her that she had to tell him everything; that he would do nothing on his own initiative. Yet he had performed impeccably, and she must be kind for Tammy's sake. Reaching over, she took another chocolate from the box and asked him to beg for it. She popped it whole into his mouth then told him to leave her. He padded out on all fours, the perfect household pet.

The first week of sybaritic indulgence passed quickly. At the back of Tammy's agenda Milly found a check list of the various pleasures that the Mistress had enjoyed at the hands of her gentlemen. It was a long list but Milly managed to get through most of them, from having her body massaged with fragrant oils and being thoroughly groomed from head to toe, to being 'serviced' by all four men at once, each assigned to a different portion of her anatomy.

The latter had not been quite as satisfying as she had hoped, however. Milly had been obliged to instruct the men at every stage, so instead of being able to lie back and think of nothing in particular she had to constantly re-direct them: 'That's enough licking, Sam, now suck! Not so fast, Julian, more slowly! Use both hands on my buttocks, Edward, and don't just stroke me but pinch a little too. Quentin, you can be a bit firmer with your finger on my button, and a bit faster.' Soon she began to feel more like Serge, directing a scene.

Serge. How long ago her life as a 'movie queen' now seemed. And it was ages since she'd seen her parents, too. One day, half-way through her second week when things were beginning to pall a little, Milly decided to pay her father a visit. She called a cab on impulse and went straight to his house but found him out. Philip was there, however, and he told her there was a letter waiting for her. 'It came last week,' he said, casually. 'From Italy, I believe. I'll get Mrs Godwin to fetch it.'

Milly seized the letter eagerly, thinking it was from Emma. Inside she did find a brief note from her godmother, but only to tell her about a second letter, enclosed with it: 'This came from that tutor of yours. I'm forwarding it to your father, in case your mother is still in Italy.'

The brevity of the note made Milly frown. Was her godmother cross with her for some reason? But she dismissed it, concentrating instead on the envelope bearing Evadne's familiar script. She was almost afraid to open it. When she did, however, she was pleasantly surprised.

'Dear Milly,' she read. 'I write to tell you of an opportunity which you may take up if you wish. An old colleague of mine at one of the training colleges affiliated to London University, Professor Alan Symes, is looking for a part-time lecturer in English. Knowing Alan, I am sure he works to the highest academic standards. If you're interested, here is his address . . .'

The letter was dated three weeks ago. Evidently Eva bore her no lasting ill-will, and for that Milly was grateful. But she cursed her own tardiness in contacting her father. Professor Symes would probably have filled the post by now. There was little point in writing to him.

Yet as Milly made her way back to Kensington, after leaving a message for her father, the idea of returning to Academia was surprisingly alluring. She had not expected to be tempted by such a post, and it had taken her completely by surprise. Now that she gave it some thought, however, she realised how much she'd been missing the intellectual life and how empty the past few months had really been for her.

As soon as she got back Milly asked Quentin to bring her writing case. She wrote a note to Professor Symes in her best handwriting, then asked him to deliver it in person to the address in Hampstead. She couldn't bring herself to pass this opportunity by.

A reply came next day. Professor Symes said the post was still unfilled, and he urgently required a lecturer to start in two weeks' time, at the beginning of the Michaelmas term. If she would care to come for an interview at ten a.m. on the twenty-fourth, he would be much obliged, etc.

Milly had just two days to prepare for her interview. She sent Quentin to her mother's house for her books, which were packed into a trunk, and set about the arduous task of oiling her rusty brain. It was a hard task. She read through her notes and essays in increasing panic, taking very little in. She had Evadne's recommendation, but she was terribly afraid she was going to let her tutor down. Whatever she felt about the woman on a personal level she greatly admired her intellectual skills and would be forever grateful for having her own mind trained in the rigours of critical analysis.

But had the intervening months of soft living and sexual indulgence addled her once-incisive brain? Milly was very much afraid so. And now she knew that if she did not get the post she would be dreadfully disappointed. After all her determination not to get sucked back into the dry world of books and note-books, of lectures and libraries, Milly was astonished at her new-born desire to re-enter it. Perhaps she was a 'bluestocking' and not a tart at heart, after all!

That same heart was thudding wildly in her chest when Milly presented herself at the Professor's elegant house. She was shown into the study of a grey-bearded man with bright brown eyes who smiled cordially as he rose from his leather chair.

'Miss Belfort! How good of you to come. I've had such an excellent report of you from Evadne. Do sit down and I'll ring for coffee.'

The interview was more like a friendly chat. He began by asking her how she'd enjoyed her time at Cambridge, and then went on to enquire about her favourite authors and poets. The time flew by as Milly talked of Keats and Shelley, Dickens and Wells. They discussed literary topics too, the effect of the Italian Renaissance on Elizabethan poetry, and the portrayal of women in Shakespeare. After around half an hour the subject was suddenly brought back to teaching.

'Evadne tells me you used to run an informal poetry reading group at Girton,' he said, his eyes twinkling. 'And once you took a tutorial for her, when she had the 'flu.'

'Oh yes, so I did!'

He laughed. 'But do you think you could manage to keep order, give lectures in a commanding tone, keep the young ladies under control, all that sort of thing?'

Remembering how she had been behaving over the

past few weeks, Milly stifled a giggle. 'Oh yes, I'm quite sure I could manage all that.'

'Well, Milly – I hope I may call you that? – I think you will probably do splendidly. You will be on probation for the first year, and on a term's notice, either side. That is normal college procedure. Your salary will be two-hundred-and-fifty pounds a year, and you will be offered the chance to live in if you so desire. Do you have any questions?'

Milly was overjoyed. They spent the rest of the day going through the syllabus, with a short break for lunch, and by the time she returned to Kensington that evening she felt far more confident about tackling the job. It amused her to think that she would be still living at Tammy Vavasour's during her first week at the college, but even that had its advantages. She wouldn't have to worry about cooking or other domestic tasks for a while.

'I suppose now I should tell Ma and Pa the good news, too,' she thought wryly. They would no doubt be relieved that she'd settled into a respectable and secure occupation at last.

There was someone else who would be pleased, but Milly didn't know whether she would tell him. Robin seemed a faded dream to her, like a pressed flower in an album, a reminder of past beauty. Well, she had too much else on her mind to worry about him now. Picking up her pile of books and papers from the seat of the taxi, Milly descended to the pavement and vowed to dedicate the next two weeks to sharpening up her mental faculties instead of indulging herself physically.

Chapter Thirteen

Milly settled back into academic life as if she had never been away from it, and enjoyed being on the other side of the fence for a change. As a member of staff she had more freedom, especially as she had declined the offer of college accommodation and found her own digs. The spacious, modern flat in Chiswick, not far from where her father lived, was easily affordable on her new salary and she loved being able to come and go as she pleased.

As she had expected, both her parents were pleased when she told them about her appointment. When she found out Kitty was back, Milly went to see her in the cramped, dark little terraced house which her mother shared with two other women.

'At least you will not be wasting your education now, Milly,' she commented, rather sourly. 'As you know I've little time for intellectuals, but anything is better than the sordid work you were involved in. I was afraid that Emma and your father were bad influences on you. They've always been the sort to put pleasure before duty.'

'I don't see why one can't have both.'

'It's a matter of getting things in proportion, dear. Still, I hope it's not all brain work for you. I must say you're looking rather peaky.'

Milly smiled wryly. 'I've not had much time for socialising so far. It was such a last-minute appointment that I was plunged into the deep end. I take each day as it comes, and I'm really just one jump ahead of the students. Still, I'll have the holidays to catch up in.'

Her father was bluff and hearty in his congratulations. 'Well done, clever girl! I suppose they pay you a decent wage too, eh? So you won't be needing that allowance from me any more, will you?'

This came as a blow to Milly, but she realised it was only fair. Her father had supported her through school and college so it was not right to expect him to continue, especially as she'd managed to build up some savings. Even so, she would miss the extra safety net of her regular bank deposit.

'How does it feel to be an independent young woman, earning your own living?' he went on. 'As long as you don't plan to become one of those fearful blue-stockinged spinster types.'

Milly laughed. 'Not me, father! I like men too much to shun their company.'

He gave her an amused, searching look. 'I dare say you won't be long out of the marriage market then, my girl. You're pretty enough. I'll give you a couple of years at most before some young whipper-snapper comes along and bowls you off your feet.'

Milly stared at him in faint horror. The thought of marriage after so short a period of independence was anathema to her. Yet it made her think of Robin. A cloud veered over her mental horizon whenever her mind turned to him. She felt horribly guilty that she had left him high and dry, and the more time passed the more dreadful she felt. It was now over three months since she last set eyes on him, but it felt more like three years.

One evening Milly sat down at her desk in her garden flat looking out on pleasant lawns and shrubs and listening to the birds' twittering evensong. She picked up her address book and found her godmother's address. Then she filled her Waterman fountain pen, took a sheet of London Bond paper and began to write her letter. Once she had blotted it and put it in the envelope she thought of Evadne. It was high time she wrote to her too.

Milly began flicking through her book in search of her old tutor's name. Suddenly her eye lighted on another entry: Robin Dupont. Her heart gave a painful lurch as she saw the familiar Paris address. Would he still be there? She gazed dreamily out of the window, forgetting all about Evadne in her reverie. Supposing she were to write now, and he were to answer. Supposing he was finishing his studies and returning to England soon . . .

She put such idle speculation aside and leafed on through her book impatiently, in search of Eva's Florentine address. But thoughts of Robin continued to haunt her even while she wrote. In the end she decided to pen him a note too. It could do no harm, after all. If he no longer wished to be in touch with her he need not reply.

For a long time Milly pondered over what to say. She opened with a 'remember me?' and went on to tell him of her college appointment, but then she was stuck. Poetry came to her rescue. She ended hoping they might remain friends, and quoting a line from Lord Byron: 'Friendship is Love without his wings!' She thought that expressed her position nicely, being unsure whether the passion they had once shared could ever be revived. All in all, friendship seemed to her to be the safer option.

221

By now she was settling in well to her life at the college. The girls were eager to learn, most of them likely to become dedicated teachers, and Milly found great satisfaction in sharing her love of literature with them, whether in the lecture hall to thirty or forty students, or in small tutorial groups. She was reminded of her own college days, and hoped that the same inspiration she had gained from Evadne and one or two other tutors would be passed on to these young women, only a few years younger than herself.

Professor Symes had the habit of sneaking in and out of her lectures from time to time, which put her on edge, but he soon pronounced himself well pleased with her.

'I have excellent reports of you from your tutorial group, and I have found your lectures to be very stimulating. I knew you would not let me down, my dear,' he smiled. 'Keep up the good work!'

But there was a missing dimension to her life and, try as she might, Milly could not dismiss it altogether. Sometimes, on dreary autumn weekends, she would find her way to Kensington where she would be received with delight by Tammy and her gentlemen. There would follow a feast of sensual indulgence which would last her through the famine of the next few weeks. Since she believed herself to be far too busy to get involved in some distracting new love affair, the arrangement suited her perfectly.

But then, just after the students had gone down for the Christmas recess, everything suddenly changed.

Milly was at home, writing her Christmas cards, when there was a ring at the doorbell. She jumped up at once and answered it. There, looking so familiar and yet so out of place, stood Robin Dupont.

'Robin!' she screeched, unable to believe it was really him.

'Hullo, Milly.'

He gave the wry smile she remembered so well, and suddenly she was back on a Parisian boulevard again. She ushered him in and took his wet raincoat to hang on a peg by the door. Her mind and heart seemed to be racing each other, each trying to divine – by reason or intuition – what his sudden reappearance might mean.

Robin followed her into the small sitting-room where her cards were still strewn on a low table. 'Were you writing one for me?' he asked, his hazel eyes twinkling at her.

'Oh Robin!' she cried, throwing herself into his arms. 'I've missed you so much!'

It was true, without her even knowing it. Seeing him now she remembered just what a companion he'd been to her, as well as a lover. She had so few real friends. Why had she been so careless as to nearly lose this one?

'I wasn't sure whether to come,' he said, hesitantly, holding her close. 'Your letter . . . I never answered it. I'm sorry.'

She pulled away and they sat down in the only two armchairs, regarding each other. 'I'm glad you did. I've been thinking about you a lot lately.'

'Have you?' Hope was written plainly on his candid brow. 'The thing is, Milly, I thought we'd parted as lovers, not just as friends. So when I got your letter . . .'

'I didn't want to presume too much. I felt guilty about not getting in touch over the summer. But then I thought you must be at Deauville, and . . .'

He held out his arms and, smiling, they linked hands across the small space that divided them. 'Never mind about that now. The main thing is we are together again. Tell me about this job of yours, Milly. I want to know everything about your life here. Are you happy?'

She wanted to say, 'I thought so, until you came back and showed me what happiness really is.' But that seemed too forward. She was still unsure of him, unsure whether this was a reconciliation between sweethearts or just a reunion of friends. But beneath her confusion Milly was sure of one thing: she was very glad he *had* come to her.

While they were drinking tea they both relaxed, laughing a good deal. Milly told him about her life at college, and he congratulated her on having found such a nice place to live.

'Yes, and I have it all to myself,' she smiled. Then blushed, because of the implication. She went on, quickly, 'It's not very proper, of course, but the people at college think I'm sharing it with another girl. I prefer to be on my own. After being at boarding school and then having to share digs at Cambridge, I relish the peace and quiet. I'm able to do what I like, when I like. Are you still in the same digs, Robin?'

He shook his head. 'I've finished in Paris. Gustave Olivier, who was supervising me, went to Germany and there's no other specialist in my field. I suppose I could have gone to Germany with him, but I wanted to come back to England. I've moved on to comparing the French Symbolists with the English Romantics, so I can continue my studies using the British Library. Gus will keep me on the right track by post.'

Milly tried not to show how excited she was at the thought of him living in London. 'But how will you live?'

'I'll have to get work of some kind, and pursue my studies in my spare time. But I'll manage, Milly. The main thing is, I shall be near you again.'

She looked into his face, relishing once more the symmetry of his brows, the rather aristocratic nose, the full red lips. She noticed once again how his brown hair had auburn glints, and rippled back in soft waves from the wide forehead. It was a face she had loved and, truth to tell, loved still. But she was wary of presuming they could take up where they had left off, with no complications. Her life had taken some strange turns since the beginning of the summer, and she was in many ways quite a different person from the one she'd been then.

'It will be nice to see more of you,' she said, stiffly.

'Milly . . .' he hesitated, and she sympathised with his apprehension for she felt it too. 'I don't quite know how to put this, but . . . there isn't anyone else, is there?'

Smiling, she shook her head. 'No, Robin. Not in the way you mean.'

'I haven't touched another woman since you, Milly, I swear it! Every night I've dreamed of you, only you. But they've been hopeless dreams. At least it seemed so in the morning, when I awoke.'

He looked so forlorn, her heart went out to him. She stood up and gathered him in her arms, his head at her waist. He clung to her like a child, and she felt an overwhelming tenderness seize her. 'Oh Robin!' she crooned, ruffling through his soft hair. 'I've missed you too! What a pair of sillies we are!'

She sat down on his lap with her arms around his neck and they began reminiscing about their time in Paris, catching up on snippets of news. Milly found it hard to pretend that she spent the summer with her parents, but she could not bring herself to reveal how she had really passed the time. It was evident that Robin still cherished his image of her as an innocent maid, whose first sexual awakening had been with him. Sometimes Milly wished it had been so, but she couldn't change her past. The most she could do was ensure he never found out about it.

They went on to talk of their families. Robin said his father owned a large house in Berkshire, and Milly thought of Maplefield, Lord Sanderford's seat, but didn't dare mention her visit there. Then he asked about her parents, and Milly found herself growing rather proud of her mother as she described her feminist activities.

'She sounds a fine-spirited woman,' Robin said. 'I should love to meet her. Maybe sometime over the Christmas season?'

Milly's heart sank. She had not thought of introducing him to her relatives. They would think she was planning to become engaged to him. Perhaps he was already thinking that, too. The warm glow that had been building up in her abruptly vanished, and a cold despair took its place. This would never work!

'Oh, mother doesn't recognise Christmas!' she said, airily. It was almost true. Emma had been the one who loved festivities, and since she had left England the celebration at her mother's had been minimal. 'And I'm not sure how father spends it. At his club, I dare say.'

Robin frowned. 'That doesn't sound like much fun for you. Why don't you come to Berkshire and spend it with my family? Oh yes, what a wonderful idea! Milly, you'd love it! We always have a big gathering, lots of children, party games. And you'd be made to feel very welcome, I can promise you that.'

Milly's heart, already sinking, felt as if it had dropped to her stomach. She'd landed herself in it good and proper now! 'Well, I'm not sure . . .' she hedged, desperately trying to think of some excuse.

'Don't worry about feeling like an outsider, Milly, because you won't be.'

He gave her a long, meaningful look and for one terrible moment she thought he was about to ask her to marry him. She had to say something. 'Look, I don't want you to be upset by this, but . . . well, I wouldn't want anyone to think I was your fiancée.'

226

He clasped her hand and kissed it, laughing. 'Don't worry! I know you've only just begun your teaching career. I wouldn't want you to give all that up yet. No, my parents are broad-minded. They will be perfectly happy to accept you as just a friend, who had nowhere else to go for Christmas. There will probably be other waifs and strays there, knowing my Mamma!'

Having cleared up that obstacle, Milly was tempted. The prospect of a real Christmas, spent with a real family, was very enticing. She hadn't had one of those since her childhood.

So it was agreed. Milly would travel down to Berkshire with Robin on Christmas Eve and stay until the day after Boxing Day. She embraced him warmly and he began kissing her, tenderly at first, but then with increasing ardour. Their tongues embraced, tasting and licking in passionate rediscovery, and suddenly their hands were everywhere, feeling the hard flesh beneath the soft skin, fingers raking and pinching and stroking. Their desire for each other became unstoppable, moved ruthlessly towards its goal, and neither had the power to put on the brakes.

Before long Milly found herself stripped to the waist, with Robin's hot lips savouring her breasts. She cried out in joy, knowing how much she had missed this exquisite feeling, and tore at his shirt trying to make him as naked as she. Her palms moved swiftly over the broad chest, the meaty biceps, and she felt the dampness of his sweat, scented the musky male aroma that issued from his armpits. She wanted him at a gutsy, animal level that had no time for the niceties of seduction.

Laughing, they found themselves tumbling to the floor as the chair gave up the struggle to contain them both. There they hastily undid buttons and pulled off each other's clothes until they were completely nude.

Milly glanced down at the instrument that had taken her virginity. It stood proudly erect, its pink head swaying towards her as if attracted by the scent of her pussy. Slowly she put out her fingers and touched it. Robin gave a sigh of bliss, closing his eyes. She took the shaft gently and began to caress it, then bent her lips to the tip. Her whole being seemed to vibrate with craving, and she felt a hollow ache inside.

'I want to sit astride you,' she murmured, hoarsely. 'May I?'

He nodded, too moved to speak. She settled with her knees outside his thighs, and slowly lowered herself on to the tall stalk of his penis. Engaging the head in her pussy, she gave a long moan of pleasure and began to sink down, inch by inch, feeling the tremulous pleasure he was giving her increase as more and more of her quim was filled with his warm, hard flesh.

'Is that good?' she cooed in his ear, wickedly.

'Mm! You don't know . . . how good!'

'Oh, I think I do!'

Milly gave him a squeeze with her inner walls that soon had him groaning. He opened his eyes and looked up at her, his gaze brimming over with love and desire. Leaning forward she kissed him on the mouth, their tongues melding sweetly. She began to experiment with her movements, sometimes making little, fast strokes, sometimes long, languid ones. She clenched her buttocks and felt her clitoris throb. She rotated her pelvis, and found it made her labia feel good. She leant right forward, so Robin could reach her swinging breasts, and found that very good too.

'Oh yes, Milly!' he murmured. 'Take your pleasure of me, dearest. I have wanted this for so long so very long!'

She plunged down hard, feeling her inner walls close over the solid length of him in a most intimate caress. Her clitoris was rubbing against the base of his shaft, taking her nearer and nearer to the height of ecstasy, and as his fingers pulled at her nipples, evoking new ripples of intense delight, she felt herself coming to a climax. Heedless of anything but her own extreme arousal, she was stunned when Robin suddenly pulled her over to one side and hastily withdrew his member. She heard him gasp out his own sudden release and realised that he had done what he had to do, even though it left her unsatisfied.

'I'm sorry, Milly,' he whispered. 'But I could not take the risk.'

'I understand.' She stroked his damp hair, pushing it back from his forehead. 'But you could help me now, if you will.'

'Anything, Milly!'

'Here.' She took his hand and placed it between her thighs. 'Rub me gently right where I show you, there's a dear.'

When she had him positioned as she wanted Milly lay back and let him bring her to orgasm. He was clumsy at first, but her whispered directions enabled him to find the right touch and when she exploded into a shattering orgasm he looked down at her glowing, ecstatic face with a proud smile. 'Oh Milly, that was wonderful!'

'I'm glad you enjoyed it,' she grinned.

'One day, my darling, I promise we shall experience that ecstasy together, each of us rejoicing in the other's pleasure, as well as our own.'

She believed him, but how long would it be before they could attain that freedom? Pulling him down beside her on the rug, she put her arm around him and told him she believed there were better methods than withdrawal.

'Something called an American sheath, I think,' she said, as if the term were strange to her. It would not do if he thought she had actually seen one, let alone made use of one!

He frowned. 'Is that the same as a Malthus sheath? The men I shared a flat with used to talk of them, and I saw one once. It looked very bulky and uncomfortable. I don't think I could ever wear one of those.'

'Not even if it let you stay in me to the end?'

'A friend of mine used one once. He said its thickness prevented all feeling, so what would be the point?'

Milly didn't want to push the idea, but she was disappointed. It looked as if they would have to use withdrawal or go back to other ways of satisfying each other. Yet now she had tasted the joys of intercourse Milly would find it hard to renounce them again. It was something special between her and Robin, something she would keep for him now that they were together again. She half regretted 'doing it' with Julian but that had been something totally different, more like using a dildo, so it hardly bore comparison. She loved the wonderful contact of Robin's silky penis with her velvety cunt, the way their flesh slipped and slid in and out, the sweet mingling of their juices. Maybe he was right after all, and it was better to have a few minutes of naked contact than have a barrier of thick rubber between them.

When they had recovered, Robin offered to take her out for a meal. They had a jolly evening at a local restaurant frequented by students. It was almost like being back in Paris. But as he walked her home Robin broke the news that he couldn't stay that night.

'I have to get back to my grandmother's house, or she'll be worrying about me.'

'Your grandmother? You haven't mentioned her. Where does she live?'

'In Bayswater. I'm staying with her until Christmas and then I plan to look for a place of my own. Oh

230

Milly, now I know we are friends again – and not just friends but lovers, too – I shall make sure I find a place as near as possible to yours!'

After he'd gone Milly made herself a cup of cocoa and sat by the gas fire, dreaming idly. It had all happened so fast, yet it had all seemed so natural, so right. She knew that she loved him, but everything else was uncertain. Although Robin seemed content to wait before making any kind of formal commitment, she wondered how it would end. What if his family disapproved of her? What if he found out about her past? How could she bear to give up her teaching career just as it was taking off?

These and a hundred other questions plagued her through the night, making her sleep fitful. When she awoke, however, she set about her preparations for Christmas with new zeal. There was scarcely a week to do all her shopping, make her family visits and post her cards. She was glad to have plenty to do so she would not sit and brood.

Her visits to her parents were rather strained. Milly was surprised at her mother's reaction when she said she was spending Christmas with 'a friend.' Kitty seemed hurt, even though she did not plan to do anything much, as usual. Her father seemed more concerned that she would be leaving her mother alone, even though Milly assured him that she would have her women friends around her.

'You know, Milly, it's a girl's duty to look after her mother at such times, make sure she is not lonely and so forth.'

She stared at him in dismay. How dare he say such a thing when he himself had abandoned his wife long ago! Equally disconcerting was the implication that if Kitty should fall ill or be unable to support herself he would expect Milly to play the 'devoted daughter' and care for her mother. The prospect was not an attractive one, yet her father seemed to have it mapped out for her. Maybe the sooner he knew about Robin the better. Yet she could not have it both ways. If she was unwilling to become engaged to him she must go on enduring talk of this dreary alternative future, of the career woman giving up her job to look after her aged parent.

The next few days slipped by in a whirl of activity. Milly treated herself to an 'off-the-peg' gown in crimson velvet and she bought some white fur trim to make it look 'Christmassey'. Yet she was still apprehensive about meeting Robin's parents, hoping they would like the presents she had bought for them: a box of Havana cigars from Dunhills for his father, and for his mother a bottle of the latest French perfume, *Narcisse Bleu*.

Milly had no trouble finding a present for Robin. A beautiful leather-bound edition of Keats' poetry fitted the bill exactly. She awaited him anxiously in her flat on Christmas Eve, her bag bulging with gaily-wrapped parcels. When he arrived she threw herself excitedly into his arms. 'Oh, I've not looked forward to Christmas this much since I was a little girl!' she exclaimed. He laughed indulgently at her and helped her, and her bags, out to the waiting cab.

They went by train from Paddington to Reading, where they were met by Robin's father in a splendid car with dark green coachwork. Milly was astonished to see how like his father Robin was. Mr Dupont had an air of Gallic charm and a twinkle in his eye that suggested he had been a one for the ladies in his heyday. Now his French accent had mellowed and his black hair was streaked with grey, but he was still a very attractive man.

'So, this is the little Milly you have so often spoken of,' Gérard Dupont said with a wink as they set off into the traffic.

'Don't embarrass her, father. She'll wonder what I've been saying about her.'

'Oh, I'm sure she can guess. You know how highly my son regards you, do you not Milly? He is like me, he has no skill in hiding his feelings.'

Milly blushed, but she was filled with dread as her old fears returned to haunt her. Had Robin told his parents that he loved her? Were they expecting their engagement to be announced? But then the conversation turned to family matters, the weather, and the state of the nation, by turns, so Milly was happy to take a back seat both literally and metaphorically.

'We shall be having a big party on Boxing Day,' Gérard said as they drew up outside an attractive manor house that had obviously been 'modernised' during the Victorian period and equipped with a few extraneous turrets. 'It's a kind of "welcome home" party for you, Robin. Your mother and I are so glad to have you back in England again.'

It was obvious by now that Robin came from a very close and happy family. Milly was surprised to feel some pangs of envy as she went through the wreathed door and into a hall hung with boughs of holly and mistletoe. Some rosy-cheeked children came running up to greet them, and then Robin's mother appeared, smiling a welcome. She was a small, pretty woman who had obviously given her son his sunny smile and temperament.

'We're so pleased to have you with us, Milly!' she smiled, kissing her cheek. 'Come on into the drawing-room, where there's a big fire. You must be frozen, sitting in the back of that dreadful contraption.'

'It's not a contraption, it's an automobile, mother!' Robin said, and the young children giggled. This was obviously a family joke.

Milly was amazed at how easily she seemed to fit in. Everyone made her very comfortable, making sure her glass and plate were always full, that she was not too hot or too cold, and that she was never left out of the conversation. She joined in the carols with gusto, tucked into the Christmas dinner with equal enthusiasm, admired the children's play, joined the ladies in a game of cards, went for a bracing walk then enjoyed roasting chestnuts round a log fire. And all the while she was aware of Robin's tender eyes upon her, making it obvious to everyone how he felt about her. At first she felt embarrassed, but everyone else seemed to take it so much for granted that she soon stopped worrying.

Since Milly had to share a room with Robin's fifteen-year-old sister there was no question of any love-making, but she didn't mind. It was enough to wallow in the warmth and friendship of his kin, to be made to feel one of the family. So when Robin asked her, on Boxing Day morning, if she were enjoying herself Milly said, with perfect sincerity, that it was the best Christmas of her life.

Chapter Fourteen

O n Boxing Night, everything suddenly livened up
as around fifty guests began arriving for the
party. A small orchestra was playing waltzes in the
drawing-room for the older generation, while a wind-
up gramophone in the long gallery belted out more
jazzy numbers for the younger set. A buffet had been
laid in the dining-room, and the family servants supple-
mented by a couple of waiters to serve the drinks.

After some rather frantic dancing, Robin and Milly
retreated to the refreshment area where quite a few
other guests were circulating. Robin was just fetching
her a glass of punch when Milly suddenly heard her
name called from across the room. Startled, she recognised a girl with dark, bobbed hair and very blue eyes
but she couldn't for the life of her remember where
they'd met before.

'It is Milly, isn't it?' the girl repeated, coming over
to peer at her. 'The English Rosebud?'

Milly quailed at the sound of her *soubriquet*. Now
she recalled where she had seen this girl: at the
Maplefield weekend. No doubt she lived locally and
went to all the parties.

'Made any good films lately?' the girl went on, with a wink. Milly wanted to sink through the floor. She cast a nervous glance towards Robin, who was carrying two over-full glasses of punch towards her with careful concentration.

'I'm sorry, I don't remember your name,' she said stiffly, wondering how on earth she could get rid of this fly in the ointment.

The girl held out her hand, but before she could say anything Robin arrived. 'Tessa!' he grinned, handing Milly her glass with a wink. Her face was frozen in a mask of horror and felt as if it were hewn from stone. 'Tessa's an old flame of mine, aren't you Tess?'

'Oh I wouldn't say that exactly!' Tessa gave a trilling laugh that set Milly's teeth on edge. 'We went to a few dances together, that's all.'

'Round here that means we're practically engaged!' he grinned, winking at Milly again. She knew he'd already had a couple of glasses of punch, and now she was seeing a different side of him. It was a side she wasn't sure she liked.

'Any girl that gets engaged to you has got to be crazy!' Tessa went on, blithely. 'But I'm not jolly well marrying anyone, at least not for ages. I intend to have a rip-roaring time before I settle down. I'm sure Milly knows what I mean!'

She gave her a wink, and Milly felt a tell-tale flush in her cheeks. She was praying that Tessa would not elaborate.

'Milly is a college lecturer,' Robin went on, a note of pride in his voice.

'Oh, really?' Tessa's thin, dark brows described two perfect upraised arches, and her mouth was pursed in amusement. 'A *lech*erer, is she? I'm sure she's frightfully good at that!'

She gave a high-pitched laugh at her own wit, which fortunately went over Robin's head.

'Some people would say she's a bluestocking,' Robin continued.

'Well, for the work she does I should think a *blue* stocking was just the job, eh Milly?'

Robin stared at her uneasily, and Milly was afraid he'd would cotton on to her double meanings. She gulped down the remainder of her drink and said, 'Robin, I think I'd like to dance again. They're playing something rather jolly in the next room.'

To her relief he didn't demur but made their excuses to Tessa. While they danced Milly was preoccupied and missed what Robin said a couple of times. Her eyes must have lost their sparkle because he pulled her close and said, 'Milly, you've gone all quiet on me. What's up?'

'Nothing, nothing at all!'

'Don't try and lie to me, darling. I can see you're upset. Is it about Tessa? She never meant anything to me, you know.'

Milly decided she would rather have him believe she was jealous than suspect the truth. 'Are you sure?'

'Oh my poor dear, did you believe all that rot about us nearly being engaged? I was seventeen at the time. If I ever felt anything for Tess, and I can't recall that I did, it was only puppy love.'

'Really?' she sniffed.

'Yes, really. God, Milly, I can't bear to see you like this. Let's go and find somewhere quiet, where we can talk properly.'

He took her up to his room. Once they were inside he locked the door, and Milly felt a brief shiver of desire as she realised that they were completely alone for the first time since they'd come to his parents' house.

'You're not going to let that silly girl upset you, are you sweetheart?' he said, embracing her.

Milly shook her head, giving a tentative smile. He

kissed first her cheek, then her lips, chaste kisses that nevertheless opened up the floodgates of their passion for each other. They were soon giving vent to all their corked-up feelings which exploded suddenly, like champagne. Ravenously they feasted on each other's lips, squeezed and stroked each other with eager hands, pressed their fluttering hearts together and intertwined their thighs. By mutual consent they moved over to the bed where, heedless of their party clothes, they began to scrabble beneath the layers to find the warm, willing flesh beneath.

'Wait, let me take this off,' Milly said, as her necklace became entangled with her hair. She quickly removed her jewellery and her dress. Robin stripped too and came to her naked, his cock more than ready for her. He pulled down the straps of her petticoat and began to nibble delicately at her breasts, making her cry out with the exquisite bliss that filled her veins.

'God, Milly, it's been hell watching you looking so happy and so lovely, and not being able to take you in my arms, let alone make love to you!'

'I've wanted you too,' she admitted, lapsing into a moan as his fumbling hands finally freed her crotch from her satin knickers and a finger probed right into her wet pussy.

Robin could hardly wait to get inside her. As soon as she felt his tumid prick between her labia Milly gave a groan of relief and when he pushed into her, her clitoris began throbbing. It didn't take her more than a few seconds to reach the very edge of orgasm.

Robin was thrusting faster and faster, pushing her towards a climax, and Milly could hardly believe how soon the first spasms started, filling her whole body with juddering currents of hot sensation that racked through her, over and over again. She cried out in delight as he increased his pace, enhancing her orgasm greatly. The ecstasy rolled through her like a giant tidal wave, sweeping her into a state of mindless bliss. It was only when she was coming down from this exalted state that she realised Robin was lying limp and spent inside her.

'God, Milly, I'm sorry. But I couldn't stop myself,' he murmured.

For a few seconds she didn't realise what he meant. Then it dawned on her, and the sticky residue that was oozing from her vagina confirmed it. 'Oh Robin!' she sighed. 'What have we done?'

'Don't fret, we may yet have a lucky escape.'

Milly did a quick calculation. 'I think you're right, love,' she said with relief. 'I'm between courses, and I read a pamphlet on birth control which said that was the safe time.'

'Whew, that's all right then.' Robin hugged her to his broad chest where she nestled, relaxed and content. 'I wouldn't want anything to spoil the way things are right now, Milly,' he told her. 'As far as I'm concerned, everything's just perfect.'

They rejoined the party and, for the rest of the evening Milly did her best to steer Robin away from the dangerous Tessa. But when she went to the bathroom the other girl cornered her as she came out. Milly felt terror grip her heart as she saw her supercilious smile and heard her say, 'Trying to hoodwink poor Robin then, are we?'

'I don't know what you mean!'

'Oh, I think you do. But women with murky pasts tend to get found out sooner or later. You'd better watch your step, Rosebud. You've made yourself a prime candidate for blackmail.'

'You wouldn't!'

'Oh, not me!' Tessa took a drag from her long cigarette holder, narrowing her eyes. 'I'm hardly one to call the kettle black! But I'm not the only local who

239

was at Sanderford's bash that night, sweetheart. If you get on to the Berkshire social scene someone else is bound to spot you sooner or later, and spill the beans. If I were you, ducky, I'd keep a very low profile – *if* you're serious about Robin, that is.'

Milly felt sickened, yet she couldn't work Tessa out. 'Why are you saying all this?'

'Just as a friend, that's all. I mean a friend of Robin's. I wouldn't want to see a nice boy like him get hurt by a heartless tart.'

She swept into the bathroom without another word, and Milly stood staring into thin air with her cheeks flaming and her heartbeat thundering in her ears. She wondered what to do. Should she tell all to Robin, come clean? It would upset him terribly, she was sure of that. And she wasn't likely to come to Berkshire again for a good while. So long as they carried on their affair in London they should be safe.

Because one thing Milly knew for sure was that she wanted to keep him. Where it would end she had no idea, but the way he made her feel was worth fighting for. If this was love, she could quite see what all the fuss was about!

There was a week or so left of the holiday before college began again, and Milly saw Robin almost every day. They explored London together and she had tea with his grandmother, but she still balked at introducing him to her parents. Even so he made her feel happy and secure. Their love-making got better and better, and Robin was able to control himself more so that it lasted longer and Milly was fully satisfied before he had to pull out. But even so, it was not quite perfect.

'I wish I could get hold of one of those female contraceptive devices,' she sighed one night as she lay in his arms. 'My mother told me Marie Stopes is advocating use of her "racial cap" to limit families, and that she plans to open a special clinic soon. She wants to make sure that the working classes don't take over the country by breeding like rabbits!'

'Is it just for poor women?' Robin asked. 'Couldn't you go along?'

'I would have to lie and say I was married. Suppose they wanted to see my marriage certificate?'

'Well I am happy as we are. But do whatever you think best, dearest. It is your body after all, and you who would have to bear the consequences.'

A chill struck her at those words. What did he mean? Was he merely referring to the social stigma of a 'shotgun wedding' and the normal trials and restrictions of motherhood? Or was he implying that if she fell for a child he would abandon her? She was too afraid that he meant the latter to ask him to clarify his statement.

Then, as they were lunching in a Lyons Corner House after visiting the National Gallery, Milly had another shock. A familiar figure began weaving her way through the tables towards them, avoiding the 'Nippies' who were dashing around at high speed in their black dresses and white caps and aprons.

'Milly! How lovely to see you again!'

'Oh, hullo Chloe,' Milly muttered, praying to sink through the floor.

'Mind if I sit down?' she asked, plonking herself on to one chair and her packages on to another. 'Oh my feet! I've been up and down Oxford Street all morning. Serge wanted me to buy some new underwear, and . . . ' She broke off, suddenly aware of Robin, who was regarding her with amused interest. 'Oh, please forgive my rudeness. Haven't we met before, in Paris?' She thrust a hand across the table. 'My name's Chloe. You might describe me as an ex-colleague of Milly's.'

As Robin re-introduced himself the room began to swim before Milly's eyes. In a voice tight with desperation, she broke in hastily. 'I . . . er . . . had a temporary job for a few weeks while I was in Paris.'

She gave Chloe a fierce glare, hoping she would get the message.

'Really? You never told me that, Milly. What job was that?'

'Oh, nothing much. Just working in a . . . milliners. It was my mother's idea,' she went on with increasing recklessness. 'She thought I should see what shop girls had to put up with. You know what a feminist she is, and all that.'

To her great relief Chloe gave her a discreet wink then said, 'We had some fun together, didn't we Milly? All that parading up and down for the customers, wearing the most extraordinary creations, so they could choose what they wanted to buy!'

Milly laughed, entering into the spirit of the game now that she was no longer worried. 'Terribly hard on the feet though.'

'And on other parts of one's anatomy. Handling all those floppy fedoras, I mean.'

Milly giggled. 'My word, yes! Hands and knees really ached by the end of the day. Not to mention one's "Boomps-a-daisy!"'

Chloe got up. 'Look, I cannot stay. I've already had my lunch, so I must get going. But here's my card. Do get in touch. I'd love to natter about old times.'

'Me too!' Milly beamed. She'd always got on well with Chloe and had missed her when she left Latour Studios. It would be nice to hear some gossip again.

Once the college term got under way, though, Milly didn't have much time. Robin found a bachelor flat a short bus ride away, but she decided to limit their meetings to weekends. Every weekday night was spent either marking or preparing lectures, but she loved the job and knew that it would become easier in subsequent years, when she'd done the groundwork. Professor Symes had already made it clear that he was keen to keep her on if she wished to stay.

But by the end of February Milly had great cause for concern. She had missed two periods and her breasts felt sore and heavy. She knew very well what these symptoms meant and, recalling what had happened in Robin's bedroom on Boxing Eve, she was thrown into panic. After weeks of secret, mounting fear she decided to pay her belated visit to Chloe. She travelled to the address on her card with a heavy heart. What she'd once imagined would be a pleasant chat to an old friend had now turned into something far more distressing, but she could think of no-one else to confide in.

Chloe was at home on that bleak Saturday afternoon in early March. She welcomed her warmly, but was soon made aware of Milly's agitated state. 'What's wrong, dear?' she asked, solicitously as she guided her to the sofa. 'You look terrible!'

'I think I may be pregnant,' she said, and at once burst into tears.

Chloe put the kettle on then came to sit beside her. 'How overdue are you, *ma chère*?'

'More than two months now.'

She put her arm around her shoulders and spoke soothingly. 'It's not the end of the world, Milly, believe me. You might almost call it an occupational hazard in our line of work.'

'But I'm not in that line of work any more!' she wailed. 'I'm supposed to be a respectable college lecturer. I'll lose my job, my career prospects, everything!'

'Was that man I met the father?' Milly nodded. 'But he looked a decent sort. Won't he stand by you?'

'I can't tell him, I daren't! He'd want to marry me, but I'm not sure that's what I want. It's all happened far too soon!'

'Don't be too hasty, dear. Many women marry in haste but not all of them end up repenting at leisure. Do you love him?'

'Yes. At least, I think so. But to be tied to him forever, and have to give up my career . . .'

As her sobbing accelerated Chloe hugged her close, then rose to make tea. Milly felt a bit better when she'd had some of the hot, sweet drink. She tried to be more rational.

'I was wondering if you knew of any . . . remedies, Chloe.'

'Oh, there's plenty on the market. I'm sure you've seen them advertised as "cures for female anaemia" and for "keeping you regular". Even Beecham's pills are supposed to do the trick.' She picked up a magazine that was lying on the table and flicked through it to the commercial pages. 'Let me see, there's bound to be some in here . . . are, here we are. "Dr Reynold's lightening pills" . . . silver-coated quinine pills, seven-and six for fifty. Or how about this? "Mère Dubois' pilules, five shillings. Guaranteed speedy and effective, work like magic in a few hours." You can get them by mail order, but I doubt they really work and you could make yourself very ill.'

'I'm desperate, Chloe! I'll try anything!'

'Well you could always try an old wives' remedy, gin and a mustard bath. Or I've heard that tansy, caraway and nutmeg can do the trick. But no-one I know has ever done away with an unwanted child except by going to an abortionist.'

Milly shuddered. 'I'd rather die than go to one of those back-street merchants.'

'You might die if you do! But think of other options Milly, please. Suppose you had the baby, somewhere secret if that's possible. You might go into one of those mother and baby homes.'

'Ugh!' Milly shuddered. 'What, be treated like dirt

by some snotty-nosed matron who thinks it's her duty to make me pay for my sins? No thank you! Anyway, they like you to give up your babies for adoption, don't they?'

'It might be the best thing. For both of you.'

Milly fell silent. It was the first time she'd really thought of her growing foetus as a fellow human being, and she felt ashamed that she'd been so selfishly concerned about herself alone. But she knew that if she went ahead and had the baby she could not bring herself to give him or her up. No matter how hard she had to struggle to make ends meet, even if she had to go on the streets, it would be preferable to knowing that her child was being reared by strangers.

'Is there no-one who can help you?' Chloe asked, gently. 'No-one in your family, I mean?'

'I couldn't possibly tell my mother. She already thinks I've failed her. My only saving grace is that I have a respectable job, and if I were to lose that she would despise me utterly.'

'Are you sure? That sounds very harsh.'

'She is so involved in the Women's Rights movement. It sounds silly, I know, but although she can pity ignorant working-class women who get into trouble, she is not so tolerant of educated ones. She thinks girls like me should know better, be more careful, and so on. She would make me feel I had let her down terribly, and I can't face that. I feel bad enough as it is.'

'What about your father?'

'He might give me money, but that would be the extent of his involvement. He hates emotional scenes or anything really personal. Besides, he might think it his duty to inform my mother.'

'Oh dear!' Chloe sighed. 'And is there no-one else, no aunts or family friends?'

'Yes!' Milly said, her spirits suddenly lifting. 'Of

course, why on earth didn't I think of her sooner? Emma, my godmother! She is living in Italy, but if I could only see her . . .'

'In Italy, eh? That sounds remarkably convenient, if you don't mind my saying so.'

For the first time in weeks Milly felt as if a ponderous burden were lifting from her shoulders. Emma, so worldly wise, so practical, would be the best person in the world to give her advice. But how could she get to see her? There were still several weeks to go before the Easter break.

'I'll write to her,' she decided. 'She may be able to come to London. I know it is several years since she visited England and she said she would like to return when I last saw her.'

'Well then, there's your answer!' Chloe smiled, pouring more tea. 'But try not to get too depressed before you see her. I know it's hard, but there is always a way round these things. It's part of human life, after all. Girls have been having babies out of wedlock ever since Eve gave birth without benefit of a wedding band!'

Milly laughed, glad to relax a little again. She was even able to push her own worries far enough into the background to enjoy Chloe's hilarious account of life at the Latour Studios.

'Serge has made another "epic masterpiece",' she said with a wry grin.

'Tell me more!'

'Well this time he is telling tales, naughty tales. It's called "Not for the Nursery – Unexpurgated Fairy Tales". Oh, and we have some new actors. Franz is still with us, but there is George to replace Richard, and another Englishman called Peter. Then there are two new girls, Sally and Bridget.'

'So Serge's company is expanding?'

246

'Yes, he's doing well. It was a good move to come to England.'

'Tell me about these naughty fairy tales. I could do with some cheering up.'

Chloe laughed. 'You wouldn't believe how ridiculous we felt doing them! First there was Red Riding Hood, who arrives at her *Grand'mère's* cottage to find her in bed with a werewolf. She climbs into bed with them and you can imagine what happens after that!'

'Knowing Serge's dirty imagination, yes I can!'

'The next scene is one I'm in. Goldilocks gets caught by Father Bear trying out Mother Bear's three dildoes . . .'

'Don't tell me, they're large, medium and small!'

'How did you guess? Anyway, he's cross with her so he gives her a spanking. Then there's Cinderella at the ball. At the stroke of midnight her ball gown disappears leaving her naked. Of course the handsome prince, played by George, doesn't mind a bit. She gets to try something out for size, but it isn't a slipper!'

'Honestly Serge is so obsessed with penis size! Makes you wonder what size he's got!'

Chloe looked knowing. 'No comment. Anyway, Sally plays the Sleeping Beauty, but it takes a bit more than a kiss to wake *her* up! And, last but not least, Pussy in Boots has me dressed in tall leather boots and nothing else. I promise Dick Whittington that if he can ring my bell I'll make him Lord Mayor of Lovedom. All very silly really, but great fun to do!'

'Yes, it must have been,' Milly said rather wistfully, getting to her feet. 'But I must get home. Robin is coming round tonight and I've promised to cook him a nice meal.'

Her eyes filled with tears as she thought of how hard it was going to be to keep her predicament a

247

secret. Chloe hugged her, saying gently, 'If you love him, Milly, you must tell him you know.'

But Milly couldn't help thinking, 'It's precisely because I love him that I must keep it a secret. I cannot marry him, it would never work. So I must bear this alone.'

As she travelled back to her flat she felt there was only one course open to her. She must tell Robin that she didn't want to see him any more. It would be the hardest thing she'd ever had to do, but she could see no other way out. Over and over she rehearsed her words, but there seemed no kind or easy way to say it. In the words of Shakespeare's Hamlet, she 'must be cruel, only to be kind'.

Seeing her lover's bright, adoring face at her door that night made her resolve waver, but after they had eaten and Robin said he would like them to visit his parents again at Easter, Milly knew she had to tell him. She blurted out, 'I'm sorry, Robin, but that won't be possible.'

'No? Why not, love?'

He looked at her with such innocent nonchalance that she almost backed out, but then she took the bit between her teeth and continued. 'I've been thinking long and hard about us, Robin, and whether we have a future together.' She saw his face fall, and had to steel herself. 'But I'm not ready for marriage. When we were with your family at Christmas I had the feeling they expected us to become engaged by the end of the year . . .'

'No, Milly, they understand that we are both starting out in our careers. There is no such expectation, I assure you.'

'But you do expect us to marry one day, don't you Robin?'

'Well, some day perhaps. When we are both good and ready.'

'But what if that day never comes? What if I am just not the marrying sort?'

He looked pained. 'Do you not want children, Milly?'

She felt a knife turn in her heart. Looking away she said, 'I don't know. All I know is that I want my freedom for now. Freedom to go where I please, to live where I please. I would like to go to Italy next summer, perhaps to live there. But I want to go alone.'

'Why, Milly? I don't understand. I thought you were happy with me!'

She was on the brink of tears. 'I have been happy with you, Robin. Please believe that. But I do not wish to tie you down when I am so uncertain of what I want out of life.'

His face twisted in torment. 'But I only want what you want. What will make you happy.'

'You don't know me, Robin. You think you do, but you don't. I am not all sweetness and light. I cannot explain exactly, but my mind is made up. It is better for us to part now than to drag on for months, even years, and then have an even more painful parting at the end of it. I'm sorry, but my mind is made up.'

Robin leapt up from the table, throwing down his serviette. 'Cruel woman!' he snarled. She shrank from him in dismay. 'You made me love you and now you do this to me. Heartless bitch!'

He'd never spoken to her in that way before and she was utterly shocked. Evidently she had cut him to the quick. He seized her roughly and she was afraid he would strike her, but he only stared wildly into her eyes as if trying to fathom her soul. At last he thrust her from him.

'I'm going!' he snapped. 'And you will not be bothered by me again. If this is the way you want it, Milly, this is how you shall have it. But I know you are making a big mistake.'

So saying he swept out of her flat like a whirlwind, leaving her stunned and bewildered. Much as she'd disliked having to tell him their affair was over, she had imagined him reacting in a cowed, sad way. His violent wrath had totally unnerved her, and she began to think that it was she who had misunderstood him, not vice-versa. She wondered if Chloe or that dreadful Tessa had said anything to him about her past, but it seemed unlikely. In that mood he would surely have thrown it back in her face if he knew the truth about her.

For most of the night Milly lay awake feeling utterly miserable. She realised that she had under-estimated the effect that breaking up with Robin would have upon her. At times she felt almost suicidal. All her hopes were pinned on her godmother to save her from this black pit of despair she'd got herself into. She would write to her first thing in the morning. When sleep obstinately refused to come, Milly started to compose the letter in her head and eventually fatigue overcame her.

Chapter Fifteen

*E*mma was wonderful. Milly had always known this, of course, but she had never needed her help so much before and now her godmother did not fail her. Soon after Milly's ambiguously-worded letter had winged its way to Florence a reply came saying that Emma would be arriving in Victoria Station on April the tenth at five-thirty and staying at the Grosvenor Hotel. If Milly liked she could dine with her there and tell her all her troubles.

Milly couldn't wait to see her. The time dragged terribly, and every day she awoke feeling sick. The sickness lasted all morning, making it difficult for her to give lectures. She always made sure she had a carafe of water to hand, but once or twice she'd had to dash out of the room and use one of the brown paper bags that she carried about with her. She was constantly terrified that someone would catch her vomiting and guess the cause of her nausea.

Fortunately her stomach was not too prominent yet, but she wondered how she would possibly manage when she began to show. By June she would be six months gone, and it would be almost impossible to conceal her condition. Yet she had to work out her term's notice. She knew how disappointed Professor Symes would be when she told him she would not be staying for another year, but if he discovered the true reason for her departure she had no doubt that he would be disgusted with her. In her low state Milly did not think she could bear to endure gossip and scathing disapproval from staff and students alike.

As she'd predicted, Professor Symes was none too pleased when she handed in her resignation, fobbing him off by saying she 'wanted to travel'. Milly hated upsetting him when he'd been so encouraging, but he promised her a good reference and once it was done she felt better. At least the way was now clear for whatever she had to face in the summer.

At last April the tenth arrived, and Milly made her way to the foyer of the Grosvenor Hotel with high hopes. She arrived early and found a seat in an unobtrusive corner from where she could watch the entrance, biting her nails. At long last she saw her godmother arrive, followed by a porter with a luggage trolley. Milly hurried up to her.

'Aunt Em! Oh, you don't know how glad I am to see you!'

'Dear girl, how are you? Your letter had me worried.'

Emma took in her appearance with a quick glance from top to toe. Milly was wearing a skirt and cardigan with a wool coat over it, but the buttons on the coat were already getting tight so she'd left it open. She'd had to let the waistband out an inch or so to fit, too. Had Emma noticed her thickening waist? Milly was almost certain she had.

She waited as patiently as she could until the key was handed over. Emma wanted to go up to her room straight away. 'I hope you don't mind, dear, but it's been a long journey and I am too tired to sit in the

252

lounge drinking tea. But we can have some sent up if you wish.'

'That would be lovely,' Milly smiled. Everything seemed easier now she was here. Somehow Emma had the knack of making everything flow smoothly. Well, that quality would be severely put to the test from now on!

The room was pleasant and spacious, allowing Milly to find a comfortable position on the sofa while Emma took off her outer clothes, shoes and stockings and soaked her feet in lavender-scented water to revive them.

'Ah, that's better,' she smiled. 'When you get older your feet are the barometer of your well-being, my dear. If your feet are refreshed and rested you can face anything.'

'That sounds a useful tip,' Milly smiled, wryly. But just then the boy came with the tea-tray so they waited until he had gone before continuing their conversation. Milly took a sip of the hot, strong brew then said, 'I'm afraid I have serious news for you, Aunty Em.'

Emma gave her a long, straight look. 'I know of only one reason why a girl would rather confide in someone other than her own mother, Milly. I presume you cannot bring yourself to go to the obvious person, your family doctor?'

Milly flushed, realising her godmother had indeed guessed her shameful secret. 'I haven't seen a doctor, but I don't need to. I am quite certain.'

'You should see a doctor all the same,' Emma said, gently. 'But first tell me how this came about. It takes two, as I'm sure you're well aware. What of the father?'

Milly burst into tears, she couldn't help herself. She had been feeling so wretched about her last encounter with Robin. Emma held out her arms and she knelt

253

with her head in her lap, sobbing. Gentle hands stroked her hair until the crying fit had passed.

'You know, I feel partly responsible for what has happened to you, dear. I am supposed to be your moral guardian, after all. Perhaps I was wrong to speak so much of the joys of love and sex. Perhaps I should have stressed the dangers. But I thought you were aware of the ways in which to prevent pregnancy.'

'It was an accident really,' Milly sniffed. 'But I thought it would not matter because I was mid-cycle.'

'But that is when you are at your most fertile, silly child. Oh dear!'

'*Most* fertile? I thought I read ... well, never mind now. Robin – he is the father – used to withdraw. But on one occasion, and only one, he was too late.'

'It only takes once! But tell me more about this Robin. Does he know?'

She shook her head, tight-lipped. 'I am no longer seeing him. I thought it best.'

'Why? Is he married, dear?'

'Oh, no!'

'Then why did you not tell him?'

'He would have been devastated. And he would have wanted to marry me, but I don't think I could have done so. Oh Aunt Em, I have only just started on my teaching career! This could not have come at a worse time.'

'So what do you want me to do about it?'

Milly stared at her, uncomprehending. She had expected Emma to have all the answers, or at least to make suggestions. To have the ball thrown back in her court like this was a shock. 'I ... I was hoping you might know what to do.'

Emma gave a weary smile. 'You are over twenty-one, a young woman. You must make up your own mind. How far on are you in your pregnancy?'

'Too far to do much about it,' she said, miserably.

'Then I'm glad you have not tried anything really stupid or we would be meeting in a hospital, not a hotel. But at least we know you are going to have the child. The next questions are, where and how? Obviously you don't want to tell your parents.'

'I can't stay here. I just don't know where to go, or what to do.'

'All right, here's what I suggest. You have the date of your last period?' Milly nodded. 'Then we can calculate roughly when the birth will be. But you must see a doctor, to ensure everything is normal. I have a very good man in Florence who will attend you if I pay him enough. He will see that you enter a hospital at the right time. I believe there is a very pleasant maternity ward, staffed by nuns. And of course I shall be on hand to see you through it.'

'Oh, you're so good to me!' Milly sobbed. 'I'm sure I don't deserve it. I've brought shame on my family . . .'

'Hush. Don't talk like that for it's not in the least how I feel about it. Everyone is capable of making a mistake. We must do what is best for both you and the baby, that is all.'

By the time Milly returned home in a taxi she was feeling much better. Now she could face the future, whereas before she had felt scarcely able to get through another day. Emma had promised to go shopping with her to buy suitably concealing clothes, then she would return to Florence and make all the arrangements. Milly would go out immediately term ended, on the pretext that Emma had found her a summer job as tutor to an English family.

Yet that was as far as Milly's future went, thus far and no further. She could not imagine how she might feel once the child had arrived, so she was unable to make plans. Emma had understood. 'We'll cross that bridge when we come to it,' she'd said.

There were a few more bridges to cross first, however. Milly had an unexpected visit from her mother, who told her she was looking 'peaky' and advised plenty of cod liver oil and malt. The true purpose of her visit was soon revealed when she invited Milly to attend a meeting where Marie Stopes was going to talk about her newly-opened Birth Control Clinic. The irony of it almost sent Milly into hysterics.

'I'm sorry, Ma, but I'm seeing Aunty Em on that day,' she said, quite truthfully. They were going on their last shopping spree before her godmother returned to Florence.

'Can't you put her off?' her mother asked, irritably. Milly knew relations between them were still strained, although Emma had visited Kitty once during her visit.

'Not really. She goes home next day, and I think she's busy until then.'

'I don't suppose she'd consider coming to the meeting too. For all her pro-feminist sentiments, your godmother shows precious little real support for the movement.'

Milly shrugged, not wanting to enter into the argument, and Kitty conceded defeat. As she looked at her mother's pinched face and dowdy clothes, Milly felt a wave of sadness envelop her. If only she had been able to marry again maybe she would have flowered, instead of withering away. But she had given her all to the Cause, and paid a high price for it.

A few days later, a parcel came from Robin. Milly recognised his handwriting and feared to open it, but when she did the volume of Keats that she had given him was inside. There was also a terse note, quoting from Shakespeare's Hamlet: 'For to the noble mind, Rich gifts wax poor when givers prove unkind.'

She recognised it as being from the scene where Hamlet spurns Ophelia. Only this time it was a woman rejecting a man. Milly felt terrible, and her eyes filled with tears. She knew she had hurt him and that he didn't deserve it, but consoled herself with the thought that she was saving him greater pain in future by seeming heartless now.

Except that she knew she wasn't heartless. She missed him dreadfully, especially at night, and sometimes fantasised about what life would have been like if she'd agreed to marry him and given her child a name. But then the doubts would set in, a deep-seated dread of repeating her mother's mistake and marrying a man who proved to be unsuitable. She felt she did not know Robin well enough, that their relationship had been based on poetry and romance rather than anything more solid.

Milly's pregnancy continued relentlessly after Emma had returned to Italy, and her bulging stomach was a constant worry to her. Somehow she managed to struggle through the term, even through the hot month of May, and to see her students through their examinations without becoming too exhausted. But when the end of term came, and she was presented with a copy of Palgrave's Golden Treasury, she burst into tears at the thought that she would have to leave the college without hope of return.

Everyone was very kind to her, but if anyone had guessed about her predicament they did not even hint at it. Milly was relieved when the day came for her to board the boat train, although she was dreading making the long journey alone. Her father saw her off at Victoria, and she was tearful as she left him, but once she was under way things did not seem too bad. At least she had a place to go, and someone to look after her at the end of the line.

The weeks leading up to her confinement passed

257

very quickly. Doctor Fantoni, a cheerful man who spoke comical English, pronounced her 'Fit as a violin, yes?' and promised that she would have 'a happy and safe birth day.' Emma had bought a layette for the baby, and had prepared a room in her villa for when Milly came out of hospital.

'They may want you to leave the baby there, to let the nuns take care of it,' she warned her. 'But if you decide you want to keep the child you should remain with it, feed it yourself if possible.'

'What do you think I should do?' Milly asked, in desperation. But her godmother would not make up her mind for her. All she would say was that if she wanted to keep the baby she would help her as much as she could.

When the pains started Milly was already in the cool, quiet hospital looking out on to a shady court-yard. The nuns were very kind and did not once censure or preach to her. Being in the peaceful birthing room had a calming influence on her, so that by the time the Doctor arrived she was halfway through her labour. She felt the growing strength of her contractions, like a cruel parody of orgasm, and did her best not to fight the bitter, cramping pains that racked her body over and over again.

Milly was amazed at the power and autonomy of her own body as it progressed through the birth without any conscious direction from her. The excruciating pain took her into another world, a world of helpless subjugation to the rhythm and drive of the biological process. Her mind was focused inside her body, imagining that tiny bundle of flesh making its first journey, feeling the muscles of her womb and vagina pushing it on its way. She gasped and groaned as the head engaged and then felt as if she would split in two, her vulva stretched almost beyond endurance.

But somehow the miracle happened. There was a

feeling of relief as the tiny head and shoulders slipped out, and then a sudden rush as the rest followed, leaving Milly with a hollow feeling between her thighs. She felt the ooze of something slimy, and lay back exhausted while the nuns got on with their work of cutting the cord. One of the sisters wiped her forehead with a damp sponge and said a brief prayer for her. Then, out of the haze of blood and sweat and tears, Milly suddenly heard a faint cry, a voice in the wilderness, announcing the child's living, breathing presence, and she sat up with tears streaming down her cheeks.

'It is a little girl,' Sister Francesca said with a smile, handing her the swaddled bundle.

The instant she looked down into that flushed, wrinkled little face Milly knew beyond all doubt that she was going to keep her baby.

'It won't be easy, but we'll manage somehow.'

Emma smiled and squeezed Milly's hand reassuringly as she lay in the big bed at the villa, in a room with a view out to the Tuscan hills. Beside her, baby Emmeline was sleeping peacefully in her cot. The name was perfect, she had decided. A combination of her own name, Emily, and Emma. There was a nice inevitability about the name evolving as it passed down the generations.

But that was all she was pleased about as she lay, for hour after hour, looking out towards the distant cypresses and umbrella pines. The baby was sweet, perfectly formed and apparently even-tempered. She fed easily, slept regularly. Everyone in the household kept telling her how lucky she was to have such a model infant. But Milly felt as if a black cloud had descended on her and never lifted, from morn till night, day in and day out.

Emma helped her to get up one day and sit in the

shady garden with a book of poetry, thinking that would cheer her up, but it had no effect. The doctor was called and pronounced her condition to be 'chronic anxiety.' In the old days, he informed her cheerfully, the doctor would have set leeches on to her to cure her 'ill humour' but in these enlightened times there was no such cure. Time would heal all, he assured her. Meanwhile she must rest and enjoy her baby as best she could.

Feeding her baby was no problem, but Milly hated to see her great swollen-veined breasts, and the huge nipples were chafed and painful. She was horrified by the folds of skin around her waist, and did not listen when she was told they would vanish in time. She felt frumpish and weak, sure she was being an inadequate mother even when everyone assured her she was doing fine.

'I worry about you, dear,' Emma admitted one day when she found her god-daughter weeping, yet again, for no apparent reason. 'If you don't get better soon I think you had better return to the hospital for a while.'

But Milly just stared listlessly at her, hardly caring where she was or who she was with. All she knew was that her life was in ruins, but the creature who had brought about all this devastation was in no way to blame. She began to think about finding someone to adopt the child after all, but when she tried to think straight her mind seemed full of wool.

One afternoon she was sitting in the garden at her godmother's insistence when she heard a carriage arrive. It was of little interest to her, but soon Emma came out looking tense and nervous. 'Milly dear, someone has come to visit you. Now I don't want you to be upset. Please understand that this is none of my doing. I think some extraordinary coincidence has occurred, but I can't help thinking it must be fate that has brought him to our door . . .'

Not even Milly, in her depressed state, could bear any more prevarication. 'For the love of God, who is it Aunt Em?'

'Well . . .'

But before any more hedging could take place, the visitor suddenly stepped boldly into the garden and Milly turned to face him. She gasped, unable to believe her eyes. How on earth had Robin discovered where she was? Anger soon replaced her shock and she turned to her godmother, but Emma shook her head and shrugged, emphasising her earlier disclaimer.

'How the hell did you find me, Robin?' Emma called out furiously, getting up out of her wicker chair so fast it almost toppled over.

'Please, Milly, don't upset yourself. The last thing in the world I want to do is upset you.'

'Then I think you have some explaining to do. I can't believe you would have the nerve to show up here.'

'At least let me explain, I beg of you. Then, if you wish, I shall go away and never trouble you again.'

She sat down, wracked with mixed feelings. Another chair was brought and Robin sat at a respectful distance, his expression grave. 'I know this is a shock to you. Milly, but when I found out you were in Florence I had to come and seek you out.'

'How did you find out I was here?'

'By chance, really. I met Professor Symes at a symposium on Keats. He showed me his edition and I said I'd had a fine one given to me by a lady friend but had returned it. He started to ask me about this friend, and I said she used to teach at his college – not realising he was the Principal. Well then he said you had left in order to travel. Things might have stopped there if another woman hadn't joined our group.'

'Don't tell me: Evadne!'

'That's right!' Robin smiled, and Milly felt as if the door of her heart had opened a chink and let some sunshine in. 'It didn't take her long to work out who we were talking about. She said you had a godmother living in a villa just outside Florence. She knew the address, so here I am! I thought even if you weren't here when I arrived your godmother might know where you were. It was a slim chance, but it was all I'd got.' He leant forward and took her hand. 'I felt I just had to see you again, Milly. We parted such bad friends and I felt so ashamed of what I'd said to you. I couldn't bear it. How are you? Please don't send me away until you have at least told me a little about yourself.'

It was so strange being with him again. Milly fought against the urge to drop back into old habits, to open her heart to him as she used to do. Evidently he knew nothing of the child, but she couldn't bring herself to tell him yet. Instead she told him she'd been ill and was convalescing.

'I thought you looked very pale. You need some sunshine in your life, my dear. Once I thought I could bring that to you, but . . .' his lips trembled, and Milly felt a rush of shame. How heartlessly she had treated him!

Emma appeared with cooling drinks and told Robin he was welcome to stay as long as he wished. He thanked her, but said he would not outstay his welcome. Milly heard the sudden shrill cry of her child and, before anyone could stop her, Maria had brought the baby out into the garden saying little Emmeline was clamouring to be fed.

There was an awful silence. Milly saw the truth dawning in Robin's eyes and didn't know where to put her blushing face. He stared incredulously at the little bundle, then at Milly. His mouth was opening and closing silently, like a fish's, and Milly had a sudden urge to giggle. She took the precious bundle from Maria with a sigh saying, 'So now you know.'

'She's mine?'

His voice was tremulous, full of awe. He peered into the bonny little face with his hazel eyes brimming. Emma ushered the maid back into the house, leaving tiny Emmeline with both her parents for the first time in her young life. Robin put out his finger and the baby gripped it. He turned to Milly, his face radiant. 'She likes me!'

Milly didn't have the heart to tell him Emmeline did that to everyone's finger. She merely smiled, undoing her blouse and taking out the nipple to nurse her child. Robin watched in silent fascination for a while, then said, 'I wish you had told me, Milly. But I am not cross with you. I can understand how you must have felt.'

'I'm not sure you can, Robin. Perhaps that is the trouble. I don't believe you really know me, so how can you know what I feel?'

He looked at her earnestly. 'I know you well enough to love you. I hoped you would believe that, but evidently you don't. I'm lost without you, Milly. I don't mind admitting it. But I won't stand in your way if you want to lead the life of an independent woman. All I ask is that you let me contribute to our child's upkeep. I don't have to see her. But I could never live with my conscience if I abandoned you both entirely.'

Milly stared at him in amazement. She had expected all kinds of reactions from him but not this one. His generosity was extraordinary and made her feel all the more guilty.

'Robin, I don't know what to say.'

'Then say nothing. Just let me sit here watching you feed her, like some medieval Madonna and child. I want to burn this image on my memory, Milly, so I never forget it. I shall conjure it up on my deathbed and carry it to my grave.'

'Oh, Robin!'

But even as she laughed at his extravagant romanticism, Milly knew that he was weaving his old spell over her, that he was seducing her with words. Already the dark cloud was starting to lift. And what was that strange commotion in her chest, beneath the milk-laden breasts: was it the excited beat of her heart, dancing?

Seeing the pair of them apparently at ease with each other, Emma invited Robin to dine with them and stay the night. Milly was secretly delighted. She was too exhausted to worry about what might come of this little interlude of peace between her and Robin. It was enough that she felt contented and relaxed for the first time since the birth. After dinner – a merry affair with Emma and Robin chatting wittily while Milly listened fondly to them both – a truckle bed was set up in the room next door to Milly's, and Emma retired to her own room with a satisfied smile on her face.

Tired as she was, Milly had no inclination to sleep. When she had checked that Emmeline was safely tucked up in the nursery, she joined Robin who was drinking a night-cap in the sitting-room. His face lit up when she appeared and he moved up to make room for her on the sofa. 'I thought you'd gone to bed,' he grinned.

'I wouldn't be able to sleep, there's too much on my mind.'

'Me too. Oh Milly, whatever happens to us I must say I'm happy about little Emmeline. You've no idea what a joy it is to know that I've helped to bring her into the world.'

'That only makes me feel more guilty about not telling you. Suppose you'd never found out where I was? Knowing how glad you are now just reminds me that I would have deprived you of that pleasure.'

'No, you mustn't feel that. Fate took a hand in bringing us together, my love. I'm sure of that now. And I want you to know that even if this is just a short visit, even if we part forever tomorrow, I still love you and always will.'

Tears sprang into her eyes as she looked into his sweet, sincere face. I have wronged him dreadfully, she thought, sobbing. He took her in his arms and relief filled her up like a tonic.

'We have this one night together,' he told her. 'This may be all we ever have. Please tell me everything that is in your heart, Milly. Then, if you want me to leave forever I shall do so, first thing tomorrow.'

'Oh Robin, I don't know where to begin!' she moaned.

But eventually she did find a way to tell him about her doubts and fears. He listened patiently at first, and then with increasing fascination as she told him about the life she'd lived before she met him.

She spared him nothing. First Milly told him about her early discovery of sex, through pleasuring herself after lights-out in the school dorm. Then she described how she made love with other girls. Observing his keen interest she grew bolder, going into more detail until he began asking questions. Did she remember her first climax? Was it self-induced or brought on by another girl? Did she give other girls the same pleasure?

'You are not shocked, then?'

He gave a chuckle. 'Really, Milly, it doesn't sound so very different from what used to go on at our school.'

She smiled wickedly at him. 'Then I think it should be your turn to tell me!'

'Later perhaps. Go on, love. I want to know what you got up to at Cambridge.'

Milly felt obliged to keep checking that he was not shocked or disgusted by her revelations. She couldn't believe he was taking it so calmly, even her affair with Evadne. He said he would like to see the naughty photos that she and her friends took on their 'picnic.'

'There were many more taken,' she confessed. 'After I came down from Cambridge I worked for a photographer for a while, here in Florence.' She smiled, remembering Leo Venuti. Was he still there in his dusty old shop, plying his old trade? Perhaps she would pay him a visit. How amazed he would be to see her. Maybe he would take some photographs of her with Emmeline. She was cheered at the thought.

Seeing her face light up, Robin gave her a brief kiss on the cheek. She was surprised by a flurry of desire that caught her completely unawares and made her blush.

He laughed. 'Tell me more, you wicked thing. Don't keep me in suspense.'

When he heard about her film rôles Robin regarded her with amazement. 'Milly, why didn't you tell me all this before? It's fascinating!'

'I was afraid you would think me cheap. No, worse. A common harlot.'

He laughed. 'It's so evident you are not that! But I must take you to task. You told me that I didn't know you. You were right, I had no idea. But only because you wouldn't tell me. Now I can justly accuse you of not knowing *me*, if you thought I'd be shocked by all this.'

'Touché!' she smiled, wryly.

But she was reluctant to tell him about her time at Tammy Vavasour's all the same. When he finally wormed it out of her he listened attentively then remarked that there had been boys at his school who seemed to fawn on the masters even when they were caned or publicly humiliated.

'I can well believe they were candidates for that sort of treatment,' he remarked. 'Isn't the sexual urge extraordinary, Milly. It takes such twists and turns in some people's psyches.'

She gazed at him archly. 'But not yours, eh?'

'Now that I wouldn't know, being so inexperienced. But I wouldn't mind finding out from an expert like you!'

She couldn't believe that he was making such light of it. When he suggested they should go up to bed she still couldn't quite believe that he meant to stay with her, but as she entered her room he followed.

'You will let me spend the night with you, won't you?' he pleaded, a humble supplicant.

She nodded. 'But I don't know if I'll be up to anything.'

'That doesn't matter. It will be enough just to hold you in my arms, truly.'

Which was what he did, for what seemed like hours more murmured conversation. Somehow Robin managed to turn the conversation from the past towards the future. He said that while Milly was away in the nursery Emma had offered to let them stay with her as a family for as long as they liked.

'Think of it, my love. Just picture how happy we could be here. Emma would look after little Emmeline while you found some teaching. It would be easy to find work in Florence, where everyone wants to learn English and study the Romantic Poets. They needn't know you have a child.'

'Or . . . a husband?' Milly whispered the dreaded word, but it didn't sound nearly as bad as she'd feared. In fact, she rather liked it.

'That would be up to you. But I'm sure I'd be able

to study here, at the University. Gus would give me a good reference. Oh Milly, surely it's worth a try, isn't it?'

'Mm. Maybe.'

She snuggled up to his warm, naked chest, revelling in the hard maleness of his flesh against her over-ripe maternal body. His penis was erect, against her belly, and she felt again the insistent stirring in her womb. It had shuddered with pain to deliver its precious burden, but now it wanted to shudder in exquisite delight once more. Her pussy was clamouring too. Having thrust new life out into the world, now it wanted life thrust back into it, the vibrant recklessness of a lusty phallus.

Helpless in the face of her body's demands, Milly reached down and took his cock in her hand. It leapt like a wild animal in her palm, another being, with a life of its own.

'I want it,' she murmured into the dark hollow of his ear. 'And I want *you!*'

'What about . . . precautions?'

His hesitant voice filled her with tenderness. Even now he was concerned for her welfare.

'I'm breast feeding. That's nature's way of preventing another pregnancy, so I've been told.'

'If you're sure.'

In the intense darkness of that Tuscan night his question took on other dimensions. There was a pause. Then she said, 'Oh yes, I'm absolutely sure. I don't think I've been so sure of anything in my life.'

He kissed her passionately, and she felt her whole body yield to him, knowing that he accepted her for what she was, loved her for just being her. What woman could ask more of a man? She took his hand and placed it on the warm, swollen slope of her breast.

'Teach me, Milly,' he said, his voice thick with emotion. 'Show me how to pleasure you.'

Then his mouth moved towards the glistening pink bud of her nipple.

BLACK LACE NEW BOOKS

Published in November

PASSION FLOWERS
Celia Parker

A revolutionary sex therapy clinic, on an idyllic Caribbean island is the mystery destination to which Katherine – a brilliant lawyer – is sent, by her boss, for a well-earned holiday. For the first time in her life, Katherine feels free to indulge in all manner of sybaritic pleasures. But will she be able to retain this sense of liberation when it's time to leave?

ISBN 0 352 33118 6

ODYSSEY
Katrina Vincenzi-Thyne

Historian Julia Symonds agrees to join the sexually sophisticated Merise and Rupert in their quest for the lost treasures of Ancient Troy. Having used her powers of seduction to extract the necessary information from the leader of a ruthless criminal fraternity, Julia soon finds herself relishing the ensuing game of erotic deception – as well as the hedonistic pleasures to which her new associates introduce her.

ISBN 0 352 33111 9

Published in December

CONTINUUM
Portia Da Costa

When Joanna takes a well-earned break from work, she also takes her first step into a new continuum of strange experiences. She discovers a clandestine, decadent parallel world of bizarre coincidences, unusual pleasures and erotic suffering. Can her working life ever be the same again?

ISBN 0 352 33120 8

THE ACTRESS
Vivienne LaFay

1920. When Milly Belfort renounces the life of a bluestocking in favour of more fleshly pleasures, her adventures in the Jazz Age take her from the risqué fringes of the film industry to the erotic excesses of the yachting set. When, however, she falls for a young man who knows nothing of her past, she finds herself faced with a crisis and a very difficult choice.

ISBN 0 352 33119 4

ÎLE DE PARADIS
Mercedes Kelly

Shipwrecked on a remote tropical island at the turn of the century, the innocent and lovely Angeline comes to enjoy the eroticism of local ways. Life is sweetly hedonistic until some of her friends and lovers are captured by a depraved band of pirates and taken to the harem of Jezebel – slave mistress of nearby Dragon Island. Angeline and her handmaidens, however, are swift to join the rescue party.

ISBN 0 352 33121 6

To be published in January

NADYA'S QUEST
Lisette Allen

Nadya's personal quest leads her to St Petersburg in the Summer of 1788. The beautiful city is in a rapturous state of decadence and its Empress, well known for her lascivious appetite, is hungry for a new lover who must by young, handsome and virile. When Nadya brings a Swedish seafarer, the magnificently-proportioned Axel, to the Imperial court, he is soon made the Empress's favourite. Nadya, determined to keep Axel for herself, is drawn into an intrigue of treachery and sedition as hostilities develop between Russia and Sweden.

ISBN 0 352 33135 6

DESIRE UNDER CAPRICORN
Louisa Francis

A shipwreck rips Dita Jones from the polite society of Sydney in the 1870s and throws her into an untamed world where Matt Warrender, a fellow castaway, develops a passion for her he will never forget. Separated after their eventual rescue, Dita is taken back into civilised life where a wealthy stud farmer, Jas McGrady, claims her for his bride. Taken to the rugged terrain of outback Australia, and a new life as Mrs McGrady, Dita realises her husband has a dark secret.

ISBN 0 352 33136 4

If you would like a complete list of plot summaries of Black Lace titles, please fill out the questionnaire overleaf or send a stamped addressed envelope to:-

Black Lace, 332 Ladbroke Grove, London W10 5AH

BLACK LACE BACKLIST

All books are prices £4.99 unless another price is given.

BLUE HOTEL	Cherri Pickford ISBN 0 352 32858 4	☐
CASSANDRA'S CONFLICT	Fredrica Alleyn ISBN 0 352 32859 2	☐
THE CAPTIVE FLESH	Cleo Cordell ISBN 0 352 32872 X	☐
PLEASURE HUNT	Sophie Danson ISBN 0 352 32880 0	☐
OUTLANDIA	Georgia Angelis ISBN 0 352 32883 5	☐
BLACK ORCHID	Roxanne Carr ISBN 0 352 32888 6	☐
ODALISQUE	Fleur Reynolds ISBN 0 352 32887 8	☐
THE SENSES BEJEWELLED	Cleo Cordell ISBN 0 352 32904 1	☐
VIRTUOSO	Katrina Vincenzi ISBN 0 352 32907 6	☐
FIONA'S FATE	Fredrica Alleyn ISBN 0 352 32913 0	☐
HANDMAIDEN OF PALMYRA	Fleur Reynolds ISBN 0 352 32919 X	☐
THE SILKEN CAGE	Sophie Danson ISBN 0 352 32928 9	☐
THE GIFT OF SHAME	Sarah Hope-Walker ISBN 0 352 32935 1	☐
SUMMER OF ENLIGHTENMENT	Cheryl Mildenhall ISBN 0 352 32937 8	☐
A BOUQUET OF BLACK ORCHIDS	Roxanne Carr ISBN 0 352 32939 4	☐
JULIET RISING	Cleo Cordell ISBN 0 352 32938 6	☐

----------✂----------------------

Please send me the books I have ticked above.

Name　　　...

Address　...

　　　　　...

　　　　　...

　　　..................　Post Code　.................

Send to: **Cash Sales, Black Lace Books, 332 Ladbroke Grove, London W10 5AH.**

Please enclose a cheque or postal order, made payable to **Virgin Publishing Ltd.** to the value of the books you have ordered plus postage and packing costs as follows:

UK and BFPO – £1.00 for the first book, 50p for each subsequent book.

Overseas (including Republic of Ireland) – £2.00 for the first book, £1.00 each subsequent book.

If you would prefer to pay by VISA or ACCESS/MASTERCARD, please write your card number and expiry date here:

....

Please allow up to 28 days for delivery.

Signature　...

----------✂----------------------

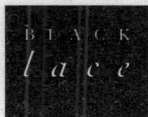

WE NEED YOUR HELP . . .
to plan the future of women's erotic fiction –

– and no stamp required!

Yours are the only opinions that matter.

Black Lace is the first series of books devoted to erotic fiction by women for women.

We intend to keep providing the best-written, sexiest books you can buy. And we'd appreciate your help and valued opinion of the books so far. Tell us what you want to read.

THE BLACK LACE QUESTIONNAIRE

SECTION ONE: ABOUT YOU

1.1 Sex (*we presume you are female, but so as not to discriminate*)
     Are you?
     Male   ☐
     Female   ☐

1.2 Age
     under 21   ☐   21–30   ☐
     31–40   ☐   41–50   ☐
     51–60   ☐   over 60   ☐

1.3 At what age did you leave full-time education?
     still in education   ☐   16 or younger   ☐
     17–19   ☐   20 or older   ☐

1.4 Occupation _____

1.5 Annual household income
          under £10,000 ☐   £10–£20,000 ☐
          £20–£30,000 ☐   £30–£40,000 ☐
          over £40,000 ☐

1.6 We are perfectly happy for you to remain anonymous;
but if you would like to receive information on other
publications available, please insert your name and
address

_____

_____

_____

_____

SECTION TWO: ABOUT BUYING BLACK LACE BOOKS

2.1 How did you acquire this copy of *The Actress*?
        I bought it myself ☐   My partner bought it ☐
        I borrowed/found it ☐

2.2 How did you find out about Black Lace books?
        I saw them in a shop ☐
        I saw them advertised in a magazine ☐
        I saw the London Underground posters ☐
        I read about them in _____
        Other _____

2.3 Please tick the following statements you agree with:
        I would be less embarrassed about buying Black
        Lace books if the cover pictures were less explicit ☐
        I think that in general the pictures on Black
        Lace books are about right ☐
        I think Black Lace cover pictures should be as
        explicit as possible ☐

2.4 Would you read a Black Lace book in a public place – on
a train for instance?
        Yes ☐   No ☐

SECTION THREE: ABOUT THIS BLACK LACE BOOK

3.1 Do you think the sex content in this book is:
Too much ☐ About right ☐
Not enough ☐

3.2 Do you think the writing style in this book is:
Too unreal/escapist ☐ About right ☐
Too down to earth ☐

3.3 Do you think the story in this book is:
Too complicated ☐ About right ☐
Too boring/simple ☐

3.4 Do you think the cover of this book is:
Too explicit ☐ About right ☐
Not explicit enough ☐

Here's a space for any other comments:

SECTION FOUR: ABOUT OTHER BLACK LACE BOOKS

4.1 How many Black Lace books have you read? ☐

4.2 If more than one, which one did you prefer?

4.3 Why?

SECTION FIVE: ABOUT YOUR IDEAL EROTIC NOVEL

We want to publish the books you want to read – so this is your chance to tell us exactly what your ideal erotic novel would be like.

5.1 Using a scale of 1 to 5 (1 = no interest at all, 5 = your ideal), please rate the following possible settings for an erotic novel:

Medieval/barbarian/sword 'n' sorcery ☐
Renaissance/Elizabethan/Restoration ☐
Victorian/Edwardian ☐
1920s & 1930s – the Jazz Age ☐
Present day ☐
Future/Science Fiction ☐

5.2 Using the same scale of 1 to 5, please rate the following themes you may find in an erotic novel:

Submissive male/dominant female ☐
Submissive female/dominant male ☐
Lesbianism ☐
Bondage/fetishism ☐
Romantic love ☐
Experimental sex e.g. anal/watersports/sex toys ☐
Gay male sex ☐
Group sex ☐

Using the same scale of 1 to 5, please rate the following styles in which an erotic novel could be written:

Realistic, down to earth, set in real life ☐
Escapist fantasy, but just about believable ☐
Completely unreal, impressionistic, dreamlike ☐

5.3 Would you prefer your ideal erotic novel to be written from the viewpoint of the main male characters or the main female characters?

Male ☐ Female ☐
Both ☐

5.4 What would your ideal Black Lace heroine be like? Tick as many as you like:

Dominant	☐	Glamorous	☐
Extroverted	☐	Contemporary	☐
Independent	☐	Bisexual	☐
Adventurous	☐	Naive	☐
Intellectual	☐	Introverted	☐
Professional	☐	Kinky	☐
Submissive	☐	Anything else?	☐
Ordinary	☐	_____	

5.5 What would your ideal male lead character be like? Again, tick as many as you like:

Rugged	☐		
Athletic	☐	Caring	☐
Sophisticated	☐	Cruel	☐
Retiring	☐	Debonair	☐
Outdoor-type	☐	Naive	☐
Executive-type	☐	Intellectual	☐
Ordinary	☐	Professional	☐
Kinky	☐	Romantic	☐
Hunky	☐		
Sexually dominant	☐	Anything else?	☐
Sexually submissive	☐	_____	

5.6 Is there one particular setting or subject matter that your ideal erotic novel would contain?

_____

SECTION SIX: LAST WORDS

6.1 What do you like best about Black Lace books?

_____

6.2 What do you most dislike about Black Lace books?

_____

6.3 In what way, if any, would you like to change Black Lace covers?

_____

6.4   Here's a space for any other comments:

_____

_____

_____

_____

_____

Thank you for completing this questionnaire. Now tear it out of the book – carefully! – put it in an envelope and send it to:

Black Lace
FREEPOST
London
W10 5BR

No stamp is required if you are resident in the U.K.